The Seven Secrets

The Seven Secrets

William Le Queux

MINT EDITIONS

The Seven Secrets was first published in 1903.

This edition published by Mint Editions 2021.

ISBN 9781513280943 | E-ISBN 9781513285962

Published by Mint Editions®

MINT
EDITIONS

minteditionbooks.com

Publishing Director: Jennifer Newens
Design & Production: Rachel Lopez Metzger
Project Manager: Micaela Clark
Typesetting: Westchester Publishing Services

Contents

I

Introduces Ambler Jevons

Ah! You don't take the matter at all seriously!" I observed, a trifle annoyed.

"Why should I?" asked my friend, Ambler Jevons, with a deep pull at his well-coloured briar. "What you've told me shows quite plainly that you have in the first place viewed one little circumstance with suspicion, then brooded over it until it has become magnified and now occupies your whole mind. Take my advice, old chap, and think nothing more about it. Why should you make yourself miserable for no earthly reason? You're a rising man—hard up like most of us—but under old Eyton's wing you've got a brilliant future before you. Unlike myself, a mere nobody, struggling against the tide of adversity, you're already a long way up the medical ladder. If you climb straight you'll end with an appointment of Physician-in-Ordinary and a knighthood thrown in as makeweight. Old Macalister used to prophesy it, you remember, when we were up at Edinburgh. Therefore, I can't, for the life of me, discover any cause why you should allow yourself to have these touches of the blues—unless it's liver, or some other internal organ about which you know a lot more than I do. Why, man, you've got the whole world before you, and as for Ethelwynn—"

"Ethelwynn!" I exclaimed, starting up from my chair. "Leave her out of the question! We need not discuss her," and I walked to the mantelshelf to light a fresh cigarette.

"As you wish, my dear fellow," said my merry, easy-going friend. "I merely wish to point out the utter folly of all this suspicion."

"I don't suspect her," I snapped.

"I didn't suggest that." Then, after a pause during which he smoked on vigorously, he suddenly asked, "Well now, be frank, Ralph, whom do you really suspect?"

I was silent. Truth to tell, his question entirely nonplussed me. I had suspicions—distinct suspicions—that certain persons surrounding me were acting in accord towards some sinister end, but which of those persons were culpable I certainly could not determine. It was that very circumstance which was puzzling me to the point of distraction.

"Ah!" I replied. "That's the worst of it. I know that the whole affair seems quite absurd, but I must admit that I can't fix suspicion upon anyone in particular."

Jevons laughed outright.

"In that case, my dear Boyd, you ought really to see the folly of the thing."

"Perhaps I ought, but I don't," I answered, facing him with my back to the fire. "To you, my most intimate friend, I've explained, in strictest confidence, the matter which is puzzling me. I live in hourly dread of some catastrophe the nature of which I'm utterly at a loss to determine. Can you define intuition?"

My question held him in pensive silence. His manner changed as he looked me straight in the face. Unlike his usual careless self—for his was a curious character of the semi-Bohemian order and Savage Club type—he grew serious and thoughtful, regarding me with critical gaze after removing his pipe from his lips.

"Well," he exclaimed at last. "I'll tell you what it is, Boyd. This intuition, or whatever you may call it, is an infernally bad thing for you. I'm your friend—one of your best and most devoted friends, old chap—and if there's anything in it, I'll render you whatever help I can."

"Thank you, Ambler," I said gratefully, taking his hand. "I have told you all this to-night in order to enlist your sympathy, although I scarcely liked to ask your aid. Your life is a busy one—busier even than my own, perhaps—and you have no desire to be bothered with my personal affairs."

"On the contrary, old fellow," he said. "Remember that in mystery I'm in my element."

"I know," I replied. "But at present there is no mystery—only suspicion."

What Ambler Jevons had asserted was a fact. He was an investigator of mysteries, making it his hobby just as other men take to collecting curios or pictures. About his personal appearance there was nothing very remarkable. When pre-occupied he had an abrupt, rather brusque manner, but at all other times he was a very easy-going man of the world, possessor of an ample income left him by his aunt, and this he augmented by carrying on, in partnership with an elder man, a profitable tea-blending business in Mark Lane.

He had entered the tea trade not because of necessity, but because he considered it a bad thing for a man to lead an idle life. Nevertheless, the chief object of his existence had always seemed to be the unravelling of mysteries of police and crime. Surely few men, even those professional investigators at Scotland Yard, held such a record of successes. He was a born detective, with a keen scent for clues, an ingenuity that was marvellous, and a patience and endurance that were inexhaustible. At Scotland Yard the name of Ambler Jevons had for several years been synonymous with all that is clever and astute in the art of detecting crime.

To be a good criminal investigator a man must be born such. He must be physically strong; he must be untiring in his search after truth; he must be able to scent a mystery as a hound does a fox, to follow up the trail with energy unflagging, and seize opportunities without hesitation; he must possess a cool presence of mind, and above all be able to calmly distinguish the facts which are of importance in the strengthening of the clue from those that are merely superfluous. All these, besides other qualities, are necessary for the successful penetration of criminal mysteries; hence it is that the average amateur, who takes up the hobby without any natural instinct, is invariably a blunderer.

Ambler Jevons, blender of teas and investigator of mysteries, was lolling back in my armchair, his dreamy eyes half-closed, smoking on in silence.

Myself, I was thirty-three, and I fear not much of an ornament to the medical profession. True, at Edinburgh I had taken my M.B. and C.M. with highest honours, and three years later had graduated M.D., but my friends thought a good deal more of my success than I did, for they overlooked my shortcomings and magnified my talents.

I suppose it was because my father had represented a county constituency in the House of Commons, and therefore I possessed that very useful advantage which is vaguely termed family influence, that I had been appointed assistant physician at Guy's. My own practice was very small, therefore I devilled, as the lawyers would term it, for my chief, Sir Bernard Eyton, knight, the consulting physician to my hospital.

Sir Bernard, whom all the smart world of London knew as the first specialist in nervous disorders, had his professional headquarters in Harley Street, but lived down at Hove, in order to avoid night work or the calls which Society made upon him. I lived a stone's-throw away from his house in Harley Street, just round the corner in Harley Place, and it was my duty to take charge of his extensive practice during his absence at night or while on holidays.

I must here declare that my own position was not at all disagreeable. True, I sometimes had night work, which is never very pleasant, but being one of the evils of the life of every medical man he accepts it as such. I had very comfortable bachelor quarters in an ancient and rather grimy house, with an old fashioned dark-panelled sitting-room, a dining-room, bedroom and dressing-room, and, save for the fact that I was compelled to be on duty after four o'clock, when Sir Bernard drove to Victoria Station, my time in the evening was very much my own.

Many a man would, I suppose, have envied me. It is not every day that a first-class physician requires an assistant, and certainly no man could have been more generous and kindly disposed than Sir Bernard himself, even though his character was something of the miser. Yet all of us find some petty shortcomings in the good things of this world, and I was no exception. Sometimes I grumbled, but generally, be it said, without much cause.

Truth to tell, a mysterious feeling of insecurity had been gradually creeping upon me through several months; indeed ever since I had returned from a holiday in Scotland in the spring. I could not define it, not really knowing what had excited the curious apprehensions within me. Nevertheless, I had that night told my secret to Ambler Jevons, who was often my visitor of an evening, and over our whiskies had asked his advice, with the unsatisfactory result which I have already written down.

II

"A Very Ugly Secret"

The consulting-room in Harley Street, where Sir Bernard Eyton saw his patients and gathered in his guineas for his ill-scribbled prescriptions, differed little from a hundred others in the same severe and depressing thoroughfare.

It was a very sombre apartment. The walls were painted dark green and hung with two or three old portraits in oils; the furniture was of a style long past, heavy and covered in brown morocco, and the big writing-table, behind which the great doctor would sit blinking at his patient through the circular gold-rimmed glasses, that gave him a somewhat Teutonic appearance, was noted for its prim neatness and orderly array. On the one side was an adjustable couch; on the other a bookcase with glass doors containing a number of instruments which were, however, not visible because of curtains of green silk behind the glass.

Into that room, on three days a week, Ford, the severely respectable footman, ushered in patients one after the other, many of them Society women suffering from what is known in these degenerate days as "nerves." Indeed, Eyton was *par excellence* a ladies' doctor, for so many of the gentler sex get burnt up in the mad rush of a London season.

I had made up my mind to consult my chief, and with that object entered his room on the following afternoon at a quarter before four.

"Well, Boyd, anything fresh?" he asked, putting off his severely professional air and lolling back in his padded writing-chair as I entered.

"No, nothing," I responded, throwing myself in the patient's chair opposite him and tossing my gloves on the table. "A hard day down at the hospital, that's all. You've been busy as usual, I suppose."

"Busy!" the old man echoed, "why, these confounded women never let me alone for a single instant! Always the same story—excitement, late hours, little worries over erring husbands, and all that sort of thing. I always know what's coming as soon as they get seated and settled. I really don't know what Society's coming to, Boyd," and he blinked over at me through his heavy-framed spectacles.

About sixty, of middle height, he was slightly inclined to rotundity, with hair almost white, a stubbly grey beard, and a pair of keen eyes rather prominently set in a bony but not unpleasant countenance. He had a peculiar habit of stroking his left ear when puzzled, and was not without those little eccentricities which run hand in hand with genius. One of them was his fondness for amateur theatricals, for he was a leading member of the Dramatic Club at Hove and nearly always took part in the performances. But he was a pronounced miser. Each day when he arrived at Victoria Station from Hove, he purchased three ham sandwiches at the refreshment bar and carried them in his black bag to Harley Street. He there concealed them in a drawer in the writing-table and stealthily ate them instead of taking half-an-hour for luncheon. Sometimes he sent Ford out to the nearest greengrocer's in the Marylebone Road for a penny apple, which he surreptitiously ate as dessert.

Indeed, he was finishing his last sandwich when I entered, and his mouth was full.

It may have been that small fact which caused me to hesitate. At any rate, sitting there with those big round eyes peering forth upon me, I felt the absurdity of the situation.

Presently, when he had finished his sandwich, carefully brushed the crumbs from his blotting-pad and cast the bag into the waste-paper basket, he raised his head and with his big eyes again blinking through his spectacles, said:

"You've had no call to poor old Courtenay, I suppose?"

"No," I responded. "Why?"

"Because he's in a bad way."

"Worse?"

"Yes," he replied. "I'm rather anxious about him. He'll have to keep to his bed, I fear."

I did not in the least doubt this. Old Mr. Henry Courtenay, one of the Devonshire Courtenays, a very wealthy if somewhat eccentric old gentleman, lived in one of those prim, pleasant, detached houses in Richmond Road, facing Kew Gardens, and was one of Sir Bernard's best patients. He had been under him for a number of years until they had become personal friends. One of his eccentricities was to insist on paying heavy fees to his medical adviser, believing, perhaps, that by so doing he would secure greater and more careful attention.

But, strangely enough, mention of the name suddenly gave me the clue so long wanting. It aroused within me a sense of impending evil regarding the very man of whom we were speaking. The sound of the name seemed to strike the sympathetic chord within my brain, and I at once became cognisant that the unaccountable presage of impending misfortune was connected with that rather incongruous household down at Kew.

Therefore, when Sir Bernard imparted to me his misgivings, I was quickly on the alert, and questioned him regarding the progress of old Mr. Courtenay's disease.

"The poor fellow is sinking, I'm afraid, Boyd," exclaimed my chief, confidentially. "He doesn't believe himself half so ill as he is. When did you see him last?"

"Only a few days ago. I thought he seemed much improved," I said.

"Ah! of course," the old doctor snapped; his manner towards me in an instant changed. "You're a frequent visitor there, I forgot. Feminine attraction and all that sort of thing. Dangerous, Boyd! Dangerous to run after a woman of her sort. I'm an older man than you. Why haven't you taken the hint I gave you long ago?"

"Because I could see no reason why I should not continue my friendship with Ethelwynn Mivart."

"My dear Boyd," he responded, in a sympathetic fatherly manner, which he sometimes assumed, "I'm an old bachelor, and I see quite sufficient of women in this room—too much of them, in fact. The majority are utterly worthless. Recollect that I have never taken away a woman's character yet, and I refuse to do so now—especially to her lover. I merely warn you, Boyd, to drop her. That's all. If you don't, depend upon it you'll regret it."

"Then there's some secret or other of her past which she conceals, I suppose?" I said hoarsely, feeling confident that being so intimate with his patient, old Mr. Courtenay, he had discovered it.

"Yes," he replied, blinking again at me through his glasses. "There is—a very ugly secret."

III

The Courtenays

I determined to spend that evening at Richmond Road with open eyes. The house was a large red-brick one, modern, gabled, and typically suburban. Mr. Courtenay, although a wealthy man with a large estate in Devonshire and extensive properties in Canada, where as a young man he had amassed a large fortune, lived in that London suburb in order to be near his old friends. Besides, his wife was young and objected to being buried in the country. With her husband an invalid she was unable to entertain, therefore she had found the country dull very soon after her marriage and gladly welcomed removal to London, even though they sank their individuality in becoming suburban residents.

Short, the prim manservant, who admitted me, showed me at once up to his master's room, and I stayed for half-an-hour with him. He was sitting before the fire in a padded dressing gown, a rather thick-set figure with grey hair, wan cheeks, and bright eyes. The hand he gave me was chill and bony, yet I saw plainly that he was much better than when I had last seen him. He was up, and that was a distinctly good sign. I examined him, questioned him, and as far as I could make out he was, contrary to my chief's opinion, very much improved.

Indeed, he spoke quite gaily, offered me a whisky and soda, and made me tell him the stories I had heard an hour earlier at the Savage. The poor old fellow was suffering from that most malignant disease, cancer of the tongue, which had caused him to develop peripheral neuritis. His doctors had recommended an operation, but knowing it to be a very serious one he had declined it, and as he had suffered great pain and inconvenience he had taken to drink heavily. He was a lonely man, and I often pitied him. A doctor can very quickly tell whether domestic felicity reigns in a household, and I had long ago seen that with the difference of age between Mrs. Courtenay and her husband—he sixty-two and she only twenty-nine—they had but few ideas in common.

That she nursed him tenderly I was well aware, but from her manner I had long ago detected that her devotedness was only assumed in order to humour him, and that she possessed little or no real affection for him. Nor was it much wonder, after all. A smart young woman, fond of society and amusement, is never the kind of wife for a snappy invalid of old Courtenay's type. She had married him, some five years before, for his money, her uncharitable enemies said. Perhaps that was so. In any case it was difficult to believe that a pretty woman of her stamp could ever entertain any genuine affection for a man of his age, and it was most certainly true that whatever bond of sympathy had existed between them at the time of their marriage had now been snapped.

Instead of remaining at home of an evening and posing as a dutiful wife as she once had done, she was now in the habit of going up to town to her friends the Penn-Pagets, who lived in Brook Street, or the Hennikers in Redcliffe Square, accompanying them to dances and theatres with all the defiance of the "covenances" allowed nowadays to the married woman. On such occasions, growing each week more frequent, her sister Ethelwynn remained at home to see that Mr. Courtenay was properly attended to by the nurse, and exhibited a patience that I could not help but admire.

Yes, the more I reflected upon it the more curious seemed that ill-assorted *ménage*. On her marriage Mary Mivart had declared that her new home in Devonshire was deadly dull, and had induced her indulgent husband to allow her sister to come and live with her, and Ethelwynn and her maid had formed part of the household ever since.

We doctors, providing we have not a brass plate in lieu of a practice, see some queer things, and being in the confidence of our patients, know of many strange and incomprehensible families. The one at Richmond Road was a case in point. I had gradually seen how young Mrs. Courtenay had tired of her wifely duties, until, by slow degrees, she had cast off the shackles altogether—until she now thought more of her new frocks, smart suppers at the Carlton, first-nights and "shows" in Mayfair than she did of the poor suffering old man whom she had not so long ago vowed to "love, honour and obey." It was to be regretted, but in my position I had no necessity nor inclination to interfere. Even Ethelwynn made no remark, although this sudden breaking forth of her sister must have pained her considerably.

When at length I shook hands with my patient, left him in the hands of the nurse and descended to the drawing room, I found Ethelwynn awaiting me.

She rose and came forward, both her slim white hands outstretched in glad welcome.

"Short told me you were here," she exclaimed. "What a long time you have been upstairs. Nothing serious, I hope," she added with a touch of anxiety, I thought.

"Nothing at all," I assured her, walking with her across to the fire and seating myself in the cosy-corner, while she threw herself upon a low lounge chair and pillowed her dark head upon a big cushion of yellow silk. "Where is Mary?" I asked.

"Out. She's dining with the Hennikers to-night, I think."

"And leaves you at home to look after the invalid?" I remarked.

"Oh, I don't mind in the least," she declared, laughing.

"And the old gentleman? What does he say to her constant absence in the evening?"

"Well, to tell the truth, Ralph, he seldom knows. He usually believes her to be at home, and I never undeceive him. Why should I?"

I grunted, for I was not at all well pleased with her connivance at her sister's deceit. The sound that escaped my lips caused her to glance across at me in quick surprise.

"You are displeased, dear," she said. "Tell me why. What have I done?"

"I'm not displeased with you," I declared. "Only, as you know, I'm not in favour of deception, and especially so in a wife."

She pursed her lips, and I thought her face went a trifle paler. She was silent for a moment, then said:

"I don't see why we should discuss that, Ralph. Mary's actions concern neither of us. It is not for us to prevent her amusing herself, neither is it our duty to create unpleasantness between husband and wife."

I did not reply, but sat looking at her, drinking in her beauty in a long, full draught. How can I describe her? Her form was graceful in every line; her face perfect in its contour, open, finely-moulded, and with a marvellous complexion—a calm, sweet countenance that reminded one of Raphael's "Madonna" in Florence, indeed almost its counterpart. Her beauty had been remarked everywhere. She had sat to a well-known R.A. for his Academy picture two years before, and the artist had declared her to be one of the most perfect types of English beauty.

Was it any wonder, then, that I was in love with her? Was it any wonder that those wonderful dark eyes held me beneath their spell, or those dark locks that I sometimes stroked from off her fair white brow should be to me the most beautiful in all the world? Man is but mortal, and a beautiful woman always enchants.

WILLIAM LE QUEUX

As she sat before me in her evening gown of some flimsy cream stuff, all frills and furbelows, she seemed perfect in her loveliness. The surroundings suited her to perfection—the old Chippendale and the palms, while the well-shaded electric lamp in its wrought-iron stand shed a mellow glow upon her, softening her features and harmonising the tints of the objects around. From beneath the hem of her skirt a neat ankle encased in its black silk stocking was thrust coquettishly forward, and her tiny patent leather slipper was stretched out to the warmth of the fire. Her pose was, however, restful and natural. She loved luxury, and made no secret of it. The hour after dinner was always her hour of laziness, and she usually spent it in that self-same chair, in that self-same position.

She was twenty-five, the youngest daughter of old Thomas Mivart, who was squire of Neneford, in Northamptonshire, a well-known hunting-man of his day, who had died two years ago leaving a widow, a charming lady, who lived alone at the Manor. To me it had always been a mystery why the craving for gaiety and amusement had never seized Ethelwynn. She was by far the more beautiful of the pair, the smartest in dress, and the wittier in speech, for possessed of a keen sense of humour, she was interesting as well as handsome—the two qualities which are *par excellence* necessary for a woman to attain social success.

She stirred slightly as she broke the silence, and then I detected in her a nervousness which I had not noticed on first entering the room.

"Sir Bernard Eyton was down here yesterday and spent over an hour with the old gentleman. They sent the nurse out of the room and talked together for a long time, upon some private business, nurse thinks. When Sir Bernard came down he told me in confidence that Mr. Courtenay was distinctly weaker."

"Yes," I said, "Sir Bernard told me that, but I must confess that to-night I find a decided improvement in him. He's sitting up quite lively."

"Very different to a month ago," my well-beloved remarked. "Do you recollect when Short went to London in a hansom and brought you down at three in the morning?"

"I gave up all hope when I saw him on that occasion," I said; "but he certainly seems to have taken a new lease of life."

"Do you think he really has?" she inquired with an undisguised eagerness which struck me as distinctly curious. "Do you believe that Sir Bernard's fears are after all ungrounded?"

I looked at her surprised. She had never before evinced such a keen interest in her sister's husband, and I was puzzled.

"I really can't give an opinion," I responded mechanically, for want of something or other to say.

It was curious, that question of hers—very curious.

Yet after all I was in love—and all lovers are fools in their jealousy.

IV

A Night Call

"Do you know, Ralph," she faltered presently, "I have a faint suspicion that you are annoyed about something. What is it? Be frank now and tell me."

"Annoyed?" I laughed. "Not at all, dearest. Nervous and impatient, perhaps. You must make allowances for me. A doctor's life is full of professional worries. I've had a trying day at the hospital, and I suppose I'm quarrelsome—eh?"

"No, not quarrelsome, but just inclined to be a little suspicious."

"Suspicious? Of what?"

Her woman's power of penetration to the innermost secrets of the heart was marvellous.

"Of me?"

"How absurd!" I exclaimed. "Why should I be suspicious—and of what?"

"Well," she laughed, "I really don't know, only your manner is peculiar. Why not be frank with me, Ralph, dear, and tell me what it is that you don't like. Have I offended you?"

"Not at all, darling," I hastened to assure her. "Why, you're the best little woman in the world. Offend me—how absurd!"

"Then who has offended you?"

I hesitated. When a woman really loves, a man can have but few secrets from her. Ethelwynn always read me like an open book.

"I'm worried over a critical case," I said, in an endeavour to evade her question.

"But your patients don't annoy you, surely," she exclaimed. "There is a distinction between annoyance and worry."

I saw that she had detected my suspicion, and at once hastened to reassure her that she had my entire confidence.

"If Mary finds her life a trifle dull with her husband it is surely no reason why I should be blamed for it," she said, in a tone of mild complaint.

"No, you entirely misunderstand me," I said. "No blame whatever attaches to you. Your sister's actions are no affair of ours. It is merely a pity that she cannot see her error. With her husband lying ill she should at least remain at home."

"She declares that she has suffered martyrdom for his sake long enough," my well-beloved said. "Perhaps she is right, for between ourselves the old gentleman is a terrible trial."

"That is only to be expected from one suffering from such a disease. Yet it can serve no excuse for his wife taking up with that gay set, the Penn-Pagets and the Hennikers. I must say I'm very surprised."

"And so am I, Ralph. But what can I do? I'm utterly powerless. She is mistress here, and does exactly as she likes. The old gentleman dotes on her and allows her to have her way in everything. She has ever been wilful, even from a child."

She did not attempt to shield her sister, and yet she uttered no condemnation of her conduct. I could not, even then, understand the situation. To me one of two things was apparent. Either she feared to displease her sister because of some power the latter held over her, or this neglect of old Mr. Courtenay was pleasing to her.

"I wonder you don't give Mary a hint that her conduct is being noticed and remarked upon. Of course, don't say that I've spoken of it. Merely put it to her in the manner of a vague suggestion."

"Very well, if you wish it," she responded promptly, for she was ever ready to execute my smallest desire.

"And you love me quite as truly and as well as you did a year ago?" I asked, eagerly, stroking the dark tendrils from her white brow.

"Love you?" she echoed. "Yes, Ralph," she went on, looking up into my face with unwavering gaze. "I may be distrait and pre-occupied sometimes, but, nevertheless, I swear to you, as I did on that summer's evening long ago when we were boating together at Shepperton, that you are the only man I have ever loved—or shall ever love."

I returned her caress with a passion that was heartfelt. I was devoted to her, and these tender words of hers confirmed my belief in her truth and purity.

"Need I repeat what I have told you so many times, dearest?" I asked, in a low voice, as her head rested upon my shoulder and she stood in my embrace. "Need I tell you how fondly I love you—how that I am entirely yours? No. You are mine, Ethelwynn—mine."

"And you will never think ill of me?" she asked, in a faltering tone. "You will never be suspicious of me as you have been to-night? You cannot tell how all this upsets me. Perfect love surely demands perfect confidence. And our love is perfect—is it not?"

"It is," I cried. "It is. Forgive me, dearest. Forgive me for my churlish conduct to-night. It is my fault—all my fault. I love you, and have every confidence in you."

"But will your love last always?" she asked, with just a tinge of doubt in her voice.

"Yes, always," I declared.

"No matter what may happen?" she asked.

"No matter what may happen."

I kissed her fervently with warm words of passionate devotion upon my lips, and went forth into the rainy winter's night with my suspicions swept away and with love renewed within me.

I had been foolish in my suspicions and apprehensions, and hated myself for it. Her sweet devotedness to me was sufficient proof of her honesty. I was not wealthy by any means, and I knew that if she chose she could, with her notable beauty, captivate a rich husband without much difficulty. Husbands are only unattainable by the blue-stocking, the flirt and the personally angular.

The rain pelted down in torrents as I walked to Kew Gardens Station, and as it generally happens to the unlucky doctor that calls are made upon him in the most inclement weather, I found, on returning to Harley Place, that Lady Langley, in Hill Street, had sent a message asking me to go round at once. I was therefore compelled to pay the visit, for her ladyship—a snappy old dowager—was a somewhat exacting patient of Sir Bernard's.

She was a fussy old person who believed herself to be much worse than she really was, and it was, therefore, not until past one o'clock that I smoked my final pipe, drained my peg, and retired to bed, full of recollections of my well-beloved.

Just before turning in my man brought me a telegram from Sir Bernard, dispatched from Brighton, regarding a case to be seen on the following day. He was very erratic about telegrams and sent them to me at all hours, therefore it was no extraordinary circumstance. He always preferred telegraphing to writing letters. I read the message, tossed it with its envelope upon the fire, and then retired with a fervent hope that I should at least be allowed to have a complete night's rest. Sir Bernard's patients were, however, of that class who call the doctor at any hour for the slightest attack of indigestion, and summonses at night were consequently very frequent.

I suppose I had been in bed a couple of hours when I was awakened by the electric bell sounding in my man's room, and a few minutes later he entered, saying:—

"There's a man who wants to see you immediately, sir. He says he's from Mr. Courtenay's, down at Kew."

"Mr. Courtenay's!" I echoed, sitting up in bed. "Bring him in here."

A few moments later the caller was shown in.

"Why, Short!" I exclaimed. "What's the matter?"

"Matter, doctor," the man stammered. "It's awful, sir!"

"What's awful?"

"My poor master, sir. He's dead—he's been murdered!"

V

Discloses a Mystery

The man's amazing announcement held me speechless.

"Murdered!" I cried when I found tongue. "Impossible!"

"Ah! sir, it's too true. He's quite dead."

"But surely he has died from natural causes—eh?"

"No, sir. My poor master has been foully murdered."

"How do you know that?" I asked breathlessly. "Tell me all the facts."

I saw by the man's agitation, his white face, and the hurried manner in which he had evidently dressed to come in search of me, that something tragic had really occurred.

"We know nothing yet, sir," was his quick response. "I entered his room at two o'clock, as usual, to see if he wanted anything, and saw that he was quite still, apparently asleep. The lamp was turned low, but as I looked over the bed I saw a small dark patch upon the sheet. This I discovered to be blood, and a moment later was horrified to discover a small wound close to the heart, and from it the blood was slowly oozing."

"Then he's been stabbed, you think?" I gasped, springing up and beginning to dress myself hastily.

"We think so, sir. It's awful!"

"Terrible!" I said, utterly dumbfounded by the man's amazing story. "After you made the discovery, how did you act?"

"I awoke the nurse, who slept in the room adjoining. And then we aroused Miss Mivart. The shock to her was terrible, poor young lady. When she saw the body of the old gentleman she burst into tears, and at once sent me to you. I didn't find a cab till I'd walked almost to Hammersmith, and then I came straight on here."

"But is there undoubtedly foul play, Short?"

"No doubt whatever, sir. I'm nothing of a doctor, but I could see the wound plainly, like a small clean cut just under the heart."

"No weapon about?"

"I didn't see anything, sir."

"Have you called the police?"

"No, sir. Miss Mivart said she would wait until you arrived. She wants your opinion."

"And Mrs. Courtenay. How does she bear the tragedy?"

"The poor lady doesn't know yet."

"Doesn't know? Haven't you told her?"

"No, sir. She's not at home."

"What? She hasn't returned?"

"No, sir," responded the man.

That fact was in itself peculiar. Yet there was, I felt sure, some strong reason if young Mrs. Courtenay remained the night with her friends, the Hennikers. Trains run to Kew after the theatres, but she had possibly missed the last, and had been induced by her friends to remain the night with them in town.

Yet the whole of the tragic affair was certainly very extraordinary. It was Short's duty to rise at two o'clock each morning and go to his master's room to ascertain if the invalid wanted anything. Generally, however, the old gentleman slept well, hence there had been no necessity for a night nurse.

When I entered the cab, and the man having taken a seat beside me, we had set out on our long night drive to Kew, I endeavoured to obtain more details regarding the Courtenay *ménage*. In an ordinary way I could scarcely have questioned a servant regarding his master and mistress, but on this drive I saw an occasion to obtain knowledge, and seized it.

Short, although a well-trained servant, was communicative. The shock he had sustained in discovering his master made him so.

After ten years' service he was devoted to his master, but from the remarks he let drop during our drive I detected that he entertained a strong dislike of the old gentleman's young wife. He was, of course, well aware of my affection for Ethelwynn, and carefully concealed his antipathy towards her, an antipathy which I somehow felt convinced existed. He regarded both sisters with equal mistrust.

"Does your mistress often remain in town with her friends at night?"

"Sometimes, when she goes to balls."

"And is that often?"

"Not very often."

"And didn't the old gentleman know of his wife's absence?"

"Sometimes. He used to ask me whether Mrs. Courtenay was at home, and then I was bound to tell the truth."

By his own admission then, this man Short had informed the invalid of his wife's frequent absences. He was an informer, and as such most probably the enemy of both Mary and Ethelwynn. I knew him to be the confidential servant of the old gentleman, but had not before suspected him of tale-telling. Without doubt Mrs. Courtenay's recent neglect had sorely grieved the old gentleman. He doted upon her, indulged her in every whim and fancy and, like many an aged husband who has a smart young wife, dared not to differ from her or complain of any of her actions. There is a deal of truth in the adage, "There's no fool like an old fool."

But the mystery was increasing, and as we drove together down that long interminable high road through Hammersmith to Chiswick, wet, dark and silent at that hour, I reflected that the strange presage of insecurity which had so long oppressed me was actually being fulfilled. Ambler Jevons had laughed at it. But would he laugh now? To-morrow, without doubt, he would be working at the mystery in the interests of justice. To try to keep the affair out of the Press would, I knew too well, be impossible. Those men, in journalistic parlance called "liners," are everywhere, hungry for copy, and always eager to seize upon anything tragic or mysterious.

From Short I gathered a few additional details. Not many, be it said, but sufficient to make it quite clear that he was intensely antagonistic towards his mistress. This struck me as curious, for as far as I had seen she had always treated him with the greatest kindness and consideration, had given him holidays, and to my knowledge had, a few months before, raised his wages of her own accord. Nevertheless, the *ménage* was a strange one, incongruous in every respect.

My chief thoughts were, however, with my love. The shock to her must, I knew, be terrible, especially as Mary was absent and she was alone with the nurse and servants.

When I sprang from the cab and entered the house she met me in the hall. She had dressed hastily and wore a light shawl over her head, probably to conceal her disordered hair, but her face was blanched to the lips.

"Oh, Ralph!" she cried in a trembling voice. "I thought you were never coming. It's terrible—terrible!"

"Come in here," I said, leading her into the dining room. "Tell me all you know of the affair."

"Short discovered him just after two o'clock. He was then quite still."

"But there may be life," I exclaimed suddenly, and leaving her I rushed up the stairs and into the room where the old man had chatted to me so merrily not many hours before.

The instant my gaze fell upon him I knew the truth. Cadaveric rigidity had supervened, and he had long been beyond hope of human aid. His furrowed face was as white as ivory, and his lower jaw had dropped in that manner that unmistakably betrays the presence of death.

As the man had described, the sheet was stained with blood. But there was not much, and I was some moments before I discovered the wound. It was just beneath the heart, cleanly cut, and about three-quarters of an inch long, evidently inflicted by some sharp instrument. He had no doubt been struck in his sleep, and with such precision that he had died without being able to raise the alarm.

The murderer, whoever he was, had carried the weapon away.

I turned and saw Ethelwynn, a pale wan figure in her light gown and shawl, standing on the threshold, watching me intently. She stood there white and trembling, as though fearing to enter the presence of the dead.

I made a hasty tour of the room, examining the window and finding it fastened. As far as I could discover, nothing whatever was disturbed.

Then I went out to her and, closing the door behind me, said—

"Short must go along to the police station. We must report it."

"But is it really necessary?" she asked anxiously. "Think of the awful exposure in the papers. Can't we hush it up? Do, Ralph—for my sake," she implored.

"But I can't give a death certificate when a person has been murdered," I explained. "Before burial there must be a *post-mortem* and an inquest."

"Then you think he has actually been murdered?"

"Of course, without a doubt. It certainly isn't suicide."

The discovery had caused her to become rigid, almost statuesque. Sudden terror often acts thus upon women of her highly nervous temperament. She allowed me to lead her downstairs and back to the dining room. On the way I met Short in the hall, and ordered him to go at once to the police station.

"Now, dearest," I said, taking her hand tenderly in mine when we were alone together with the door closed, "tell me calmly all you know of this awful affair."

"I—I know nothing," she declared. "Nothing except what you already know. Short knocked at my door and I dressed hastily, only to discover that the poor old gentleman was dead."

"Was the house still locked up?"

"I believe so. The servants could, I suppose, tell that."

"But is it not strange that Mary is still absent?" I remarked, perplexed.

"No, not very. Sometimes she has missed her last train and has stopped the night with the Penn-Pagets or the Hennikers. It is difficult, she says, to go to supper after the theatre and catch the last train. It leaves Charing Cross so early."

Again there seemed a distinct inclination on her part to shield her sister.

"The whole thing is a most profound mystery," she went on. "I must have slept quite lightly, for I heard the church clock strike each quarter until one o'clock, yet not an unusual sound reached me. Neither did nurse hear anything."

Nurse Kate was an excellent woman whom I had known at Guy's through several years. Both Sir Bernard and myself had every confidence in her, and she had been the invalid's attendant for the past two years.

"It certainly is a mystery—one which we must leave to the police to investigate. In the meantime, however, we must send Short to Redcliffe Square to find Mary. He must not tell her the truth, but merely say that her husband is much worse. To tell her of the tragedy at once would probably prove too great a blow."

"She ought never to have gone to town and left him," declared my well-beloved in sudden condemnation of her sister's conduct. "She will never forgive herself."

"Regrets will not bring the poor fellow to life again," I said with a sigh. "We must act, and act promptly, in order to discover the identity of the murderer and the motive of the crime. That there is a motive is certain; yet it is indeed strange that anyone should actually kill a man suffering from a disease which, in a few months at most, must prove fatal. The motive was therefore his immediate decease, and that fact will probably greatly assist the police in their investigations."

"But who could have killed him?"

"Ah! that's the mystery. If, as you believe, the house was found to be still secured when the alarm was raised, then it would appear that someone who slept beneath this roof was guilty."

"Oh! Impossible! Remember there are only myself and the servants. You surely don't suspect either of them?"

"I have no suspicion of anyone at present," I answered. "Let the police search the place, and they may discover something which will furnish them with a clue."

I noticed some telegraph-forms in the stationery rack on a small writing-table, and taking one scribbled a couple of lines to Sir Bernard, at Hove, informing him of the mysterious affair. This I folded and placed in my pocket in readiness for the re-opening of the telegraph office at eight o'clock.

Shortly afterwards we heard the wheels of the cab outside, and a few minutes later were joined by a police inspector in uniform and an officer in plain clothes.

In a few brief sentences I explained to them the tragic circumstances, and then led them upstairs to the dead man's room.

After a cursory glance around, they went forth again out upon the landing in order to await the arrival of two other plain-clothes officers who had come round on foot, one of them the sergeant of the Criminal Investigation Department attached to the Kew station. Then, after giving orders to the constable on the beat to station himself at the door and allow no one to enter or leave without permission, the three detectives and the inspector entered the room where the dead man lay.

VI

In Which I Make a Discovery

Having explained who I was, I followed the men in and assisted them in making a careful and minute examination of the place.

Search for the weapon with which the crime had been committed proved fruitless; hence it was plain that the murderer had carried it away. There were no signs whatever of a struggle, and nothing to indicate that the blow had been struck by any burglar with a motive of silencing the prostrate man.

The room was a large front one on the first floor, with two French windows opening upon a balcony formed by the big square portico. Both were found to be secured, not only by the latches, but also by long screws as an extra precaution against thieves, old Mr. Courtenay, like many other elderly people, being extremely nervous of midnight intruders. The bedroom itself was well furnished in genuine Sheraton, which he had brought up from his palatial home in Devonshire, for the old man denied himself no personal comfort. The easy chair in which he had sat when I had paid my visit was still in its place at the fireside, with the footstool just as he had left it; the drawers which we opened one after another showed no sign of having been rummaged, and the sum result of our investigations was absolutely *nil*.

"It looks very much as though someone in the house had done it," whispered the inspector seriously to me, having first glanced at the door to ascertain that it was closed.

"Yes," I admitted, "appearances certainly do point to that."

"Who was the young lady who met us downstairs?" inquired the detective sergeant, producing a small note-book and pencil.

"Miss Ethelwynn Mivart, sister to Mrs. Courtenay."

"And is Mrs. Courtenay at home?" he inquired, making a note of the name.

"No. We have sent for her. She's staying with friends in London."

"Hulloa! There's an iron safe here!" exclaimed one of the men rummaging at the opposite side of the room. He had pulled away a chest of drawers from the wall, revealing what I had never noticed before, the door of a small fireproof safe built into the wall.

"Is it locked?" inquired the inspector.

The man, after trying the knob and examining the keyhole, replied in the affirmative.

"Keeps his deeds and jewellery there, I suppose," remarked one of the other detectives. "He seems to have been very much afraid of burglars. I wonder whether he had any reason for that?"

"Like many old men he was a trifle eccentric," I replied. "Thieves once broke into his country house years ago, I believe, and he therefore entertained a horror of them."

We all examined the keyhole of the safe, but there was certainly no evidence to show that it had been tampered with. On the contrary, the little oval brass plate which closed the hole was rusty, and had not apparently been touched for weeks.

While they were searching in other parts of the room I directed my attention to the position and appearance of my late patient. He was lying on his right side with one arm slightly raised in quite a natural attitude for one sleeping. His features, although the pallor of death was upon them and they were relaxed, showed no sign of suffering. The blow had been unerring, and had no doubt penetrated to the heart. The crime had been committed swiftly, and the murderer had escaped unseen and unheard.

The eider-down quilt, a rich one of Gobelin blue satin, had scarcely been disturbed, and save for the small spot of blood upon the sheet, traces of a terrible crime were in no way apparent.

While, however, I stood at the bedside, at the same spot most probably where the murderer had stood, I suddenly felt something uneven between the sole of my boot and the carpet. So intent was I upon the examination I was making that at first my attention was not attracted by it, but on stepping on it a second time I looked down and saw something white, which I quickly picked up.

The instant I saw it I closed my hand and hid it from view.

Then I glanced furtively around, and seeing that my action had been unobserved I quickly transferred it to my vest pocket, covering the movement by taking out my watch to glance at it.

I confess that my heart beat quickly, and in all probability the colour at that moment had left my face, for I had, by sheer accident, discovered a clue.

To examine it there was impossible, for of such a character was it that I had no intention, as yet, to arouse the suspicions of the police.

WILLIAM LE QUEUX

I intended at the earliest moment to apprise my friend, Ambler Jevons, of the facts and with him pursue an entirely independent inquiry.

Scarcely had I safely pocketed the little object I had picked up from where the murderer must have stood when the inspector went out upon the landing and called to the constable in the hall:

"Four-sixty-two, lock that door and come up here a moment."

"Yes, sir," answered a gruff voice from below, and in a few moments the constable entered, closing the door after him.

"How many times have you passed this house on your beat to-night, four-sixty-two?" inquired the inspector.

"About eight, sir. My beat's along the Richmond Road, from the Lion Gate down to the museum, and then around the back streets."

"Saw nothing?"

"I saw a man come out of this house hurriedly, soon after I came on duty. I was standing on the opposite side, under the wall of the Gardens. The lady what's downstairs let him out and told him to fetch the doctor quickly."

"Ah! Short, the servant," I observed.

"Where is he?" asked the inspector, while the detective with the ready note-book scribbled down the name.

"He came to fetch me, and Miss Mivart has now sent him to fetch her sister. He was the first to make the discovery."

"Oh, was he?" exclaimed the detective-sergeant, with some suspicion. "It's rather a pity that he's been sent out again. He might be able to tell us something."

"He'll be back in an hour, I should think."

"Yes, but every hour is of consequence in a matter of this sort," remarked the sergeant. "Look here, Davidson," he added, turning to one of the plain-clothes men, "just go round to the station and send a wire to the Yard, asking for extra assistance. Give them a brief outline of the case. They'll probably send down Franks or Moreland. If I'm not mistaken, there's a good deal more in this mystery than meets the eye."

The man addressed obeyed promptly, and left.

"What do you know of the servants here?" asked the inspector of the constable.

"Not much, sir. Six-forty-eight walks out with the cook, I've heard. She's a respectable woman. Her father's a lighterman at Kew Bridge. I know 'em all here by sight, of course. But there's nothing against them, to my knowledge, and I've been a constable in this sub-division for eighteen years."

"The man—what's his name?—Short. Do you know him?"

"Yes, sir. I've often seen him in the 'Star and Garter' at Kew Bridge."

"Drinks?"

"Not much, sir. He was fined over at Brentford six months ago for letting a dog go unmuzzled. His greatest friend is one of the gardeners at the Palace—a man named Burford, a most respectable fellow."

"Then there's no suspicion of anyone as yet?" remarked the inspector, with an air of dissatisfaction. In criminal mysteries the police often bungle from the outset, and to me it appeared as though, having no clue, they were bent on manufacturing one.

I felt in my vest pocket and touched the little object with a feeling of secret satisfaction. How I longed to be alone for five minutes in order to investigate it!

The inspector, having dismissed the constable and sent him back to his post to unlock the door for the detective to pass out, next turned his attention to the servants and the remainder of the house. With that object we all descended to the dining-room.

Ethelwynn met us at the foot of the stairs, still wearing the shawl about her head and shoulders. She placed a trembling hand upon my arm as I passed, asking in a low anxious voice:

"Have you found anything, Ralph? Tell me."

"No, nothing," I replied, and then passed into the dining-room, where the nurse and domestics had been assembled.

The nurse, a plain matter-of-fact woman, was the first person to be questioned. She explained to us how she had given her patient his last dose of medicine at half-past eleven, just after Miss Mivart had wished her good-night and retired to her room. Previously she had been down in the drawing-room chatting with the young lady. The man Short was then upstairs with his master.

"Was the deceased gentleman aware of his wife's absence?" the inspector asked presently.

"Yes. He remarked to me that it was time she returned. I presume that Short had told him."

"What time was this?"

"Oh! about half-past ten, I should think," replied Nurse Kate. "He said something about it being a bad night to go out to a theatre, and hoped she would not take cold."

"He was not angry?"

"Not in the least. He was never angry when she went to town. He used to say to me, 'My wife's a young woman, nurse. She wants a little amusement sometimes, and I'm sure I don't begrudge it to her.'"

This puzzled me quite as much as it puzzled the detective. I had certainly been under the impression that husband and wife had quarrelled over the latter's frequent absences from home. Indeed, in a household where the wife is young and the husband elderly, quarrels of that character are almost sure to occur sooner or later. As a doctor I knew the causes of domestic infelicity in a good many homes. Men in my profession see a good deal, and hear more. Every doctor could unfold strange tales of queer households if he were not debarred by the bond of professional secrecy.

"You heard no noise during the night?" inquired the inspector.

"None. I'm a light sleeper as a rule, and wake at the slightest sound," the woman replied. "But I heard absolutely nothing."

"Anyone, in order to enter the dead man's room, must have passed your door, I think?"

"Yes, and what's more, the light was burning and my door was ajar. I always kept it so in order to hear if my patient wanted anything."

"Then the murderer could see you as he stood on the landing?"

"No. There's a screen at the end of my bed. He could not see far into the room. But I shudder to think that to-night I've had an assassin a dozen feet from me while I slept," she added.

Finding that she could throw no light upon the mysterious affair, the officer turned his attention to the four frightened domestics, each in turn.

All, save one, declared that they heard not a single sound. The one exception was Alice, the under housemaid, a young fair-haired girl, who stated that during the night she had distinctly heard a sound like the low creaking of light shoes on the landing below where they slept.

This first aroused our interest, but on full reflection it seemed so utterly improbable that an assassin would wear a pair of creaky boots when on such an errand that we were inclined to disregard the girl's statement as a piece of imagination. The feminine mind is much given to fiction on occasions of tragic events.

But the girl over and over again asserted that she had heard it. She slept alone in a small room at the top of the second flight of stairs and had heard the sound quite distinctly.

"When you heard it what did you do?"

"I lay and listened."

"For how long?"

"Oh, quite a quarter of an hour, I should think. It was just before half-past one when I heard the noise, for the church clock struck almost immediately afterwards. The sound of the movement was such as I had never before heard at night, and at first I felt frightened. But I always lock my door, therefore I felt secure. The noise was just like someone creeping along very slowly, with one boot creaking."

"But if it was so loud that you could hear it with your door closed, it is strange that no one else heard it," the detective-sergeant remarked dubiously.

"I don't care what anybody else heard, I heard it quite plainly," the girl asserted.

"How long did it continue?" asked the detective.

"Oh, only just as though someone was stealing along the corridor. We often hear movements at nights, because Short is always astir at two o'clock, giving the master his medicine. If it hadn't ha' been for the creaking I should not have taken notice of it. But I lay quite wide awake for over half an hour—until Short came banging at our doors, telling us to get up at once, as we were wanted downstairs."

"Well," exclaimed the inspector, "now, I want to ask all of you a very simple question, and wish to obtain an honest and truthful reply. Was any door or window left unfastened when you went to bed?"

"No, sir," the cook replied promptly. "I always go round myself, and see that everything is fastened."

"The front door, for example?"

"I bolted it at Miss Ethelwynn's orders."

"At what time?"

"One o'clock. She told me to wait up till then, and if mistress did not return I was to lock up and go to bed."

"Then the tragedy must have been enacted about half an hour later?"

"I think so, sir."

"You haven't examined the doors and windows to see if any have been forced?"

"As far as I can see, they are just as I left them when I went to bed, sir."

"That's strange—very strange," remarked the inspector, turning to us. "We must make an examination and satisfy ourselves."

The point was one that was most important in the conduct of the inquiry. If all doors and windows were still locked, then the assassin was one of that strange household.

Led by the cook, the officers began a round of the lower premises. One of the detectives borrowed the constable's bull's-eye and, accompanied by a second officer, went outside to make an examination of the window sashes, while we remained inside assisting them in their search for any marks.

Ethelwynn had been called aside by one of the detectives, and was answering some questions addressed to her, therefore for an instant I found myself alone. It was the moment I had been waiting for, to secretly examine the clue I had obtained.

I was near the door of the morning room, and for a second slipped inside and switched on the electric light.

Then I took from my vest pocket the tiny little object I had found and carefully examined it.

My heart stood still. My eyes riveted themselves upon it. The mystery was solved.

I alone knew the truth!

VII

The Man Short and His Story

A light footstep sounded behind me, and scarcely had I time to thrust the little object hastily back into my pocket when my well-beloved entered in search of me.

"What do the police think, Ralph?" she asked eagerly. "Have they any clue? Do tell me."

"They have no clue," I answered, in a voice which I fear sounded hard and somewhat abrupt.

Then I turned from her, as though fully occupied with the investigations at which I was assisting, and went past her, leaving her standing alone.

The police were busy examining the doors and windows of the back premises, kitchens, scullery, and pantry, but could find no evidence of any lock or fastening having been tampered with. The house, I must explain, was a large detached red brick one, standing in a lawn that was quite spacious for a suburban house, and around it ran an asphalte path which diverged from the right hand corner of the building and ran in two parts to the road, one a semi-circular drive which came up to the portico from the road, and the other, a tradesmen's path, that ran to the opposite extremity of the property.

From the back kitchen a door led out upon this asphalted tradesmen's path, and as I rejoined the searchers some discussion was in progress as to whether the door in question had been secured. The detective-sergeant had found it unbolted and unlocked, but the cook most positively asserted that she had both locked and bolted it at half-past ten, when the under housemaid had come in from her "evening out." None of the servants, however, recollected having undone the door either before the alarm or after. Perhaps Short had done so, but he was absent, in search of the dead man's widow.

The police certainly spared no pains in their search. They turned the whole place upside down. One man on his hands and knees, and carrying a candle, carefully examined the blue stair-carpet to see if he could find the marks of unusual feet. It was wet outside, and if an intruder had been there, there would probably remain marks of muddy feet. He found many, but they were those of the constable and detectives. Hence the point was beyond solution.

The drawing-room, the dining-room, the morning-room, and the big conservatory were all closely inspected, but without any satisfactory result. My love followed us everywhere, white-faced and nervous, with the cream chenille shawl still over her shoulders. She had hastily put up her wealth of dark hair, and now wore the shawl wrapped lightly about her.

That shawl attracted me. I managed to speak with her alone for a moment, asking her quite an unimportant question, but nevertheless with a distinct object. As we stood there I placed my hand upon her shoulder—and upon the shawl. It was for that very reason—in order to feel the texture of the silk—that I returned to her.

The contact of my hand with the silk was convincing. I turned from her once again, and rejoined the shrewd men whose object it was to fasten the guilt upon the assassin.

Presently we heard the welcome sound of cab wheels outside, and a few minutes later young Mrs. Courtenay, wild eyed and breathless, rushed into the hall and dashed headlong up the stairs. I, however, barred her passage.

"Let me pass!" she cried wildly. "Short has told me he is worse and has asked for me. Let me pass!"

"No, Mary, not so quickly. Let me tell you something," I answered gravely, placing my hand firmly upon her arm. The police were again re-examining the back premises below, and only Ethelwynn was present at the top of the stairs, where I arrested her progress to the dead man's room.

"But is there danger?" she demanded anxiously. "Tell me."

"The crisis is over," I responded ambiguously. "But is not your absence to-night rather unusual?"

"It was entirely my own fault," she admitted. "I shall never forgive myself for this neglect. After the theatre we had supper at the Savoy, and I lost my last train. Dolly Henniker, of course, asked me to stay, and I could not refuse." Then glancing from my face to that of her sister she asked: "Why do you both look so strange? Tell me," she shrieked. "Tell me the worst. Is he—is he *dead*?"

I nodded in the affirmative.

For a second she stood dumb, then gave vent to a long wail, and would have fallen senseless if I had not caught her in my arms and laid her back upon the long settee placed in an alcove on the landing.

She, like all the others, had dressed hurriedly. Her hair was dishevelled beneath her hat, but her disordered dress was concealed by her long ulster heavily lined with silver fox, a magnificent garment which her doting husband had purchased through a friend at Moscow, and presented to her as a birthday gift.

From her manner it was only too plain that she was filled with remorse. I really pitied her, for she was a light-hearted, flighty, little woman who loved gaiety, and, without an evil thought, had no doubt allowed her friends to draw her into that round of amusement. They sympathised with her—as every woman who marries an old man is sympathised with—and they gave her what pleasures they could. Alas! that such a clanship between women so often proves fatal to domestic happiness. Judged from a logical point of view it was merely natural that young Mrs. Courtenay should, after a year or two with an invalid husband, aged and eccentric, beat her wings against the bars. She was a pretty woman, almost as pretty as her sister, but two years older, with fair hair, blue eyes, and a pink and white, almost doll-like complexion. Indeed, I knew quite well that she had long had a host of admirers, and that just prior to her marriage with Courtenay it had been rumoured that she was to marry the heir to an earldom, a rather rakish young cavalry officer up at York.

To restore her to consciousness was not a difficult matter, but after she had requested me to tell her the whole of the ghastly truth she sat speechless, as though turned to stone.

Her manner was unaccountable. She spoke at last, and to me it seemed as though the fainting fit had caused her an utter loss of memory. She uttered words at random, allowing her tongue to ramble on in strange disjointed sentences, of which I could make nothing.

"My head! Oh! my head!" she kept on exclaiming, passing her hand across her brow as though to clear her brain.

"Does it pain you?" I inquired.

"It seems as though a band of iron were round it. I can't think. I—I can't remember!" And she glanced about her helplessly, her eyes with a wild strange look in them, her face so haggard and drawn that it gave her a look of premature age.

"Oh! Mary, dear!" cried Ethelwynn, taking both her cold hands. "Why, what's the matter? Calm yourself, dear." Then turning to me she asked, "Can nothing be done, Ralph? See—she's not herself. The shock has unbalanced her brain."

"Ralph! Ethelwynn!" gasped the unfortunate woman, looking at us with an expression of sudden wonder. "What has happened? Did I understand you aright? Poor Henry is dead?"

"Unfortunately that is the truth." I was compelled to reply. "It is a sad affair, Mary, and you have all our sympathy. But recollect he was an invalid, and for a long time his life has been despaired of."

I dared not yet tell her the terrible truth that he had been the victim of foul play.

"It is my fault!" she cried. "My place was here—at home. But—but why was I not here?" she added with a blank look. "Where did I go?"

"Don't you remember that you went to London with the Hennikers?" I said.

"Ah! of course!" she exclaimed. "How very stupid of me to forget. But do you know, I've never experienced such a strange sensation before. My memory is a perfect blank. How did I return here?"

"Short fetched you in a cab."

"Short? I—I don't recollect seeing him. Somebody knocked at my door and said I was wanted, because my husband had been taken worse, so I dressed and went down. But after that I don't recollect anything."

"Her mind is a trifle affected by the shock," I whispered to my love. "Best take her downstairs into one of the rooms and lock the door. Don't let her see the police. She didn't notice the constable at the door. She'll be better presently."

I uttered these words mechanically, but, truth to tell, these extraordinary symptoms alarmed and puzzled me. She had fainted at hearing of the death of her husband, just as many other wives might have fainted; but to me there seemed no reason whatsoever why the swoon should be followed by that curious lapse of memory. The question she had put to me showed her mind to be a blank. I could discern nothing to account for the symptoms, and the only remedy I could suggest was perfect quiet. I intended that, as soon as daylight came, both women should be removed to the house of some friend in the vicinity.

The scene of the tragedy was no place for two delicate women.

Notwithstanding Mrs. Courtenay's determination to enter her husband's room I managed at last to get them both into the morning-room and called the nurse and cook to go in and assist in calming her, for her lapse of memory had suddenly been followed by a fit of violence.

"I must see him!" she shrieked. "I will see him! You can't prevent me. I am his wife. My place is at his side!"

My love exchanged looks with me. Her sister's extraordinary manner utterly confounded us.

"You shall see him later," I promised, endeavouring to calm her. "At present remain quiet. No good can possibly be done by this wild conduct."

"Where is Sir Bernard?" she inquired suddenly. "Have you telegraphed for him? I must see him."

"As soon as the office is open I shall wire."

"Yes, telegraph at the earliest moment. Tell him of the awful blow that has fallen upon us."

Presently, by dint of much persuasion, we managed to quiet her. The nurse removed her hat, helped her out of her fur-lined coat, and she sat huddled up in a big "grandfather" chair, her handsome evening gown crushed and tumbled, the flowers she had worn in her corsage on the previous night drooping and withered.

For some time she sat motionless, her chin sunk upon her breast, the picture of dejection, until, of a sudden, she roused herself, and before we were aware of her intention she had torn off her marriage ring and cast it across the room, crying wildly:

"It is finished. He is dead—dead!"

And she sank back again, among the cushions, as though exhausted by the effort.

What was passing through her brain at that moment I wondered. Why should a repulsion of the marriage bond seize her so suddenly, and cause her to tear off the golden fetter under which she had so long chafed? There was some reason, without a doubt; but at present all was an enigma—all save one single point.

When I returned to the police to urge them not to disturb Mrs. Courtenay, I found them assembled in the conservatory discussing an open window, by which anyone might easily have entered and left. The mystery of the kitchen door had been cleared up by Short, who admitted that after the discovery he had unlocked and unbolted it, in order to go round the outside of the house and see whether anyone was lurking in the garden.

When I was told this story I remarked that he had displayed some bravery in acting in such a manner. No man cares to face an assassin unarmed.

The man looked across at me with a curious apprehensive glance, and replied:

"I was armed, sir. I took down one of the old Indian daggers from the hall."

"Where is it now?" inquired the inspector, quickly, for at such a moment the admission that he had had a knife in his possession was sufficient to arouse a strong suspicion.

"I hung it up again, sir, before going out to call the doctor," he replied quite calmly.

"Show me which it was," I said; and he accompanied me out to the hall and pointed to a long thin knife which formed part of a trophy of antique Indian weapons.

In an instant I saw that such a knife had undoubtedly inflicted the wound in the dead man's breast.

"So you armed yourself with this?" I remarked, taking down the knife with affected carelessness, and examining it.

"Yes, doctor. It was the first thing that came to hand. It's sharp, for I cut myself once when cleaning it."

I tried its edge, and found it almost as keen as a razor. It was about ten inches long, and not more than half an inch broad, with a hilt of carved ivory, yellow with age, and inlaid with fine lines of silver. Certainly a very dangerous weapon. The sheath was of purple velvet, very worn and faded.

I walked back to where the detectives were standing, and examined the blade beneath the light. It was bright, and had apparently been recently cleaned. It might have been cleaned and oil smeared upon it after the commission of the crime. Yet as far as I could discern with the naked eye there was no evidence that it had recently been used.

It was the man's curious apprehensive glance that had first aroused my suspicion, and the admissions that he had opened the back door, and that he had been armed, both increased my mistrust. The detectives, too, were interested in the weapon, but were soon satisfied that, although a dangerous knife, it bore no stain of blood.

So I put it back in its case and replaced it. But I experienced some difficulty in getting the loop of wire back upon the brass-headed nail from which it was suspended; and it then occurred to me that Short, in the excitement of the discovery, and ordered by Ethelwynn to go at once in search of me, would not without some motive remain there, striving to return the knife to its place. Such action was unnatural. He would probably have cast it aside and dashed out in search of a cab. Indeed, the constable on the beat had seen him rush forth hurriedly and, urged by Ethelwynn, run in the direction of Kew Bridge.

No. Somehow I could not rid myself of the suspicion that the man was lying. To my professional eye the weapon with which the wound had been inflicted was the one which he admitted had been in his possession.

The story that he had unlocked the door and gone in search of the assassin struck the inspector, as it did myself, as a distinctly lame tale.

I longed for the opening of the telegraph office, so that I might summon my friend Jevons to my aid. He revelled in mysteries, and if the present one admitted of solution I felt confident that he would solve it.

VIII

Ambler Jevons is Inquisitive

P eople were about me the whole time. Hence I had no opportunity of re-examining the little object I had picked up from the spot where the murderer must have stood.

When morning dawned two detectives from Scotland Yard arrived, made notes of the circumstances, examined the open window in the conservatory, hazarded a few wise remarks, and closely scrutinised the dagger in the hall.

Ethelwynn had taken her sister to a friend in the vicinity, accompanied by the nurse and the cook. The house was now in the possession of the police, and it had already become known in the neighbourhood that old Mr. Courtenay was dead. In all probability early passers-by, men on their way to work, had noticed a constable in uniform enter or leave, and that had excited public curiosity. I hoped that Ambler Jevons would not delay, for I intended that he should be first in the field. If ever he had had a good mystery before him this certainly was one. I knew how keen was his scent for clues, and how carefully and ingeniously he worked when assisting the police to get at the bottom of any such affair.

He came a little after nine in hot haste, having driven from Hammersmith in a hansom. I was upstairs when I heard his deep cheery voice crying to the inspector from Scotland Yard:

"Hulloa, Thorpe. What's occurred? My friend Doctor Boyd has just wired to me."

"Murder," responded the inspector. "You'll find the doctor somewhere about. He'll explain it all to you. Queer case—very queer case, sir, it seems."

"Is that you, Ambler?" I called over the banisters. "Come up here."

He came up breathlessly, two steps at a time, and gripping my hand, asked:

"Who's been murdered?"

"Old Mr. Courtenay."

"The devil!" he exclaimed.

"A most mysterious affair," I went on. "They called me soon after three, and I came down here, only to find the poor old gentleman stone dead—stabbed to the heart."

"Let me see him," my friend said in a sharp business-like tone, which showed that he intended to lose no time in sifting the matter. He had his own peculiar methods of getting at the bottom of a mystery. He worked independently, and although he assisted the police and was therefore always welcomed by them, his efforts were always apart, and generally marked by cunning ingenuity and swift logical reasoning that were alike remarkable and marvellous.

I gave him a brief terse outline of the tragedy, and then, unlocking the door of the room where the dead man still lay in the same position as when discovered, allowed him in.

The place was in darkness, so I drew up the Venetian blinds, letting in the grey depressing light of the wintry morning.

He advanced to the bed, stood in the exact spot where I had stood, and where without doubt the murderer had stood, and folding his arms gazed straight and long upon the dead man's features.

Then he gave vent to a kind of dissatisfied grunt, and turned down the coverlet in order to examine the wound, while I stood by his side in silence.

Suddenly he swung round on his heel, and measured the paces between the bed and the door. Then he went to the window and looked out; afterwards making a tour of the room slowly, his dark eyes searching everywhere. He did not open his lips in the presence of the dead. He only examined everything, swiftly and yet carefully, opening the door slowly and closing it just as slowly, in order to see whether it creaked or not.

It creaked when closed very slowly. The creaking was evidently what the under-housemaid had heard and believed to be the creaking of boots. The murderer, finding that it creaked, had probably closed it by degrees; hence it gave a series of creaks, which to the girl had sounded in the silence of the night like those of new boots.

Ambler Jevons had, almost at the opening of his inquiry, cleared up one point which had puzzled us.

When he had concluded his examination of the room and re-covered the dead face with the sheet, we emerged into the corridor. Then I told him of the servant's statement.

"Boots!" he echoed in a tone of impatience. "Would a murderer wear creaking boots? It was the door, of course. It opens noiselessly, but when closed quietly it creaks. Curious, however, that he should have risked the creaking and the awakening of the household in order to close it. He had some strong motive in doing so."

"He evidently had a motive in the crime," I remarked. "If we could only discover it, we might perhaps fix upon the assassin."

"Yes," he exclaimed, thoughtfully. "But to tell the truth, Ralph, old chap, the fact which is puzzling me most of all at this moment is that extraordinary foreboding of evil which you confessed to me the day before yesterday. You had your suspicions aroused, somehow. Cudgel your brains, and think what induced that very curious presage of evil."

"I've tried and tried over again, but I can fix on nothing. Only yesterday afternoon, when Sir Bernard incidentally mentioned old Mr. Courtenay, it suddenly occurred to me that the curious excitement within me had some connection with him. Of course he was a patient, and I may have studied his case and given a lot of thought to it, but that wouldn't account for such an oppression as that from which I've been suffering."

"You certainly did have the blues badly the night before last," he said frankly. "And by some unaccountable manner your curious feeling was an intuition of this tragic occurrence. Very odd and mysterious, to say the least."

"Uncanny, I call it," I declared.

"Yes, I agree with you," he answered. "It is an uncanny affair altogether. Tell me about the ladies. Where are they?"

I explained how Mrs. Courtenay had been absent, and how she had been prostrated by the news of his death.

He stroked his moustache slowly, deeply reflecting.

"Then at present she doesn't know that he's been murdered? She thinks that he was taken ill, and expired suddenly?"

"Exactly."

And I went on to describe the wild scene which followed my admission that her husband was dead. I explained it to him in detail, for I saw that his thoughts were following in the same channel as my own. We both pitied the unfortunate woman. My friend knew her well, for he had often accompanied me there and had spent the evening with us. Ethelwynn liked him for his careless Bohemianism, and for the fund of stories always at his command. Sometimes he used to entertain us for hours together, relating details of mysteries upon which he had at one time or another been engaged. Women are always fond of mysteries, and he often held both of them breathless by his vivid narratives.

Thorpe, the detective from Scotland Yard, a big, sturdily-built, middle-aged man, whose hair was tinged with grey, and whose round, rosy face made him appear the picture of good health, joined us a moment later. In a low, mysterious tone he explained to my friend the circumstance of Short having admitted possession of the knife hanging in the hall.

In it Ambler Jevons at once scented a clue.

"I never liked that fellow!" he exclaimed, turning to me. "My impression has always been that he was a sneak, and told old Courtenay everything that went on, either in drawing-room or kitchen."

Thorpe, continuing, explained how the back door had been found unfastened, and how Short had admitted unfastening it in order to go forth to seek the assassin.

"A ridiculous story—utterly absurd!" declared Jevons. "A man doesn't rush out to shed blood for blood like that!"

"Of course not," agreed the detective. "To my mind appearances are entirely against this fellow. Yet, we have one fact to bear in mind, namely, that being sent to town twice he was afforded every opportunity for escape."

"He was artful," I remarked. "He knew that his safest plan was to remain and face it. If, as seems very probable, the crime was planned, it was certainly carried out at a most propitious moment."

"It certainly was," observed my friend, carefully scrutinising the knife, which Thorpe had brought to him. "This," he said, "must be examined microscopically. You can do that, Boyd. It will be easy to see if there are any traces of blood upon it. To all appearances it has been recently cleaned and oiled."

"Short admits cleaning it, but he says he did so three days ago," I exclaimed.

He gave vent to another low grunt, from which I knew that the explanation was unsatisfactory, and replaced the knife in its faded velvet sheath.

Save for the man upon whom suspicion had thus fallen, the servants had all gone to the house where their mistress was lodged, after being cautioned by the police to say nothing of the matter, and to keep their mouths closed to all the reporters who would no doubt very soon be swarming into the district eager for every scrap of information. Their evidence would be required at the inquest, and the police forbade them, until then, to make any comment, or to give any explanation of the mysterious affair. The tongues of domestics wag quickly and wildly in such cases, and have many times been the means of defeating the ends of justice by giving away important clues to the Press.

Ambler Jevons, however, was a practised hand at mysteries. He sat down in the library, and with his crabbed handwriting covered two sheets of paper with notes upon the case. I watched as his pencil went swiftly to work, and when he had finished I saw him underline certain words he had written.

"Thorpe appears to suspect that fellow Short," he remarked, when I met him again in the library a quarter of an hour later. "I've just been chatting with him, and to me his demeanour is not that of a guilty man. He's actually been upstairs with the coroner's officer in the dead man's room. A murderer generally excuses himself from entering the presence of his victim."

"Well," I exclaimed, after a pause, "you know the whole circumstances now. Can you see any clue which may throw light on the affair?"

He slowly twisted his moustache again; then twisted his plain gold ring slowly round the little finger on the left hand—a habit of his when perplexed.

"No, Ralph, old chap; can't say I do," he answered. "There's an unfathomable mystery somewhere, but in what direction I'm utterly at a loss to distinguish."

"But do you think that the assassin is a member of the household? That seems to me our first point to clear up."

"That's just where we're perplexed. Thorpe suspects Short; but the police so often rush to conclusions on a single suspicion. Before condemning him it is necessary to watch him narrowly, and note his demeanour and his movements. If he is guilty he'll betray himself sooner or later. Thorpe was foolish to take down that knife a second time. The fellow might have seen him and had his suspicions aroused thereby. That's the worst of police inquiries. They display so little ingenuity. It is all method—method—method. Everything must be done by rule. They appear to overlook the fact that a window in the conservatory was undoubtedly left open," he added.

"Well?" I asked, noticing that he was gazing at me strangely, full in the face.

"Well, has it not occurred to you that that window might have been purposely left open?"

"You mean that the assassin entered and left by that window?"

"I mean to suggest that the murder might have been connived at by one of the household, if the man we suspect were not the actual assassin himself."

The theory was a curious one, but I saw that there were considerable grounds for it. As in many suburban houses, the conservatory joined the drawing-room, an unlocked glass door being between them. The window that had been left unfastened was situated at the further end, and being low down was in such a position that any intruder might easily have entered and left. Therefore the suggestion appeared a sound one—more especially so because the cook had most solemnly declared that she had fastened it securely before going up to bed.

In that case someone must have crept down and unfastened it after the woman had retired, and done so with the object of assisting the assassin.

But Ambler Jevons was not a man to remain idle for a single moment when once he became interested in a mystery. To his keen perception and calm logical reasoning had been due the solution of "The Mornington Crescent Mystery," which, as all readers of this narrative will remember, for six months utterly perplexed Scotland Yard; while in a dozen other notable cases his discoveries had placed the police on the scent of the guilty person. Somehow he seemed to possess a peculiar facility in the solving of enigmas. At ordinary times he struck one as a rather careless, easy-going man, who drifted on through life, tasting and dealing in tea, with regular attendance at Mark Lane each day. Sometimes he wore a pair of cheap pince-nez, the frames of which were rusty, but these he seldom assumed unless he was what he termed "at work." He was at work now, and therefore had stuck the pince-nez on the bridge of his nose, giving him a keener and rather more intelligent appearance.

"Excuse me," he exclaimed, suddenly twisting his ring again round his finger. "I've just thought of something else. I won't be a moment," and he rushed from the library and ran upstairs to the floor above.

His absence gave me an opportunity to re-examine the little object which I had picked up from the floor at the earlier stages of the inquiry; and advancing to the window I took it from my pocket and looked again at it, utterly confounded.

Its appearance presented nothing extraordinary, for it was merely a soft piece of hard-knotted cream-coloured chenille about half-an-inch long. But sight of it lying in the palm of my hand held me spellbound in horror.

It told me the awful truth. It was nothing less than a portion of the fringe of the cream shawl which my love had been wearing, and just as chenille fringes will come to pieces, it had become detached and fallen where she had stood at that spot beside the victim's bed.

There was a smear of blood upon it.

I recollected her strangely nervous manner, her anxiety to ascertain what clue we had discovered and to know the opinion of the police. Yes, if guilt were ever written upon a woman's face, it was upon hers.

Should I show the tiny fragment to my friend? Should I put it into his hands and tell him the bitter truth—the truth that I believed my love to be a murderess?

IX

SHADOWS

The revelation held me utterly dumfounded.

Already I had, by placing my hand in contact with the shawl, ascertained its exact texture, and saw that both its tint and its fabric were unquestionably the same as the knotted fragment I held in my hand. Chenille shawls, as every woman knows, must be handled carefully or the lightly-made fringe will come asunder; for the kind of cord of floss silk is generally made upon a single thread, which will break with the slightest strain.

By some means the shawl in question had accidentally become entangled—or perhaps been strained by the sudden uplifting of the arm of the wearer. In any case the little innocent-looking fragment had snapped, and dropped at the bedside of the murdered man.

The grave suspicions of Ethelwynn which I had held on the previous night when she endeavoured to justify her sister's neglect again crowded upon me, and Sir Bernard's hint at the secret of her past thrust the iron deeply into my heart.

My eyes were fixed upon the little object in my palm—the silent but damning evidence—and my mind became filled by bitterest regrets. I saw how cleverly I had been duped—I recognised that this woman, whom I thought an angel, was only a cunning assassin.

No, believe me: I was not prejudging her! The thought had already occurred to me that she might have entered the room wearing that shawl perhaps to wish the invalid good-night. She had, however, in answer to my question, declared that she had retired to bed without seeing him—for Nurse Kate had told her that he was sleeping. She had therefore not disturbed him.

Then, yet another thought had occurred to me. She might have worn the shawl when she entered after the raising of the alarm. In order to clear up that point I had questioned the servants, one by one, and all had told me the same story, namely, that Miss Ethelwynn had not entered the room at all. She had only come to the door and glanced in, then turned away in horror and shut herself in her own room. As far as anyone knew, she had not summoned sufficient courage to go in and look upon the dead man's face. She declared herself horrified, and dared not to enter the death chamber.

In the light of my discovery all these facts as related to me made the truth only too apparent. She had entered there unknown to anyone, and that her presence had been with a fell purpose I could no longer doubt.

If I gave the clue into Ambler Jevons' hands he would, I knew, quickly follow it, gathering up the threads of the tangled skein one by one, until he could openly charge her with the crime. I stood undecided how to act. Should I leave my friend to make his own investigations independently and unbiassed, or should I frankly tell him of my own startling discovery?

I carefully went through the whole of the circumstances, weighing point after point, and decided at last to still retain the knowledge I had gained. The point which outbalanced my intention was that curious admission of Short regarding the possession of the knife. So I resolved to say nothing to my friend until after the inquest.

As may be imagined, the London papers that afternoon were full of the mystery. Nothing like a first-class "sensation," sub-editors will tell you. There is art in alliterative headlines and startling "cross-heads." The inevitable interview with "a member of the family"—who is generally anonymous, be it said—is sure to be eagerly devoured by the public. The world may sneer at sensational journalism, but after all it loves to have its curiosity excited over the tragic dénouement of some domestic secret. As soon as the first information reached the Central News and Press Association, therefore, reporters crowded upon us. Representatives, not only of the metropolitan press, but those of the local newspapers, the "Richmond and Twickenham Times," the "Independent," over at Brentford, the "Middlesex Chronicle" at Hounslow, and the "Middlesex Mercury," of Isleworth, all vied with each other in obtaining the most accurate information.

"Say nothing," Jevons urged. "Be civil, but keep your mouth closed tight. There are one or two friends of mine among the crowd. I'll see them and give them something that will carry the story further. Remember, you mustn't make any statement whatsoever."

I obeyed him, and although the reporters followed me about all the morning, and outside the house the police had difficulty in preventing a crowd assembling, I refused to express any opinion or describe anything I had witnessed.

At eleven o'clock I received a wire from Sir Bernard at Hove as follows:—

"Much shocked at news. Unfortunately very unwell, but shall endeavour to be with you later in the day."

At mid-day I called at the neighbour's house close to Kew Gardens Station, where the widow and her sister had taken refuge. Mrs. Courtenay was utterly broken down, for Ethelwynn had told her the terrible truth that her husband had been murdered, and both women pounced upon me eagerly to ascertain what theory the police now held.

I looked at the woman who had held me so long beneath her spell. Was it possible that one so open-faced and pure could be the author of so dastardly and cowardly a crime? Her face was white and anxious, but the countenance had now reassumed its normal innocence of expression, and in her eyes I saw the genuine love-look of old. She had arranged her hair and dress, and no longer wore the shawl.

"It's terrible—terrible, Ralph," she cried. "Poor Mary! The blow has utterly crushed her."

"I am to blame—it is my own fault!" exclaimed the young widow, hoarsely. "But I had no idea that his end was so near. I tried to be a dutiful wife, but oh—only Ethelwynn knows how hard it was, and how I suffered. His malady made him unbearable, and instead of quarrelling I thought the better plan was to go out and leave him with the nurse. What people have always said, was, alas! too true. Owing to the difference of our ages our marriage was a ghastly failure. And now it has ended in a tragedy."

I responded in words as sympathetic as I could find tongue to utter. Her eyes were red with crying, and her pretty face was swollen and ugly. I knew that she now felt a genuine regret at the loss of her husband, even though her life had been so dull and unhappy.

While she sat in a big armchair bowed in silence, I turned to Ethelwynn and discussed the situation with her. Their friends were most kind, she said. The husband was churchwarden at Kew Church, and his wife was an ardent church worker, hence they had long ago become excellent friends.

"You have your friend, Mr. Jevons, with you, I hear. Nurse has just returned and told me so."

"Yes," I responded. "He is making an independent inquiry."

"And what has he found?" she inquired breathlessly.

"Nothing."

Then, as I watched her closely, I saw that she breathed again more freely. By the manner in which she uttered Ambler's name I detected that she was not at all well-disposed towards him. Indeed, she spoke as though she feared that he might discover the truth.

After half-an-hour I left, and more puzzled than ever, returned to the house in Richmond Road. Sometimes I felt entirely convinced that my love was authoress of the foul deed; yet at others there seemed something wanting in the confirmation of my suspicions. Regarding the latter I could not overlook the fact that Short had told a story which was false on the face of it, while the utter absence of any motive on my love's part in murdering the old gentleman seemed to point in an entirely opposite direction.

Dr. Diplock, the coroner, had fixed the inquest for eleven o'clock on the morrow; therefore I assisted Dr. Farmer, of Kew, the police surgeon, to make the post-mortem.

We made the examination in the afternoon, before the light faded, and if the circumstances of the crime were mysterious, the means by which the unfortunate man was murdered were, we found, doubly so.

Outwardly, the wound was an ordinary one, one inch in breadth, inflicted by a blow delivered from left to right. The weapon had entered between the fourth and fifth ribs, and the heart had been completely transfixed by some sharp cutting instrument. The injuries we discovered within, however, increased the mystery ten-fold, for we found two extraordinary lateral incisions, which almost completely divided the heart from side to side, the only remaining attachment of the upper portion to the lower being a small portion of the anterior wall of the heart behind the sternum.

Such a wound was absolutely beyond explanation.

The instrument with which the crime had been committed by striking between the ribs had penetrated to the heart with an unerring precision, making a terrible wound eight times the size within, as compared with the exterior puncture. And yet the weapon had been withdrawn, and was missing!

For fully an hour we measured and discussed the strange discovery, hoping all the time that Sir Bernard would arrive. The knife which the man Short confessed he had taken down in self-defence we compared with the exterior wound and found, as we anticipated, that just such a wound could be caused by it. But the fact that the exterior cut was cleanly done, while the internal injuries were jagged and the tissues torn in a most terrible manner, caused a doubt to arise whether the Indian knife, which was double-edged, had actually been used. To be absolutely clear upon this point it would be necessary to examine it microscopically, for the corpuscles of human blood are easily distinguished beneath the lens.

We were about to conclude our examination in despair, utterly unable to account for the extraordinary wound, when the door opened and Sir Bernard entered.

He looked upon the body of his old friend, not a pleasing spectacle indeed, and then grasped my hand without a word.

"I read the evening paper on my way up," he said at last in a voice trembling with emotion. "The affair seems very mysterious. Poor Courtenay! Poor fellow!"

"It is sad—very sad," I remarked. "We have just concluded the post-mortem;" and then I introduced the police surgeon to the man whose name was a household word throughout the medical profession.

I showed my chief the wound, explained its extraordinary features, and asked his opinion. He removed his coat, turned up his shirt-cuffs, adjusted his big spectacles, and, bending beside the board upon which the body lay, made a long and careful inspection of the injury.

"Extraordinary!" he exclaimed. "I've never known of such a wound before. One would almost suspect an explosive bullet, if it were not for the clean incised wound on the exterior. The ribs seem grazed, yet the manner in which such a hurt has been inflicted is utterly unaccountable."

"We have been unable to solve the enigma," Dr. Farmer observed. "I was an army surgeon before I entered private practice, but I have never seen a similar case."

"Nor have I," responded Sir Bernard. "It is most puzzling."

"Do you think that this knife could have been used?" I asked, handing my chief the weapon.

He looked at it, raised it in his hand as though to strike, felt its edge, and then shook his head, saying: "No, I think not. The instrument used was only sharp on one edge. This has both edges sharpened."

It was a point we had overlooked, but at once we agreed with him, and abandoned our half-formed theory that the Indian dagger had caused the wound.

With Sir Bernard we made an examination of the tongue and other organs, in order to ascertain the progress of the disease from which the deceased had been suffering, but a detailed account of our discoveries can have no interest for the lay reader.

In a word, our conclusions were that the murdered man could easily have lived another year or more. The disease was not so advanced as we had believed. Sir Bernard had a patient to see in Grosvenor Square; therefore he left at about four o'clock, regretting that he had not time to call round at the neighbour's and express his sympathy with the widow.

"Give her all my sympathies, poor young lady," he said to me. "And tell her that I will call upon her to-morrow." Then, after promising to attend the inquest and give evidence regarding the post-mortem, he shook hands with us both and left.

At eight o'clock that evening I was back in my own rooms in Harley Place, eating my dinner alone, when Ambler Jevons entered.

He was not as cheery as usual. He did not exclaim, as was his habit, "Well, my boy, how goes it? Whom have you killed to-day?" or some such grim pleasantry.

On the contrary, he came in with scarcely a word, threw his hat upon a side table, and sank into his usual armchair with scarcely a word, save the question uttered in almost a growl:

"May I smoke?"

"Of course," I said, continuing my meal. "Where have you been?"

"I left while you were cutting up the body," he said. "I've been about a lot since then, and I'm a bit tired."

"You look it. Have a drink?"

"No," he responded, shaking his head. "I don't drink when I'm bothered. This case is an absolute mystery." And striking a match he lit his foul pipe and puffed away vigorously, staring straight into the fire the while.

"Well," I asked, after a long silence. "What's your opinion now?"

"I've none," he answered, gloomily. "What's yours?"

"Mine is that the mystery increases hourly."

"What did you find at the cutting-up?"

In a few words I explained the unaccountable nature of the wound, drawing for him a rough diagram on the back of an old envelope, which I tossed over to where he sat.

He looked at it for a long time without speaking, then observed:

"H'm! Just as I thought. The police theory regarding that fellow Short and the knife is all a confounded myth. Depend upon it, Boyd, old chap, that gentleman is no fool. He's tricked Thorpe finely—and with a motive, too."

"What motive do you suspect?" I inquired, eagerly, for this was an entirely fresh theory.

"One that you'd call absurd if I were to tell it to you now. I'll explain later on, when my suspicions are confirmed—as I feel sure they will be before long."

"You're mysterious, Ambler," I said, surprised. "Why?"

"I have a reason, my dear chap," was all the reply he vouchsafed. Then he puffed again vigorously at his pipe, and filled the room with clouds of choking smoke of a not particularly good brand of tobacco.

X

Which Puzzles the Doctors

At the inquest held in the big upstair room of the Star and Garter Hotel at Kew Bridge there was a crowded attendance. By this time the public excitement had risen to fever-heat. It had by some unaccountable means leaked out that at the post-mortem we had been puzzled; therefore the mystery was much increased, and the papers that morning without exception gave prominence to the startling affair.

The coroner, seated at the table at the head of the room, took the usual formal evidence of identification, writing down the depositions upon separate sheets of blue foolscap.

Samuel Short was the first witness of importance, and those in the room listened breathlessly to the story of how his alarum clock had awakened him at two o'clock; how he had risen as usual and gone to his master's room, only to discover him dead.

"You noticed no sign of a struggle?" inquired the coroner, looking sharply up at the witness.

"None, sir. My master was lying on his side, and except for the stain of blood which attracted my attention it looked as though he had died in his sleep."

"And what did you do?"

"I raised the alarm," answered Short; and then he went on to describe how he switched on the electric light, rushed downstairs, seized the knife hanging in the hall, opened one of the back doors and rushed outside.

"And why did you do that, pray?" asked the coroner, looking at him fixedly.

"I thought that someone might be lurking in the garden," the man responded, a trifle lamely.

The solicitor of Mrs. Courtenay's family, to whom she had sent asking him to be present on her behalf, rose at this juncture and addressing the coroner, said:

"I should like to put a question to the witness, sir. I represent the deceased's family."

"As you wish," replied the coroner. "But do you consider such a course wise at this stage of the inquiry? There must be an adjournment."

He understood the coroner's objection and, acquiescing, sat down.

Nurse Kate and the cook were called, and afterwards Ethelwynn, who, dressed in black and wearing a veil, looked pale and fragile as she drew off her glove in order to take the oath.

As she stood there our eyes met for an instant; then she turned towards her questioner, bracing herself for the ordeal.

"When did you last see the deceased alive?" asked the coroner, after the usual formal inquiry as to her name and connection with the family.

"At ten o'clock in the evening. Dr. Boyd visited him, and found him much better. After the doctor had gone I went upstairs and found the nurse with him, giving him his medicine. He was still sitting before the fire."

"Was he in his usual spirits?"

"Quite."

"What was the character of your conversation with him? I understand that Mrs. Courtenay, your sister, was out at the time. Did he remark upon her absence?"

"Yes. He said it was a wet night, and he hoped she would not take cold, for she was so careless of herself."

The coroner bent to his paper and wrote down her reply.

"And you did not see him alive again."

"No."

"You entered the room after he was dead, I presume?"

"No. I—I hadn't the courage," she faltered. "They told me that he was dead—that he had been stabbed to the heart."

Again the coroner bent to his writing. What, I wondered, would those present think if I produced the little piece of stained chenille which I kept wrapped in tissue paper and hidden in my fusee-box?

To them it, of course, seemed quite natural that a delicate woman should hesitate to view a murdered man. But if they knew of my discovery they would detect that she was an admirable actress—that her horror of the dead was feigned, and that she was not telling the truth. I, who knew her countenance so well, saw even through her veil how agitated she was, and with what desperate resolve she was concealing the awful anxiety consuming her.

"One witness has told us that the deceased was very much afraid of burglars," observed the coroner. "Had he ever spoken to you on the subject?"

"Often. At his country house some years ago a burglary was committed, and one of the burglars fired at him but missed. I think that unnerved him, for he always kept a loaded revolver in the drawer of a table beside his bed. In addition to this he had electrical contrivances attached to the windows, so as to ring an alarm."

"But it appears they did not ring," said the coroner, quickly.

"They were out of order, the servants tell me. The bells had been silent for a fortnight or so."

"It seems probable, then, that the murderer knew of that," remarked Dr. Diplock, again writing with his scratchy quill. Turning to the solicitor, he asked, "Have you any questions to put to the witness?"

"None," was the response.

And then the woman whom I had loved so fervently and well, turned and re-seated herself. She glanced across at me. Did she read my thoughts?

Her glance was a glance of triumph.

Medical evidence was next taken, Sir Bernard Eyton being the first witness. He gave his opinion in his habitual sharp, snappy voice, terse and to the point.

In technical language he explained the disease from which his patient had been suffering, and then proceeded to describe the result of the post-mortem, how the wound inside was eight times larger than the exterior incision.

"That seems very remarkable!" exclaimed the coroner, himself a surgeon of no mean repute, laying down his pen and regarding the physician with interest suddenly aroused. "Have you ever seen a similar wound in your experience, Sir Bernard?"

"Never!" was the reply. "My friends, Doctor Boyd and Doctor Farmer, were with me, and we are agreed that it is utterly impossible that the cardiac injuries I have described could have been caused by the external wound."

"Then how were they caused?" asked the coroner.

"I cannot tell."

There was no cross-examination. I followed, merely corroborating what my chief had said. Then, after the police surgeon had given his evidence, Dr. Diplock turned to the twelve Kew tradesmen who had been "summoned and sworn" as jurymen, and addressing them said:

"I think, gentlemen, you have heard sufficient to show you that this is a more than usually serious case. There are certain elements both extraordinary and mysterious, and that being so I would suggest an adjournment, in order that the police should be enabled to make further enquiries into the matter. The deceased was a gentleman whose philanthropy was probably well known to you all, and we must all therefore regret that he should have come to such a sudden and tragic end. You may, of course, come to a verdict to-day if you wish, but I would strongly urge an adjournment—until, say, this day week."

The jury conferred for a few moments, and after some whispering the foreman, a grocer at Kew Bridge, announced that his fellow jurymen acquiesced in the coroner's suggestion, and the public rose and slowly left, more puzzled than ever.

Ambler Jevons had been present, sitting at the back of the room, and in order to avoid the others we lunched together at an obscure public-house in Brentford, on the opposite side of the Thames to Kew Gardens. It was the only place we could discover, save the hotel where the inquest had been held, and we had no desire to be interrupted, for during the inquiry he had passed me a scrap of paper upon which he had written an earnest request to see me alone afterwards.

Therefore when I had put Ethelwynn into a cab, and had bade farewell to Sir Bernard and received certain private instructions from him, we walked together into the narrow, rather dirty High Street of Brentford, the county town of Middlesex.

The inn we entered was close to a soap works, the odour from which was not conducive to a good appetite, but we obtained a room to ourselves and ate our meal of cold beef almost in silence.

"I was up early this morning," Ambler observed at last. "I was at Kew at eight o'clock."

"Why?"

"In the night an idea struck me, and when such ideas occur I always seek to put them promptly into action."

"What was the idea?" I asked.

"I thought about that safe in the old man's bedroom," he replied, laying down his knife and fork and looking at me.

"What about it? There's surely nothing extraordinary in a man having a safe in his room?"

"No. But there's something extraordinary in the key of that safe being missing," he said. "Thorpe has apparently overlooked the point; therefore this morning I went down to Kew, and finding only a constable in charge, I made a thorough search through the place. In the dead man's room I naturally expected to find it, and after nearly a couple of hours searching in every nook and every crack I succeeded. It was hidden in the mould of a small pot-fern, standing in the corridor outside the room."

"You examined the safe, then?"

"No, I didn't. There might be money and valuables within, and I had no right to open it without the presence of a witness. I've waited for you to accompany me. We'll go there after luncheon and examine its contents."

"But the executors might have something to say regarding such an action," I remarked.

"Executors be hanged! I saw them this morning, a couple of dry-as-dust old fossils—city men, I believe, who only think of house property and dividends. Our duty is to solve this mystery. The executors can have their turn, old chap, when we've finished. At present they haven't the key, or any notion where it is. One of them mentioned it, and said he supposed it was in the widow's possession."

"Well," I remarked, "I must say that I don't half like the idea of turning out a safe without the presence of the executors."

"Police enquiries come before executors' inventories," he replied. "They'll get their innings all in good time. The house is, at present, in the occupation of the police, and nobody therefore can disturb us."

"Have you told Thorpe?"

"No. He's gone up to Scotland Yard to make his report. He'll probably be down again this afternoon. Let's finish, and take the ferry across."

Thus persuaded I drained my ale, and together we went down to the ferry, landing at Kew Gardens, and crossing them until we emerged by the Unicorn Gate, almost opposite the house.

There were loiterers still outside, men, women, and children, who lounged in the vicinity, staring blankly up at the drawn blinds. A constable in uniform admitted us. He had his lunch, a pot of beer and some bread and cheese which his wife had probably brought him, on the dining-room table, and we had disturbed him with his mouth full.

He was the same man whom Ambler Jevons had seen in the morning, and as we entered he saluted, saying:

"Inspector Thorpe has left a message for you, sir. He'll be back from the Yard about half-past three, and would very much like to see you."

"Do you know why he wants to see me?"

"It appears, sir, that one of the witnesses who gave evidence this morning is missing."

"Missing!" he cried, pricking up his ears. "Who's missing?"

"The manservant, sir. My sergeant told me an hour ago that as soon as the man had given evidence he went out, and was seen hurrying towards Gunnersbury Station. They believe he's absconded."

I exchanged significant glances with my companion, but neither of us uttered a word. Ambler gave vent to his habitual grunt of dissatisfaction, and then led the way upstairs.

The body had been removed from the room in which it had been found, and the bed was dismantled. When inside the apartment, he turned to me calmly, saying:

"There seems something in Thorpe's theory regarding that fellow Short, after all."

"If he has really absconded, it is an admission of guilt," I remarked.

"Most certainly," he replied. "It's a suspicious circumstance, in any case, that he did not remain until the conclusion of the inquiry."

We pulled the chest of drawers, a beautiful piece of old Sheraton, away from the door of the safe, and before placing the key in the lock my companion examined the exterior minutely. The key was partly rusted, and appeared as though it had not been used for many months.

Could it be that the assassin was in search of that key and had been unsuccessful?

He showed me the artful manner in which it had been concealed. The small hardy fern had been rooted up and stuck back again heedlessly into its pot. Certainly no one would ever have thought to search for a safe-key there. The dampness of the mould had caused the rust, hence before we could open the iron door we were compelled to oil the key with some brilliantine which was discovered on the dead man's dressing table.

The interior, we found, was a kind of small strong-room—built of fire-brick, and lined with steel. It was filled with papers of all kinds neatly arranged.

We drew up a table, and the first packet my friend handed out was a substantial one of five pound notes, secured by an elastic band, beneath which was a slip on which the amount was pencilled. Securities of various sorts followed, and then large packets of parchment deeds which, on examination, we found related to his Devonshire property and his farms in Canada.

"Here's something!" cried Ambler at length, tossing across to me a small packet methodically tied with pink tape. "The old boy's love-letters—by the look of them."

I undid the loop eagerly, and opened the first letter. It was in a feminine hand, and proved a curious, almost unintelligible communication.

I glanced at the signature. My heart ceased its beating, and a sudden cry involuntarily escaped me, although next moment I saw that by it I had betrayed myself, for Ambler Jevons sprang to my side in an instant.

But next instant I covered the signature with my hand, grasped the packet swift as thought, and turned upon him defiantly, without uttering a word.

XI

CONCERNS MY PRIVATE AFFAIRS

W hat have you found there?" inquired Ambler Jevons, quickly interested, and yet surprised at my determination to conceal it from him.

"Something that concerns me," I replied briefly.

"Concerns you?" he exclaimed. "I don't understand. How can anything among the old man's private papers concern you?"

"This concerns me personally," I answered. "Surely that is sufficient explanation."

"No," my friend said. "Forgive me, Ralph, for speaking quite plainly, but in this affair we are both working towards the same end—namely, to elucidate the mystery. We cannot hope for success if you are bent upon concealing your discoveries from me."

"This is a private affair of my own," I declared doggedly. "What I have found only concerns myself."

He shrugged his shoulders with an air of distinct dissatisfaction.

"Even if it is a purely private matter we are surely good friends enough to be cognisant of one another's secrets," he remarked.

"Of course," I replied dubiously. "But only up to a certain point."

"Then, in other words, you imply that you can't trust me?"

"I can trust you, Ambler," I answered calmly. "We are the best of friends, and I hope we shall always be so. Will you not forgive me for refusing to show you these letters?"

"I only ask you one question. Have they anything to do with the matter we are investigating?"

I hesitated. With his quick perception he saw that a lie was not ready upon my lips.

"They have. Your silence tells me so. In that case it is your duty to show me them," he said, quietly.

I protested again, but he overwhelmed my arguments. In common fairness to him I ought not, I knew, keep back the truth. And yet it was the greatest and most terrible blow that had ever fallen upon me. He saw that I was crushed and stammering, and he stood by me wondering.

"Forgive me, Ambler," I urged again. "When you have read this letter

WILLIAM LE QUEUX

you will fully understand why I have endeavoured to conceal it from you; why, if you were not present here at this moment, I would burn them all and not leave a trace behind."

Then I handed it to him.

He took it eagerly, skimmed it through, and started just as I had started when he saw the signature. Upon his face was a blank expression, and he returned it to me without a word.

"Well?" I asked. "What is your opinion?"

"My opinion is the same as your own, Ralph, old fellow," he answered slowly, looking me straight in the face. "It is amazing—startling—tragic."

"You think, then, that the motive of the crime was jealousy?"

"The letter makes it quite plain," he answered huskily. "Give me the others. Let me examine them. I know how severe this blow must be to you, old fellow," he added, sympathetically.

"Yes, it has staggered me," I stammered. "I'm utterly dumfounded by the unexpected revelation!" and I handed him the packet of correspondence, which he placed upon the table, and, seating himself, commenced eagerly to examine letter after letter.

While he was thus engaged I took up the first letter, and read it through—right to the bitter end.

It was apparently the last of a long correspondence, for all the letters were arranged chronologically, and this was the last of the packet. Written from Neneford Manor, Northamptonshire, and vaguely dated "Wednesday," as is a woman's habit, it was addressed to Mr. Courtenay, and ran as follows:—

"Words cannot express my contempt for a man who breaks his word as easily as you break yours. A year ago, when you were my father's guest, you told me that you loved me, and urged me to marry you. At first I laughed at your proposal; then when I found you really serious, I pointed out the difference of our ages. You, in return, declared that you loved me with all the ardour of a young man; that I was your ideal; and you promised, by all you held most sacred, that if I consented I should never regret. I believed you, and believed the false words of feigned devotion which you wrote to me later under seal of strictest secrecy. You went to Cairo, and none knew of our secret—the secret that you intended to make me your wife. And how have you kept your promise? To-day my father has informed me that you are to marry Mary! Imagine the blow to me! My father expects me to rejoice, little dreaming how I have been fooled; how lightly you have treated a woman's affections and aspirations. Some there are who, finding themselves in my position, would place in Mary's hands the packet of your correspondence which is before me as I write, and thus open her eyes to the fact that she is but the dupe of a man devoid of honour. Shall I do so? No. Rest assured that I shall not. If my sister is happy, let her remain so. My vendetta lies not in that direction. The fire of hatred may be stifled, but it can never be quenched. We shall be quits some day, and you will regret bitterly that you have broken your word so lightly. My revenge—the vengeance of a jealous woman—will fall upon you at a moment and in a manner you will little dream of. I return you your letters, as you may not care for them to fall into other hands, and from to-day I shall never again refer to what has passed. I am young, and may still obtain an upright and honourable man as husband. You are old, and are tottering slowly to your doom. Farewell.

ETHELWYNN MIVART

The letter fully explained a circumstance of which I had been entirely ignorant, namely, that the woman I had loved had actually been engaged to old Mr. Courtenay before her sister had married him. Its tenor showed how intensely antagonistic she was towards the man who had fooled her, and in the concluding sentence there was a distinct if covert threat—a threat of bitter revenge.

She had returned the old man's letters apparently in order to show that in her hand she held a further and more powerful weapon; she had not sought to break off his marriage with Mary, but had rather stood by, swallowed her anger, and calmly calculated upon a fierce vendetta at a moment when he would least expect it.

Truly those startling words spoken by Sir Bernard had been full of truth. I remembered them now, and discerned his meaning. He was at least an honest upright man who, although sometimes a trifle eccentric, had my interests deeply at heart. In the progress I had made in my profession I owed much to him, and even in my private affairs he had sought to guide me, although I had, alas! disregarded his repeated warnings.

I took up one after another of the letters my friend had examined, and found them to be the correspondence of a woman who was either angling after a wealthy husband, or who loved him with all the strength of her affection. Some of the communications were full of passion, and betrayed that poetry of soul that was innate in her. The letters were dated from Neneford, from Oban, and from various Mediterranean ports, where she had gone yachting with her uncle, Sir Thomas Heaton, the great Lancashire coal-owner. Sometimes she addressed him as "Dearest," at others as "Beloved," usually signing herself "Your Own." So full were they of the ardent passion characteristic of her that they held me in amazement. It was passion developed under its most profound and serious aspects; they showed the calm and thoughtful, not the brilliant side of intellect.

In Ethelwynn's character the passionate and the imaginative were blended equally and in the highest conceivable degree as combined with delicate female nature. Those letters, although written to a man in whose heart romance must long ago have been dead, showed how complex was her character, how fervent, enthusiastic and self-forgetting her love. At first I believed that those passionate outpourings were merely designed to captivate the old gentleman for his money; but when I read on I saw how intense her passion became towards the end, and how the culmination of it all was that wild reproachful missive written when the crushing blow fell so suddenly upon her.

Ethelwynn was a woman of extraordinary character, full of picturesque charm and glowing romance. To be tremblingly alive to the gentle impressions, and yet be able to preserve, when the prosecution of a design requires it, an immovable heart, amidst even the most imperious causes of subduing emotion, is perhaps not an impossible constitution of mind, but it is the utmost and rarest endowment of humanity. I knew her as a woman of highest mental powers touched with a melancholy sweetness. I was now aware of the cause of that melancholy.

Yet it was apparent that the serious and energetic part of her character was founded on deep passion, for after her sister's marriage with the man she had herself loved and had threatened, she had actually come there beneath their roof, and lived as her sister's companion, stifling all the hatred that had entered her heart, and preserving an outward calm that had no doubt entirely disarmed him.

Such a circumstance was extraordinary. To me, as to Ambler Jevons who knew her well, it seemed almost inconceivable that old

Mr. Courtenay should allow her to live there after receiving such a wild communication as that final letter. Especially curious, too, that Mary had never suspected or discovered her sister's jealousy. Yet so skilfully had Ethelwynn concealed her intention of revenge that both husband and wife had been entirely deceived.

Love, considered under its poetical aspect, is the union of passion and imagination. I had foolishly believed that this calm, sweet-voiced woman had loved me, but those letters made it plain that I had been utterly fooled. "Le mystère de l'existence," said Madame de Stael to her daughter, "c'est la rapport de nos erreurs avec nos peines."

And although there was in her, in her character, and in her terrible situation, a concentration of all the interests that belong to humanity, she was nevertheless a murderess.

"The truth is here," remarked my friend, laying his hand upon the heap of tender correspondence which had been brought to such an abrupt conclusion by the letter I have printed in its entirety. "It is a strange, romantic story, to say the least."

"Then you really believe that she is guilty?" I exclaimed, hoarsely.

He shrugged his shoulders significantly, but no word escaped his lips.

In the silence that fell between us, I glanced at him. His chin was sunk upon his breast, his brows knit, his thin fingers toying idly with the plain gold ring.

"Well?" I managed to exclaim at last. "What shall we do?"

"Do?" he echoed. "What can we do, my dear fellow? That woman's future is in your hands."

"Why in mine?" I asked. "In yours also, surely?"

"No," he answered resolutely, taking my hand and grasping it warmly. "No, Ralph; I know—I can see how you are suffering. You believed her to be a pure and honest woman—one above the common run—a woman fit for helpmate and wife. Well, I, too, must confess myself very much misled. I believed her to be all that you imagined; indeed, if her face be any criterion, she is utterly unspoiled by the world and its wickedness. In my careful studies in physiognomy I have found that very seldom does a perfect face like hers cover an evil heart. Hence, I confess, that this discovery has amazed me quite as much as it has you. I somehow feel—"

"I don't believe it!" I cried, interrupting him. "I don't believe, Ambler, that she murdered him—I can't believe it. Her's is not the face of a murderess."

"Faces sometimes deceive," he said quietly. "Recollect that a clever woman can give a truthful appearance to a lie where a man utterly fails."

"I know—I know. But even with this circumstantial proof I can't and won't believe it."

"Please yourself, my dear fellow," he answered. "I know it is hard to believe ill of a woman whom one loves so devotedly as you've loved Ethelwynn. But be brave, bear up, and face the situation like a man."

"I am facing it," I said resolutely. "I will face it by refusing to believe that she killed him. The letters are plain enough. She was engaged secretly to old Courtenay, who threw her over in favour of her sister. But is there anything so very extraordinary in that? One hears of such things very often."

"But the final letter?"

"It bears evidence of being written in the first moments of wild anger on realising that she had been abandoned in favour of Mary. Probably she has by this time quite forgotten the words she wrote. And in any case the fact of her living beneath the same roof, supervising the household, and attending to the sick man during Mary's absence, entirely negatives any idea of revenge."

Jevons smiled dubiously, and I myself knew that my argument was not altogether logical.

"Well?" I continued. "And is not that your opinion?"

"No. It is not," he replied, bluntly.

"Then what is to be done?" I asked, after a pause.

"The matter rests entirely with you, Ralph," he replied. "I know what I should do in a similar case."

"What would you do? Advise me," I urged eagerly.

"I should take the whole of the correspondence, just as it is, place it in the grate there, and burn it," he said.

I was not prepared for such a suggestion. A similar idea had occurred to me, but I feared to suggest to him such a mode of defeating the ends of justice.

"But if I do that will you give me a vow of secrecy?" I asked, quickly. "Recollect that such a step is a serious offence against the law."

"When I pass out of this room I shall have no further recollection of ever having seen any letters," he answered, again giving me his hand. "In this matter my desire is only to help you. If, as you believe, Ethelwynn is innocent, then no harm can be done in destroying the letters, whereas if she is actually the assassin she must, sooner or later, betray her guilt.

A woman may be clever, but she can never successfully cover the crime of murder."

"Then you are willing that I, as finder of those letters, shall burn them? And further, that no word shall pass regarding this discovery?"

"Most willing," he replied. "Come," he added, commencing to gather them together. "Let us lose no time, or perhaps the constable on duty below or one of the plain-clothes men may come prying in here."

Then at his direction and with his assistance I willingly tore up each letter in small pieces, placed the whole in the grate where dead cinders still remained, and with a vesta set a light to them. For a few moments they blazed fiercely up the chimney, then died out, leaving only black tinder.

"We must make a feint of having tried to light the fire," said Jevons, taking an old newspaper, twisting it up, and setting light to it in the grate, afterwards stirring up the dead tinder with the tinder of the letters. "I'll remark incidentally to the constable that we've tried to get a fire, and didn't succeed. That will prevent Thorpe poking his nose into it."

So when the whole of the letters had been destroyed, all traces of their remains effaced and the safe re-locked, we went downstairs—not, however, before my companion had made a satisfactory explanation to the constable and entirely misled him as to what we had been doing.

XII

I Receive a Visitor

The adjourned inquest was resumed on the day appointed in the big room at the Star and Garter at Kew, and the public, eager as ever for sensational details, overflowed through the bar and out into the street, until the police were compelled to disperse the crowd. The evening papers had worked up all kinds of theories, some worthy of attention, others ridiculous; hence the excitement and interest had become intense.

The extraordinary nature of the wound which caused Mr. Courtenay's death was the chief element of mystery. Our medical evidence had produced a sensation, for we had been agreed that to inflict such a wound with any instrument which could pass through the exterior orifice was an absolute impossibility. Sir Bernard and myself were still both bewildered. In the consulting room at Harley Street we had discussed it a dozen times, but could arrive at no definite conclusion as to how such a terrible wound could possibly have been caused.

I noticed a change in Sir Bernard. He seemed mopish, thoughtful, and somewhat despondent. Usually he was a busy, bustling man, whose manner with his patients was rather brusque, and who, unlike the majority of my own profession, went to the point at once. There is no profession in which one is compelled to exercise so much affected patience and courtesy as in the profession of medicine. Patients will bore you to death with long and tedious histories of all their ailments since the days when they chewed a gutta-percha teething-ring, and to appear impatient is to court a reputation for flippancy and want of attention. Great men may hold up their hands and cry "Enough!" But small men must sit with pencil poised, apparently intensely interested, and listen through until the patient has exhausted his long-winded recollections of all his ills.

Contrary to his usual custom, Sir Bernard did not now return to Hove each evening, but remained at Harley Street—dining alone off a chop or a steak, and going out afterwards, probably to his club. His change of manner surprised me. I noticed in him distinct signs of nervous disorder; and on several afternoons he sent round to me at the

Hospital, saying that he could not see his patients, and asking me to run back to Harley Street and take his place.

On the evening before the adjourned inquest I remarked to him that he did not appear very well, and his reply, in a strained, desponding voice, was:

"Poor Courtenay has gone. He was my best friend."

Yes, it was as I expected, he was sorrowing over his friend.

When we had re-assembled at the Star and Garter, he entered quietly and took a seat beside me just before the commencement of the proceedings.

The Coroner, having read over all the depositions taken on the first occasion, asked the police if they had any further evidence to offer, whereupon the local inspector of the T Division answered with an air of mystery:

"We have nothing, sir, which we can make public. Active inquiries are still in progress."

"No further medical evidence?" asked the coroner.

I turned towards Sir Bernard inquiringly, and as I did so my eye caught a face hidden by a black veil, seated among the public at the far side of the room. It was Ethelwynn herself—come there to watch the proceedings and hear with her own ears whether the police had obtained traces of the assassin!

Her anxious countenance shone through her veil haggard and white; her eyes were fixed upon the Coroner. She hung breathlessly upon his every word.

"We have no further evidence," replied the inspector.

There was a pause. The public who were there in search of some solution of the bewildering mystery which had been published in every paper through the land, were disappointed. They had expected at least to hear some expert evidence—which, if not always reliable, is always interesting. But there seemed an inclination on the part of the police to maintain a silence which increased rather than lessened the mystery.

"Well, gentlemen," exclaimed Dr. Diplock, turning at last to the twelve local tradesmen who formed the jury, "you have heard the evidence in this curious case, and your duty is to decide in what manner the deceased came by his death, whether by accidental means, or by foul play. I think in the circumstances you will have very little difficulty in deciding. The case is a mysterious one—a very mysterious one. The deceased was a gentleman of means who was suffering from a malignant disease, and that disease must have proved fatal within a short time. Now this fact appears to have been well known to himself, to the members of his household, and probably to most of his friends. Nevertheless, he was found dead in circumstances which point most strongly to wilful murder. If he was actually murdered, the assassin, whoever he was, had some very strong incentive in killing him at once, because he might well have waited another few months for the fatal termination of the disease. That fact, however, is not for you to consider, gentlemen. You are here for the sole purpose of deciding whether or not this case is one of murder. If, in your opinion it is, then it becomes your duty to return a verdict to that effect and leave it to the police to discover the assassin. To comment at length on the many mysterious circumstances surrounding the tragedy is, I think, needless. The depositions I have just read are sufficiently full and explanatory, especially the evidence of Sir Bernard Eyton and of Doctor Boyd, both of whom, besides being well-known in the profession, were personal friends of the deceased. In considering your verdict I would further beg of you not to heed any theories you may have read in the newspapers, but adjudge the matter from a fair and impartial standpoint, and give your verdict as you honestly believe the truth to be."

The dead silence which had prevailed during the Coroner's address was at once broken by the uneasy moving of the crowd. I glanced across at Ethelwynn, and saw her sitting immovable, breathless, statuesque.

She watched the foreman of the jury whispering to two or three of his colleagues in the immediate vicinity. The twelve tradesmen consulted together in an undertone, while the reporters at the table conversed audibly. They, too, were disappointed at being unable to obtain any sensational "copy."

"If you wish to retire in order to consider your verdict, gentlemen, you are quite at liberty to do so," remarked the coroner.

"That is unnecessary," replied the foreman. "We are agreed unanimously."

"Upon what?"

"Our verdict is that the deceased was wilfully murdered by some person or persons unknown."

"Very well, gentlemen. Of course in my position I am not permitted to give you advice, but I think that you could have arrived at no other verdict. The police will use every endeavour to discover the identity of the assassin."

I glanced at Ethelwynn, and at that instant she turned her head, and her eyes met mine. She started quickly, her face blanched to the lips; then she rose unsteadily, and with the crowd went slowly out.

Ambler Jevons, who had been seated at the opposite side of the room, got up and rushed away; therefore I had no chance to get a word with him. He had glanced at me significantly, and I knew well what passed through his mind. Like myself, he was thinking of that strange letter we had found among the dead man's effects and had agreed to destroy.

About nine o'clock that same night I had left Sir Bernard's and was strolling slowly round to my rooms, when my friend's cheery voice sounded behind me. He was on his way to have a smoke with me as usual, he explained. So we entered together, and after I had turned up the light and brought out the drinks he flung himself into his habitual chair, and stretching himself wearily said—

"The affair becomes more mysterious hourly."

"How?" I inquired quickly.

"I've been down to Kew this afternoon," was his rather ambiguous response. "I had to go to my office directly after the inquest, but I returned at once."

"And what have you discovered? Anything fresh?"

"Yes," he responded slowly. "A fresh fact or two—facts that still increase the mystery."

"What are they? Tell me," I urged.

"No, Ralph, old chap. When I am certain of their true importance I'll explain them to you. At present I desire to pursue my own methods until I arrive at some clear conclusion."

This disinclination to tell me the truth was annoying. He had always been quite frank and open, explaining all his theories, and showing to me any weak points in the circumstantial evidence. Yet suddenly, as it seemed to me, he had become filled with a strange mistrust. Why, I could not conceive.

"But surely you can tell me the nature of your discoveries?" I said. "There need be no secrets between us in this affair."

"No, Ralph. But I'm superstitious enough to believe that ill-luck follows a premature exposure of one's plans," he said.

His excuse was a lame one—a very lame one. I smiled—in order to show him that I read through such a transparent attempt to mislead me.

"I might have refused to show you that letter of Ethelwynn's," I protested. "Yet our interests being mutual I handed it to you."

"And it is well that you did."

"Why?"

"Because knowledge of it has changed the whole course of my inquiries."

"Changed them from one direction to another?"

He nodded.

"And you are now prosecuting them in the direction of Ethelwynn?"

"No," he answered. "Not exactly."

I looked at his face, and saw upon it an expression of profound mysteriousness. His dark, well-marked countenance was a complex one always, but at that moment I was utterly unable to discern whether he spoke the truth, or whether he only wished to mislead my suspicions into a different channel. That he was the acme of shrewdness, that his powers of deduction were extraordinary, and that his patience in unravelling a secret was almost beyond comprehension I knew well. Even those great trackers of criminals, Shaw and Maddox, of New Scotland Yard, held him in respect, and admired his acute intelligence and marvellous power of perception.

Yet his attempt to evade a question which so closely concerned my own peace of mind and future happiness tried my patience. If he had really discovered some fresh facts I considered it but right that I should be acquainted with them.

"Has your opinion changed as to the identity of the person who committed the crime?" I asked him, rather abruptly.

"Not in the least," he responded, slowly lighting his foul pipe. "How can it, in the face of the letter we burnt?"

"Then you think that jealousy was the cause of the tragedy? That she—"

"No, not jealousy," he interrupted, speaking quite calmly. "The facts I have discovered go to show that the motive was not jealousy."

"Hatred, then?"

"No, not hatred."

"Then what?"

"That's just where I fail to form a theory," he answered, after a brief silence, during which he watched the blue smoke curl upward to the sombre ceiling of my room. "In a few days I hope to discover the motive."

"You will let me assist you?" I urged, eagerly. "I am at your disposal at any hour."

"No," he answered, decisively. "You are prejudiced, Ralph. You unfortunately still love that woman."

A sigh escaped me. What he said was, alas! too true. I had adored her through those happy months prior to the tragedy. She had come into my lonely bachelor life as the one ray of sunlight that gave me hope and happiness, and I had lived for her alone. Because of her I had striven to rise in the profession, and had laboured hard so that in a little while I might be in a position to marry and buy that quiet country practice that was my ideal existence. And even now, with my idol broken by the knowledge of her previous engagement to the man now dead, I confess that I nevertheless still entertained a strong affection for her. The memory of a past love is often more sweet than the love itself—and to men it is so very often fatal.

I had risen to pour out some whiskey for my companion when, of a sudden, my man opened the door and announced:

"There's a lady to see you, sir."

"A lady?" we both exclaimed, with one voice.

"Yes, sir," and he handed me a card.

I glanced at it. My visitor was the very last person I desired to meet at that moment, for she was none other than Ethelwynn herself.

"I'll go, old chap," Jevons cried, springing to his feet, and draining his glass at a single draught. "She mustn't meet me here. Good-bye till to-morrow. Remember, betray no sign to her that you know the truth. It's certainly a curious affair, as it now stands; but depend upon it that there's more complication and mystery in it than we have yet suspected."

XIII

MY LOVE

As soon as Ambler Jevons had slipped out through my little study my love came slowly forward, as though with some unwillingness.

She was dressed, as at the inquest, in deep mourning, wearing a smartly-cut tailor-made dress trimmed with astrachan and a neat toque, her pale countenance covered with a thick spotted veil.

"Ralph," she exclaimed in a low voice, "forgive me for calling upon you at this hour. I know it's indiscreet, but I am very anxious to see you."

I returned her greeting, rather coldly I am afraid, and led her to the big armchair which had only a moment before been vacated by my friend.

When she seated herself and faced me I saw how changed she was, even though she did not lift her veil. Her dark eyes seemed haggard and sunken, her cheeks, usually pink with the glow of health, were white, almost ghastly, and her slim, well-gloved hand, resting upon the chair arm, trembled perceptibly.

"You have not come to me for two whole days, Ralph," she commenced in a tone of complaint. "Surely you do not intend to desert me in these hours of distress?"

"I must apologise," I responded quickly, remembering Jevons' advice. "But the fact is I myself have been very upset over the sad affair, and, in addition, I've had several serious cases during the past few days. Sir Bernard has been unwell, and I've been compelled to look after his practice."

"Sir Bernard!" she exclaimed, in a tone which instantly struck me as strange. It was as though she held him in abhorrence. "Do you know, Ralph, I hate to think of you in association with that man."

"Why?" I asked, much surprised, while at that same moment the thought flashed through my mind how often Sir Bernard had given me vague warnings regarding her.

They were evidently bitter enemies.

"I have no intention to give my reasons," she replied, her brows slightly knit. "I merely give it as my opinion that you should no longer remain in association with him."

"But surely you are alone in that opinion!" I said. "He bears a high character, and is certainly one of the first physicians in London. His practice is perhaps the most valuable of any medical man at the present moment."

"I don't deny that," she said, her gloved fingers twitching nervously. "A man may be a king, and at the same time a knave."

I smiled. It was apparent that her intention was to separate me from the man to whom I owed nearly all, if not quite all, my success. And why? Because he knew of her past, and she feared that he might, in a moment of confidence, betray all to me.

"Vague hints are always irritating," I remarked. "Cannot you give me some reason for your desire that my friendship with him should end?"

"No. If I did, you would accuse me of selfish motives," she said, fixing her dark eyes upon me.

Could a woman with a Madonna-like countenance be actually guilty of murder? It seemed incredible. And yet her manner was that of a woman haunted by the terrible secret of her crime. At that moment she was seeking, by ingenious means, to conceal the truth regarding the past. She feared that my intimate friendship with the great physician might result in her unmasking.

"I can't see that selfish motives enter into this affair at all," I remarked. "Whatever you tell me, Ethelwynn, is, I know, for my own benefit. Therefore you should at least be explicit."

"I can't be more explicit."

"Why not?"

"Because I have no right to utter a libel without being absolutely certain of the facts."

"I don't quite follow you," I said, rather puzzled.

"I mean that at present the information I have is vague," she replied. "But if it is the truth, as I expect to establish it, then you must dissociate yourself from him, Ralph."

"You have only suspicions?"

"Only suspicions."

"Of what?"

"Of a fact which will some day astound you."

Our eyes met again, and I saw in hers a look of intense earnestness that caused me to wonder. To what could she possibly be referring?

"You certainly arouse my curiosity," I said, affecting to laugh. "Do you really think Sir Bernard such a very dreadful person, then?"

"Ah! You do not take my words seriously," she remarked. "I am warning you, Ralph, for your own benefit. It is a pity you do not heed me."

"I do heed you," I declared. "Only your statement is so strange that it appears almost incredible."

"Incredible it may seem; but one day ere long you will be convinced that what I say to-night is the truth."

"What do you say?"

"I say that Sir Bernard Eyton, the man in whom you place every confidence, and whose example as a great man in his profession you are so studiously following, is not your friend."

"Nor yours, I suppose?"

"No, neither is he mine."

This admission was at least the truth. I had known it long ago. But what had been the cause of difference between them was hidden in deepest mystery. Sir Bernard, as old Mr. Courtenay's most intimate friend, knew, in all probability, of his engagement to her, and of its rupture in favour of her sister Mary. It might even be that Sir Bernard had had a hand in the breaking of the engagement. If so, that would well account for her violent hostility towards him.

Such thoughts, with others, flashed through my mind as I sat there facing her. She was leaning back, her hands fallen idly upon her lap, peering straight at me through that spotted veil which, half-concealing her wondrous beauty, imparted to her an additional air of mystery.

"You have quarrelled with Sir Bernard, I presume?" I hazarded.

"Quarrelled!" she echoed. "We were never friends."

Truly she possessed all a clever woman's presence of mind in the evasion of a leading question.

"He was an acquaintance of yours?"

"An acquaintance—yes. But I have always distrusted him."

"Mary likes him, I believe," I remarked. "He was poor Courtenay's most intimate friend for many years."

"She judges him from that standpoint alone. Any of her husband's friends were hers, and she was fully cognisant of Sir Bernard's unceasing attention to the sufferer."

"If that is so it is rather a pity that she was recently so neglectful," I said.

"I know, Ralph—I know the reason of it all," she faltered. "I can't explain to you, because it is not just that I should expose my sister's secret. But I know the truth which, when revealed, will make it clear to the world that her apparent neglect was not culpable. She had a motive."

"A motive in going to town of an evening and enjoying herself!" I exclaimed. "Of course, the motive was to obtain relaxation. When a man is more than twice the age of his wife, the latter is apt to chafe beneath the golden fetter. It's the same everywhere—in Mayfair as in Mile End; in Suburbia as in a rural village. Difference of age is difference of temperament; and difference of temperament opens a breach which only a lover can fill."

She was silent—her eyes cast down. She saw that the attempt to vindicate her sister had, as before, utterly and ignominiously failed.

"Yes, Ralph, you are right," she admitted at last. "Judged from a philosophic standpoint a wife ought not to be more than ten years her husband's junior. Love which arises out of mere weakness is as easily fixed upon one object as another; and consequently is at all times transferable. It is so pleasant to us women to be admired, and so soothing to be loved that the grand trial of constancy to a young woman married to an elderly man is not to add one more conquest to her triumphs, but to earn the respect and esteem of the man who is her husband. And it is difficult. Of that I am convinced."

There was for the first time a true ring of earnestness in her voice, and I saw by her manner that her heart was overburdened by the sorrow that had fallen upon her sister. Her character was a complex one which I had failed always to analyse, and it seemed just then as though her endeavour was to free her sister of all the responsibilities of her married life. She had made that effort once before, prior to the tragedy, but its motive was hidden in obscurity.

"Women are often very foolish," she went on, half-apologetically. "Having chosen their lover for his suitability they usually allow the natural propensity of their youthful minds to invest him with every ideal of excellence. That is a fatal error committed by the majority of women. We ought to be satisfied with him as he is, rather than imagine him what he never can be."

"Yes," I said, smiling at her philosophy. "It would certainly save them a world of disappointment in after life. It has always struck me that the extravagant investiture of fancy does not belong, as is commonly supposed, to the meek, true and abiding attachment which it is woman's highest virtue and noblest distinction to feel. I strongly suspect it is vanity, and not affection, which leads a woman to believe her lover perfect; because it enhances her triumph to be the choice of such a man."

"Ah! I'm glad that we agree, Ralph," she said with a sigh and an air of deep seriousness. "The part of the true-hearted woman is to be satisfied with her lover such as he is, old or young, and to consider him, with all his faults, as sufficiently perfect for her. No after development of character can then shake her faith, no ridicule or exposure can weaken her tenderness for a single moment; while, on the other hand, she who has blindly believed her lover to be without a fault, must ever be in danger of awaking to the conviction that her love exists no longer."

"As in your own case," I added, in an endeavour to obtain from her the reason of this curious discourse.

"My own case!" she echoed. "No, Ralph. I have never believed you to be a perfect ideal. I have loved you because I knew that you loved me. Our tastes are in common, our admiration for each other is mutual, and our affection strong and ever-increasing—until—until—"

And faltering, she stopped abruptly, without concluding her sentence.

"Until what?" I asked.

Tears sprang to her eyes. One drop rolled down her white cheek until it reached her veil, and stood there sparkling beneath the light.

"You know well," she said hoarsely. "Until the tragedy. From that moment, Ralph, you changed. You are not the same to me as formerly. I feel—I feel," she confessed, covering her face with her hands and sobbing bitterly, "I feel that I have lost you."

"Lost me! I don't understand," I said, feigning not to comprehend her.

"I feel as though you no longer hold me in esteem," she faltered through her tears. "Something tells me, Ralph, that—that your love for me has vanished, never to return!"

With a sudden movement she raised her veil, and I saw how white and anxious was her fair countenance. I could not bring myself to believe that such a perfect face could conceal a heart blackened by the crime of murder. But, alas! all men are weak where a pretty woman is concerned. After all, it is feminine wiles and feminine graces that rule our world. Man is but a poor mortal at best, easily moved to sympathy by a woman's tears, and as easily misled by the touch of a soft hand or a passionate caress upon the lips. Diplomacy is inborn in woman, and although every woman is not an adventuress, yet one and all are clever actresses when the game of love is being played.

The thought of that letter I had read and destroyed again recurred to me. Yes, she had concealed her secret—the secret of her attempt to marry Courtenay for his money. And yet if, as seemed so apparent, she had nursed her hatred, was it not but natural that she should assume a hostile attitude towards her sister—the woman who had eclipsed her in the old man's affections? Nevertheless, on the contrary, she was always apologetic where Mary was concerned, and had always sought to conceal her shortcomings and domestic infelicity. It was that point which so sorely puzzled me.

"Why should my love for you become suddenly extinguished?" I asked, for want of something other to say.

"I don't know," she faltered. "I cannot tell why, but I have a distinct distrust of the future, a feeling that we are drifting apart."

She spoke the truth. A woman in love is quick of perception, and no feigned affection on the man's part can ever blind her.

I saw that she read my heart like an open book, and at once strove to reassure her, trying to bring myself to believe that I had misjudged her.

"No, no, dearest," I said, rising with a hollow pretence of caressing her tears away. "You are nervous, and upset by the tragedy. Try to forget it all."

"Forget!" she echoed in a hard voice, her eyes cast down despondently. "Forget that night! Ah, no, I can never forget it—never!"

XIV

Is Distinctly Curious

The dark days of the London winter brightened into spring, but the mystery of old Mr. Courtenay's death remained an enigma inexplicable to police and public. Ambler Jevons had prosecuted independent inquiries assiduously in various quarters, detectives had watched the subsequent movements of Short and the other servants, but all to no purpose. The sudden disappearance of Short was discovered to be due to the illness of his brother.

The identity of the assassin, as well as the mode in which the extraordinary wound had been inflicted, both remained mysteries impenetrable.

At Guy's we were a trifle under-staffed, and my work was consequently heavy; while, added to that, Sir Bernard was suffering from the effects of a severe chill, and had not been able to come to town for nearly a month. Therefore, I had been kept at it practically night and day, dividing my time between the hospital, Harley Street, and my own rooms. I saw little of my friend Jevons, for his partner had been ordered to Bournemouth for his health, and therefore his constant attendance at his office in Mark Lane was imperative. Ambler had now but little leisure save on Sundays, when we would usually dine together at the Cavour, the Globe, the Florence, or some other foreign restaurant.

Whenever I spoke to him of the tragedy, he would sigh, his face would assume a puzzled expression, and he would declare that the affair utterly passed his comprehension. Once or twice he referred to Ethelwynn, but it struck me that he did not give tongue to what passed within his mind for fear of offending me. His methods were based on patience, therefore I often wondered whether he was still secretly at work upon the case, and if so, whether he had gained any additional facts. Yet he told me nothing. It was a mystery, he said—that was all.

Of Ethelwynn I saw but little, making my constant occupation with Sir Bernard's patients my excuse. She had taken up her abode with Mrs. Henniker—the cousin at whose house Mary had stayed on the night of the tragedy. The furniture at Richmond Road had been removed and the house advertised for sale, young Mrs. Courtenay having moved to her aunt's house in the country, a few miles from Bath.

On several occasions I had dined at Redcliffe Square, finding both Mrs. Henniker and her husband extremely agreeable. Henniker was partner in a big brewing concern at Clapham, and a very good fellow; while his wife was a middle-aged, fair-haired woman, of the type who shop of afternoons in High Street, Kensington. Ethelwynn had always been a particular favourite with both, hence she was a welcome guest at Redcliffe Square. Old Mr. Courtenay had had business relations with Henniker a couple of years before, and a slight difference had led to an open quarrel. For that reason they had not of late visited at Kew.

On the occasions I had spent the evening with Ethelwynn at their house I had watched her narrowly, yet neither by look nor by action did she betray any sign of a guilty secret. Her manner had during those weeks changed entirely; for she seemed perfectly calm and self-possessed, and although she alluded but seldom to our love, she treated me with that same sweet tenderness as before the fatal night of her brother-in-law's assassination.

I must admit that her attitude, although it inspired me with a certain amount of confidence, nevertheless caused me to ponder deeply. I knew enough of human nature to be aware that it is woman's métier to keep up appearances. Was she keeping up an appearance of innocence, although her heart was blackened by a crime?

One evening, when we chanced to be left alone in the little smoking-room after dinner, she suddenly turned to me, saying:

"I've often thought how strange you must have thought my visit to your rooms that night, Ralph. It was unpardonable, I know—only I wanted to warn you of that man."

"Of Sir Bernard?" I observed, laughing.

"Yes. But it appears that you have not heeded me," she sighed. "I fear, Ralph, that you will regret some day."

"Why should I regret? Your fears are surely baseless."

"No," she answered decisively. "They are not baseless. I have reasons— strong ones—for urging you to break your connexion with him. He is no friend to you."

I smiled. I knew quite well that he was no friend of hers. Once or twice of late he had said in that peevish snappy voice of his:

"I wonder what that woman, Mrs. Courtenay's sister, is doing? I hear nothing of her."

WILLIAM LE QUEUX

I did not enlighten him, for I had no desire to hear her maligned. I knew the truth myself sufficiently well.

But turning to her I looked straight into her dark luminous eyes, those eyes that held me always as beneath their spell, saying:

"He has proved himself my best friend, up to the present. I have no reason to doubt him."

"But you will have. I warn you."

"In what manner, then, is he my enemy?"

She hesitated, as though half-fearing to respond to my question. Presently she said:

"He is my enemy—and therefore yours."

"Why is he your enemy?" I asked, eager to clear up a point which had so long puzzled me.

"I cannot tell," she responded. "One sometimes gives offence and makes enemies without being aware of it."

The evasion was a clever one. Another illustration of tactful ingenuity.

By dint of careful cross-examination I endeavoured to worm from her the secret of my chief's antagonism, but she was dumb to every inquiry, fencing with me in a manner that would have done credit to a police-court solicitor. Though sweet, innocent, and intensely charming, yet there was a reverse side of her character, strong, firm-minded, almost stern in its austerity.

I must here say that our love, once so passionate and displayed by fond kisses and hand-pressing, in the usual manner of lovers, had gradually slackened. A kiss on arrival and another on departure was all the demonstration of affection that now passed between us. I doubted her; and though I strove hard to conceal my true feelings, I fear that my coldness was apparent, not only to her but to the Hennikers also. She had complained of it when she called at my rooms, and certainly she had full reason for doing so. I am not one of those who can feign love. Some men can; I cannot.

Thus it will be seen that although a certain coolness had arisen between us, in a manner that seemed almost mutual, we were nevertheless the best of friends. Once or twice she dined with me at a restaurant, and went to a play afterwards, on such occasions remarking that it seemed like "old times," in the early days of our blissful love. And sometimes she would recall those sweet halcyon hours, until I felt a pang of regret that my trust in her had been shaken by that letter found among the dead man's effects and that tiny piece of chenille. But I steeled my heart, because I felt assured that the truth must out some day.

Mine was a strange position for any man. I loved this woman, remember; loved her with all my heart and with all my soul. Yet that letter penned by her had shown me that she had once angled for larger spoils, and was not the sweet unsophisticated woman I had always supposed her to be. It showed me, too, that in her heart had rankled a fierce, undying hatred.

Because of this I did not seek her society frequently, but occupied myself diligently with my patients—seeking solace in my work, as many another professional man does where love or domestic happiness is concerned. There are few men in my profession who have not had their affairs of the heart, many of them serious ones. The world never knows how difficult it is for a doctor to remain heart-whole. Sometimes his lady patients deliberately set themselves to capture him, and will speak ill-naturedly of him if he refuses to fall into their net. At others, sympathy with a sufferer leads to a flirtation during convalescence, and often a word spoken in jest in order to cheer is taken seriously by romantic girls who believe that to marry a doctor is to attain social status and distinction.

Heigho! When I think of all my own little love episodes, and of the ingenious diplomacy to which I have been compelled to resort in order to avoid tumbling into pitfalls set by certain designing Daughters of Eve, I cannot but sympathise with every other medical man who is on the right side of forty and sound of wind and limb. There is not a doctor in all the long list in the medical register who could not relate strange stories of his own love episodes—romances which have sometimes narrowly escaped developing into tragedies, and plots concocted by women to inveigle and to allure. It is so easy for a woman to feign illness and call in the doctor to chat to her and amuse her. Lots of women in London do that regularly. They will play with a doctor's heart as a sort of pastime, while the unfortunate medico often cannot afford to hold aloof for fear of offending. If he does, then evil gossip will spread among his patients and his practice may suffer considerably; for in no profession does a man rely so entirely upon his good name and a reputation for care and integrity as in that of medicine.

I do not wish it for a moment to be taken that I am antagonistic to women, or that I would ever speak ill of them. I merely refer to the mean method of some of the idling class, who deliberately call in the doctor for the purpose of flirtation and then boast of it to their intimates. To such, a man's heart or a man's future are of no consequence. The doctor is easily visible, and is therefore the easiest prey to all and sundry.

In my own practice I had had a good deal of experience of it. And I am not alone. Every other medical man, if not a grey-headed fossil or a wizened woman-hater, has had similar episodes; many strange—some even startling.

Reader, in this narrative of curious events and remarkable happenings, I am taking you entirely and completely into my confidence. I seek to conceal nothing, nor to exaggerate in any particular, but to present the truth as a plain matter-of-fact statement of what actually occurred. I was a unit among a hundred thousand others engaged in the practice of medicine, not more skilled than the majority, even though Sir Bernard's influence and friendship had placed me in a position of prominence. But in this brief life of ours it is woman who makes us dance as puppets on our miniature stage, who leads us to brilliant success or to black ruin, who exalts us above our fellows or hurls us into oblivion. Woman—always woman.

Since that awful suspicion had fallen upon me that the hand that had struck old Mr. Courtenay was that soft delicate one that I had so often carried to my lips, a blank had opened in my life. Consumed by conflicting thoughts, I recollected how sweet and true had been our affection; with what an intense passionate love-look she had gazed upon me with those wonderful eyes of hers; with what wild fierce passion her lips would meet mine in fond caress.

Alas! it had all ended. She had acted a lie to me. That letter told the bitter truth. Hence, we were gradually drifting apart.

One Sunday morning in May, just as I had finished my breakfast and flung myself into an armchair to smoke, as was my habit on the day of rest, my man entered, saying that Lady Twickenham had sent to ask if I could go round to Park Lane at once. Not at all pleased with this call, just at a moment of laziness, I was, nevertheless, obliged to respond, because her ladyship was one of Sir Bernard's best patients; and suffering as she was from a malignant internal complaint, I knew it was necessary to respond at once to the summons.

On arrival at her bedside I quickly saw the gravity of the situation; but, unfortunately, I knew very little of the case, because Sir Bernard himself always made a point of attending her personally. Although elderly, she was a prominent woman in society, and had recommended many patients to my chief in earlier days, before he attained the fame he had now achieved. I remained with her a couple of hours; but finding myself utterly confused regarding her symptoms, I resolved to take the afternoon train down to Hove and consult Sir Bernard. I suggested this course to her ladyship, who was at once delighted with the suggestion. Therefore, promising to return at ten o'clock that night, I went out, swallowed a hasty luncheon, and took train down to Brighton.

The house was one of those handsome mansions facing the sea at Hove, and as I drove up to it on that bright, sunny afternoon, it seemed to me an ideal residence for a man jaded by the eternal worries of a physician's life. The sea-breeze stirred the sun-blinds before the windows, and the flowers in the well-kept boxes were already gay with bloom. I knew the place well, for I had been down many times before; therefore, when the page opened the door he showed me at once to the study, a room which lay at the back of the big drawing-room.

"Sir Bernard is in, sir," the page said. "I'll tell him at once you're here," and he closed the door, leaving me alone.

I walked towards the window, which looked out upon a small flower garden, and in so doing, passed the writing table. A sheet of foolscap lay upon it, and curiosity prompted me to glance at it.

What I saw puzzled me considerably; for beside the paper was a letter of my own that I had sent him on the previous day, while upon the foolscap were many lines of writing in excellent imitation of my own!

He had been practising the peculiarities of my own handwriting. But with what purpose was a profound mystery.

I was bending over, closely examining the words and noting how carefully they had been traced in imitation, when, of a sudden, I heard a voice in the drawing-room adjoining—a woman's voice.

I pricked my ears and listened—for the eccentric old fellow to entertain was most unusual. He always hated women, because he saw too much of their wiles and wilfulness as patients.

Nevertheless it was apparent that he had a lady visitor in the adjoining room, and a moment later it was equally apparent that they were not on the most friendly terms; for, of a sudden, the voice sounded again quite distinctly—raised in a cry of horror, as though at some sudden and terrible discovery.

"Ah! I see—I see it all now!" shrieked the unknown woman. "You have deceived me! Coward! You call yourself a man—you, who would sell a woman's soul to the devil!"

"Hold your tongue!" cried a gruff voice which I recognised as Sir Bernard's. "You may be overheard. Recollect that your safety can only be secured by your secrecy."

"I shall tell the truth!" the woman declared.

"Very well," laughed the man who was my chief in a tone of defiance. "Tell it, and condemn yourself."

XV

I am Called for Consultation

The incident was certainly a puzzling one, for when, a few minutes later, my chief entered the study, his face, usually ashen grey, was flushed with excitement.

"I've been having trouble with a lunatic," he explained, after greeting me, and inquiring why I had come down to consult him. "The woman's people are anxious to place her under restraint; yet, for the present, there is not quite sufficient evidence of insanity to sign the certificate. Did you overhear her in the next room?" And, seating himself at his table, he looked at me through his glasses with those keen penetrating eyes that age had not dimmed or time dulled.

"I heard voices," I admitted, "that was all." The circumstance was a strange one, and those words were so ominous that I was determined not to reveal to him the conversation I had overheard.

"Like many other women patients suffering from brain troubles, she has taken a violent dislike to me, and believes that I'm the very devil in human form," he said, smiling. "Fortunately, she had a friend with her, or she might have attacked me tooth and nail just now," and leaning back in his chair he laughed at the idea—laughed so lightly that my suspicions were almost disarmed.

But not quite. Had you been in my place you would have had your curiosity and suspicion aroused to no mean degree—not only by the words uttered by the woman and Sir Bernard's defiant reply, but also by the fact that the female voice sounded familiar.

A man knows the voice of his love above all. The voice that I had heard in that adjoining room was, to the best of my belief, that of Ethelwynn.

With a resolution to probe this mystery slowly, and without unseemly haste, I dropped the subject, and commenced to ask his advice regarding the complicated case of Lady Twickenham. The history of it, and the directions he gave can serve no purpose if written here; therefore suffice it to say that I remained to dinner and caught the nine o'clock express back to London.

While at dinner, a meal served in that severe style which characterised the austere old man's daily life, I commenced to talk of the antics of insane persons and their extraordinary antipathies, but quickly discerned that he had neither intention nor desire to speak of them. He replied in those snappy monosyllables which told me plainly that the subject was distasteful to him, and when I bade him good-bye and drove to the station I was more puzzled than ever by his strange behaviour. He was eccentric, it was true; but I knew all his little odd ways, the eccentricity of genius, and could plainly see that his recent indisposition, which had prevented him from attending at Harley Street, was due to nerves rather than to a chill.

The trains from Brighton to London on Sunday evenings are always crowded, mainly by business people compelled to return to town in readiness for the toil of the coming week. Week-end trippers and day excursionists fill the compartments to overflowing, whether it be chilly spring or blazing summer, for Brighton is ever popular with the jaded Londoner who is enabled to "run down" without fatigue, and get a cheap health-giving sea-breeze for a few hours after the busy turmoil of the Metropolis.

On this Sunday night it was no exception. The first-class compartment was crowded, mostly be it said, by third-class passengers who had "tipped" the guard, and when we had started I noticed in the far corner opposite me a pale-faced young girl of about twenty or so, plainly dressed in shabby black. She was evidently a third-class passenger, and the guard, taking compassion upon her fragile form in the mad rush for seats, had put her into our carriage. She was not good-looking, indeed rather plain; her countenance wearing a sad, pre-occupied expression as she leaned her chin upon her hand and gazed out upon the lights of the town we were leaving.

I noticed that her chest rose and fell in a long-drawn sigh, and that she wore black cotton gloves, one finger of which was worn through. Yes, she was the picture of poor respectability.

The other passengers, two of whom were probably City clerks with their loves, regarded her with some surprise that she should be a first-class passenger, and there seemed an inclination on the part of the loudly-dressed females to regard her with contempt.

Presently, when we had left the sea and were speeding through the open country, she turned her sad face from the window and examined her fellow passengers one after the other until, of a sudden, her eyes met mine. In an instant she dropped them modestly and busied herself in the pages of the sixpenny reprint of a popular novel which she carried with her.

In that moment, however, I somehow entertained a belief that we had met before. Under what circumstances, or where, I could not recollect. The wistfulness of that white face, the slight hollowness of the cheeks, the unnaturally dark eyes, all seemed familiar to me; yet although for half an hour I strove to bring back to my mind where I had seen her, it was to no purpose. In all probability I had attended her at Guy's. A doctor in a big London hospital sees so many faces that to recollect all is utterly impossible. Many a time I have been accosted and thanked by people whom I have had no recollection of ever having seen in my life. Men do not realise that they look very different when lying in bed with a fortnight's growth of beard to when shaven and spruce, as is their ordinary habit: while women, when smartly dressed with fashionable hats and flimsy veils, are very different to when, in illness, they lie with hair unbound, faces pinched and eyes sunken, which is the only recollection their doctor has of them. The duchess and the servant girl present very similar figures when lying on a sick bed in a critical condition.

There was an element of romantic mystery in that fragile little figure huddled up in the far corner of the carriage. Once or twice, when she believed my gaze to be averted, she raised her eyes furtively as though to reassure herself of my identity, and in her restless manner I discerned a desire to speak with me. It was very probable that she was some poor girl of the lady's maid or governess class to whom I had shown attention during an illness. We have so many in the female wards at Guy's.

But during that journey a further and much more important matter recurred to me, eclipsing all thought of the sad-faced girl opposite. I recollected those words I had overheard, and felt convinced that the speaker had been none other than Ethelwynn herself.

Sometimes when a man's mind is firmly fixed upon an object the events of his daily life curiously tend towards it. Have you never experienced that strange phenomenon for which medical science has never yet accounted, namely, the impression of form upon the imagination? You have one day suddenly thought of a person long absent. You have not seen him for years, when, without any apparent cause, you have recollected him. In the hurry and bustle of city life a thousand faces are passing you hourly. Like a flash one man passes, and you turn to look, for the countenance bears a striking resemblance to your absent friend. You are disappointed, for it is not the man. A second face appears in the human phantasmagoria of the street, and the similarity is almost startling. You are amazed that two persons should pass so very like your friend. Then, an hour after, a third face—actually that of your long-lost friend himself. All of us have experienced similar vagaries of coincidence. How can we account for them?

And so it was in my own case. So deeply had my mind been occupied by thoughts of my love that several times that day, in London and in Brighton, I had been startled by striking resemblances. Thus I wondered whether that voice I had heard was actually hers, or only a distorted hallucination. At any rate, the woman had expressed hatred of Sir Bernard just as Ethelwynn had done, and further, the old man had openly defied her, with a harsh laugh, which showed confidence in himself and an utter disregard for any statement she might make.

At Victoria the pale-faced girl descended quickly, and, swallowed in a moment in the crowd on the platform, I saw her no more.

She had, before descending, given me a final glance, and I fancied that a faint smile of recognition played about her lips. But in the uncertain light of a railway carriage the shadows are heavy, and I could not see sufficiently distinctly to warrant my returning her salute. So the wan little figure, so full of romantic mystery, went forth again into oblivion.

I was going my round at Guy's on the following morning when a telegram was put into my hand. It was from Ethelwynn's mother— Mrs. Mivart, at Neneford—asking me to go down there without delay, but giving no reason for the urgency. I had always been a favourite with the old lady, and to obey was, of course, imperative—even though I were compelled to ask Bartlett, one of my colleagues, to look after Sir Bernard's private practice in my absence.

Neneford Manor was an ancient, rambling old Queen Anne place, about nine miles from Peterborough on the high road to Leicester. Standing in the midst of the richest grass country in England, with its grounds sloping to the brimming river that wound through meadows which in May were a blaze of golden buttercups, it was a typical English home, with quaint old gables, high chimney stacks and old-world garden with yew hedges trimmed fantastically as in the days of wigs and patches. I had snatched a week-end several times to be old Mrs. Mivart's guest; therefore I knew the picturesque old place well, and had been entranced by its many charms.

Soon after five o'clock that afternoon I descended from the train at the roadside station, and, mounting into the dog-cart, was driven across the hill to the Manor. In the hall the sweet-faced, silver-haired old lady, in her neat black and white cap greeted me, holding both my hands and pressing them for a moment, apparently unable to utter a word. I had expected to find her unwell; but, on the contrary, she seemed quite as active as usual, notwithstanding the senile decay which I knew had already laid its hand heavily upon her.

"You are so good to come to me, Doctor. How can I sufficiently thank you?" she managed to exclaim at last, leading me into the drawing-room, a long old-fashioned apartment with low ceiling supported by black oak beams, and quaint diamond-paned windows at each end.

"Well?" I inquired, when she had seated herself, and, with the evening light upon her face, I saw how blanched and anxious she was.

"I want to consult you, Doctor, upon a serious and confidential matter," she began, leaning forward, her thin white hands clasped in her lap. "We have not met since the terrible blow fell upon us—the death of poor Mary's husband."

"It must have been a great blow to you," I said sympathetically, for I liked the old lady, and realised how deeply she had suffered.

"Yes, but to poor Mary most of all," she said. "They were so happy together; and she was so devoted to him."

This was scarcely the truth; but mothers are often deceived as to their daughters' domestic felicity. A wife is always prone to hide her sorrows from her parents as far as possible. Therefore the old lady had no doubt been the victim of natural deception.

"Yes," I agreed; "it was a tragic and terrible thing. The mystery is quite unsolved."

"To me, the police are worse than useless," she said, in her slow, weak voice; "they don't seem to have exerted themselves in the least after that utterly useless inquest, with its futile verdict. As far as I can gather, not one single point has been cleared up."

"No," I said; "not one."

"And my poor Mary!" exclaimed old Mrs. Mivart; "she is beside herself with grief. Time seems to increase her melancholy, instead of bringing forgetfulness, as I hoped it would."

"Where is Mrs. Courtenay?" I asked.

"Here. She's been back with me for nearly a month. It was to see her, speak with her, and give me an opinion that I asked you to come down."

"Is she unwell?"

"I really don't know what ails her. She talks of her husband incessantly, calls him by name, and sometimes behaves so strangely that I have once or twice been much alarmed."

Her statement startled me. I had no idea that the young widow had taken the old gentleman's death so much to heart. As far as I had been able to judge, it seemed very much as though she had every desire to regain her freedom from a matrimonial bond that galled her. That she was grief-stricken over his death showed that I had entirely misjudged her character.

"Is she at home now?" I asked.

"Yes, in her own sitting-room—the room we used as a schoolroom when the girls were at home. Sometimes she mopes there all day, only speaking at meals. At others, she takes her dressing-bag and goes away for two or three days—just as the fancy takes her. She absolutely declines to have a maid."

"You mean that she's just a little—well, eccentric," I remarked seriously.

"Yes, Doctor," answered the old lady, in a strange voice quite unusual to her, and fixing her eyes upon me. "To tell the truth I fear her mind is slowly giving way."

I remained silent, thinking deeply; and as I did not reply, she added:

"You will meet her at dinner. I shall not let her know you are here. Then you can judge for yourself."

The situation was becoming more complicated. Since the conclusion of the inquest I had seen nothing of the widow. She had stayed several days with Ethelwynn at the Hennikers', then had visited her aunt near Bath. That was all I knew of her movements, for, truth to tell, I held her in some contempt for her giddy pleasure-seeking during her husband's illness. Surely a woman who had a single spark of affection for the man she had married could not go out each night to theatres and supper parties, leaving him to the care of his man and a nurse. That one fact alone proved that her professions of love had been hollow and false.

While the twilight fell I sat in that long, sombre old room that breathed an air of a century past, chatting with old Mrs. Mivart, and learning from her full particulars of Mary's eccentricities. My hostess told me of the proving of the will, which left the Devonshire estate to her daughter, and of the slow action of the executors. The young widow's actions, as described to me, were certainly strange, and made me strongly suspect that she was not quite responsible for them. That Mary's remorse was overwhelming was plain; and that fact aroused within my mind a very strong suspicion of a circumstance I had not before contemplated, namely, that during the life of her husband there had been a younger male attraction. The acuteness of her grief seemed proof of this. And yet, if argued logically, the existence of a secret lover should cause her to congratulate herself upon her liberty.

The whole situation was an absolute enigma.

XVI

Reveals an Astounding Fact

Dinner was announced, and I took Mrs. Mivart into the room on the opposite side of the big old-fashioned hall, a long, low-ceilinged apartment the size of the drawing-room, and hung with some fine old family portraits and miniatures. Old Squire Mivart had been an enthusiastic collector of antique china, and the specimens of old Montelupo and Urbino hanging upon the walls were remarkable as being the finest in any private collection in this country. Many were the visits he had made to Italy to acquire those queer-looking old mediæval plates, with their crude colouring and rude, inartistic drawings, and certainly he was an acknowledged expert in antique porcelain.

The big red-shaded lamp in the centre of the table shed a soft light upon the snowy cloth, the flowers and the glittering silver; and as my hostess took her seat she sighed slightly, and for the first time asked of Ethelwynn.

"I haven't seen her for a week," I was compelled to admit. "Patients have been so numerous that I haven't had time to go out to see her, except at hours when calling at a friend's house was out of the question."

"Do you like the Hennikers?" her mother inquired, raising her eyes inquiringly to mine.

"Yes, I've found them very agreeable and pleasant."

"H'm," the old lady exclaimed dubiously. "Well, I don't. I met Mrs. Henniker once, and I must say that I did not care for her in the least. Ethelwynn is very fond of her, but to my mind she's fast, and not at all a suitable companion for a girl of my daughter's disposition. It may be that I have an old woman's prejudices, living as I do in the country always, but somehow I can never bring myself to like her."

Mrs. Mivart, like the majority of elderly widows who have given up the annual visit to London in the season, was a trifle behind the times. More charming an old lady could not be, but, in common with all who vegetate in the depths of rural England, she was just a trifle narrow-minded. In religion, she found fault constantly with the village parson, who, she declared, was guilty of ritualistic practices, and on the subject of her daughters she bemoaned the latter-day emancipation of women, which allowed them to go hither and thither at their own free will. Like all such mothers, she considered wealth a necessary adjunct to happiness, and it had been with her heartiest approval that Mary had married the unfortunate Courtenay, notwithstanding the difference between the ages of bride and bridegroom. In every particular the old lady was a typical specimen of the squire's widow, as found in rural England to-day.

Scarcely had we seated ourselves and I had replied to her question when the door opened and a slim figure in deep black entered and mechanically took the empty chair. She crossed the room, looking straight before her, and did not notice my presence until she had seated herself face to face with me.

Of a sudden her thin wan face lit up with a smile of recognition, and she cried:

"Why, Doctor! Wherever did you come from? No one told me you were here," and across the table she stretched out her hand in greeting.

"I thought you were reposing after your long walk this morning, dear; so I did not disturb you," her mother explained.

But, heedless of the explanation, she continued putting to me questions as to when I had left town, and the reason of my visit there. To the latter I returned an evasive answer, declaring that I had run down because I had heard that her mother was not altogether well.

"Yes, that's true," she said. "Poor mother has been very queer of late. She seems so distracted, and worries quite unnecessarily over me. I wish you'd give her advice. Her state causes me considerable anxiety."

"Very well," I said, feigning to laugh, "I must diagnose the ailment and see what can be done."

The soup had been served, and as I carried my spoon to my mouth I examined her furtively. My hostess had excused me from dressing, but her daughter, neat in her widow's collar and cuffs, sat prim and upright, her eyes now and then raised to mine in undisguised inquisitiveness.

She was a trifle paler than heretofore, but her pallor was probably rendered the more noticeable by the dead black she wore. Her hands seemed thin, and her fingers toyed nervously with her spoon in a manner that betrayed concealed agitation. Outwardly, however, I detected no extraordinary signs of either grief or anxiety. She spoke calmly, it was true, in the tone of one upon whom a great calamity had fallen, but that was only natural. I did not expect to find her bright, laughing, and light-hearted, like her old self in Richmond Road.

As dinner proceeded I began to believe that, with a fond mother's solicitude for her daughter's welfare, Mrs. Mivart had slightly exaggerated Mary's symptoms. They certainly were not those of a woman plunged in inconsolable grief, for she was neither mopish nor artificially gay. As far as I could detect, not even a single sigh escaped her.

She inquired of Ethelwynn and of the Hennikers, remarking that she had seen nothing of them for over three weeks; and then, when the servants had left the room, she placed her elbows upon the table, at the risk of a breach of good manners, and resting her chin upon her hands, looked me full in the face, saying:

"Now, tell me the truth, Doctor. What has been discovered regarding my poor husband's death? Have the police obtained any clue to the assassin?"

"None—none whatever, I regret to say," was my response.

"They are useless—worse than useless!" she burst forth angrily; "they blundered from the very first."

"That's entirely my own opinion, dear," her mother said. "Our police system nowadays is a mere farce. The foreigners are far ahead of us, even in the detection of crime. Surely the mystery of your poor husband's death might have been solved, if they had worked assiduously."

"I believe that everything that could be done has been done," I remarked. "The case was placed in the hands of two of the smartest and most experienced men at Scotland Yard, with personal instructions from the Superintendent of the Criminal Investigation Department to leave no stone unturned in order to arrive at a successful issue."

"And what has been done?" asked the young widow, in a tone of discontent; "why, absolutely nothing! There has, I suppose, been a pretence at trying to solve the mystery; but, finding it too difficult, they have given it up, and turned their attention to some other crime more open and plain-sailing. I've no faith in the police whatever. It's scandalous!"

I smiled; then said:

"My friend, Ambler Jevons—you know him, for he dined at Richmond Road one evening—has been most active in the affair."

"But he's not a detective. How can he expect to triumph where the police fail?"

"He often does," I declared. "His methods are different from the hard-and-fast rules followed by the police. He commences at whatever point presents itself, and laboriously works backwards with a patience that is absolutely extraordinary. He has unearthed a dozen crimes where Scotland Yard has failed."

"And is he engaged upon my poor husband's case?" asked Mary, suddenly interested.

"Yes."

"For what reason?"

"Well—because he is one of those for whom a mystery of crime has a fascinating attraction."

"But he must have some motive in devoting time and patience to a matter which does not concern him in the least," Mrs. Mivart remarked.

"Whatever is the motive, I can assure you that it is an entirely disinterested one," I said.

"But what has he discovered? Tell me," Mary urged.

"I am quite in ignorance," I said. "We are most intimate friends, but when engaged on such investigations he tells me nothing of their result until they are complete. All I know is that so active is he at this moment that I seldom see him. He is often tied to his office in the City, but has, I believe, recently been on a flying visit abroad for two or three days."

"Abroad!" she echoed. "Where?"

"I don't know. I met a mutual friend in the Strand yesterday, and he told me that he had returned yesterday."

"Has he been abroad in connection with his inquiries, do you think?" Mrs. Mivart inquired.

"I really don't know. Probably he has. When he takes up a case he goes into it with a greater thoroughness than any detective living."

"Yes," Mary remarked, "I recollect, now, the stories you used to tell us regarding him—of his exciting adventures—of his patient tracking of the guilty ones, and of his marvellous ingenuity in laying traps to get them to betray themselves. I recollect quite well that evening he came to Richmond Road with you. He was a most interesting man."

"Let us hope he will be more successful than the police," I said.

"Yes, Doctor," she remarked, sighing for the first time. "I hope he will—for the mystery of it all drives me to distraction." Then placing both hands to her brow, she added, "Ah! if we could only discover the truth—the real truth!"

"Have patience," I urged. "A complicated mystery such as it is cannot be cleared up without long and careful inquiry."

"But in the months that have gone by surely the police should have at least made some discovery?" she said, in a voice of complaint; "yet they have not the slightest clue."

"We can only wait," I said. "Personally, I have confidence in Jevons. If there is a clue to be obtained, depend upon it he will scent it out."

I did not tell them of my misgivings, nor did I explain how Ambler, having found himself utterly baffled, had told me of his intention to relinquish further effort. The flying trip abroad might be in connection with the case, but I felt confident that it was not. He knew, as well as I did, that the truth was to be found in England.

Again we spoke of Ethelwynn; and from Mary's references to her sister I gathered that a slight coolness had fallen between them. She did not, somehow, speak of her in the same terms of affection as formerly. It might be that she shared her mother's prejudices, and did not approve of her taking up her abode with the Hennikers. Be it how it might, there were palpable signs of strained relations.

Could it be possible, I wondered, that Mary had learnt of her sister's secret engagement to her husband?

I looked full at her as that thought flashed through my mind. Yes, she presented a picture of sweet and interesting widowhood. In her voice, as in her countenance, was just that slight touch of grief which told me plainly that she was a heart-broken, remorseful woman—a woman, like many another, who knew not the value of a tender, honest and indulgent husband until he had been snatched from her. Mother and daughter, both widows, were a truly sad and sympathetic pair.

As we spoke I watched her eyes, noted her every movement attentively, but failed utterly to discern any suggestion of what her mother had remarked.

Once, at mention of her dead husband, she had of a sudden exclaimed in a low voice, full of genuine emotion:

"Ah, yes. He was so kind, so good always. I cannot believe that he will never come back," and she burst into tears, which her mother, with a word of apology to me, quietly soothed away.

When we arose I accompanied them to the drawing-room; but without any music, and with Mary's sad, half-tragic countenance before us, the evening was by no means a merry one; therefore I was glad when, in pursuance of the country habit of retiring early, the maid brought my candle and showed me to my room.

It was not yet ten o'clock, and feeling in no mood for sleep, I took from my bag the novel I had been reading on my journey and, throwing myself into an armchair, first gave myself up to deep reflection over a pipe, and afterwards commenced to read.

The chiming of the church clock down in the village aroused me, causing me to glance at my watch. It was midnight. I rose, and going to the window, pulled aside the blind, and looked out upon the rural view lying calm and mysterious beneath the brilliant moonlight.

How different was that peaceful aspect to the one to which I was, alas! accustomed—that long blank wall in the Marylebone Road. There the cab bells tinkled all night, market wagons rumbled through till dawn, and the moonbeams revealed drunken revellers after "closing time."

A strong desire seized me to go forth and enjoy the splendid night. Such a treat of peace and solitude was seldom afforded me, stifled as I was by the disinfectants in hospital wards and the variety of perfumes and pastilles in the rooms of wealthy patients. Truly the life of a London doctor is the most monotonous and laborious of any of the learned professions, and little wonder is it that when the jaded medico finds himself in the country or by the sea he seldom fails to take his fill of fresh air.

At first a difficulty presented itself in letting myself out unheard; but I recollected that in the new wing of the house, in which I had been placed, there were no other bedrooms, therefore with a little care I might descend undetected. So taking my hat and stick I opened the door, stole noiselessly down the stairs, and in a few minutes had made an adventurous exit by a window—fearing the grating bolts of the door—and was soon strolling across the grounds by the private path, which I knew led through the churchyard and afterwards down to the river-bank.

With Ethelwynn I had walked across the meadows by that path on several occasions, and in the dead silence of the brilliant night vivid recollections of a warm summer's evening long past came back to me—sweet remembrances of days when we were childishly happy in each other's love.

Nothing broke the quiet save the shrill cry of some night bird down by the river, and the low roar of the distant weir. The sky was cloudless, and the moon so bright that I could have read a newspaper. I strolled on slowly, breathing the refreshing air, and thinking deeply over the complications of the situation. In the final hour I had spent in the drawing-room I had certainly detected in the young widow a

WILLIAM LE QUEUX

slight eccentricity of manner, not at all accentuated, but yet sufficient to show me that she had been strenuously concealing her grief during my presence there.

Having swung myself over the stile I passed round the village churchyard, where the moss-grown gravestones stood grim and ghostly in the white light, and out across the meadows down to where the waters of the Nene, rippling on, were touched with silver. The river-path was wide, running by the winding bank away to the fen-lands and beyond. As I gained the river's edge and walked beneath the willows I heard now and then a sharp, swift rustling in the sedges as some water-rat or otter, disturbed by my presence, slipped away into hiding. The rural peace of that brilliant night attracted me, and finding a hurdle I seated myself upon it, and taking out my pipe enjoyed a smoke.

Ever since my student days I had longed for a country life. The pleasures of the world of London had no attraction for me, my ideal being a snug country practice with Ethelwynn as my wife. But alas! my idol had been shattered, like that of many a better man.

With this bitter reflection still in my mind, my attention was attracted by low voices—as though of two persons speaking earnestly together. Surprised at such interruption, I glanced quickly around, but saw no one.

Again I listened, when, of a sudden, footsteps sounded, coming down the path I had already traversed. Beneath the deep shadow I saw the dark figures of two persons. They were speaking together, but in a tone so low that I could not catch any word uttered.

Nevertheless, as they emerged from the semi-darkness the moon shone full upon them, revealing to me that they were a man and a woman.

Next instant a cry of blank amazement escaped me, for I was utterly unprepared for the sight I witnessed. I could not believe my eyes; nor could you, my reader, had you been in my place.

The woman walking there, close to me, was young Mrs. Courtenay—the man was none other than her dead husband!

XVII

Discusses Several Matters

Reader, I know that what I have narrated is astounding. It astounded me just as it astounded you.

There are moments when one's brain becomes dulled by sudden bewilderment at sight of the absolutely impossible.

It certainly seemed beyond credence that the man whose fatal and mysterious wound I had myself examined should be there, walking with his wife in lover-like attitude. And yet there was no question that the pair were there. A small bush separated us, so that they passed arm-in-arm within three feet of me. As I have already explained, the moon was so bright that I could see to read; therefore, shining full upon their faces, it was impossible to mistake the features of two persons whom I knew so well.

Fortunately they had not overheard my involuntary exclamation of astonishment, or, if they had, both evidently believed it to be one of the many distorted sounds of the night. Upon Mary's face there was revealed a calm expression of perfect content, different indeed from the tearful countenance of a few hours before, while her husband, grey-faced and serious, just as he had been before his last illness, had her arm linked in his, and walked with her, whispering some low indistinct words which brought to her lips a smile of perfect felicity.

Now had I been a superstitious man I should have promptly declared the whole thing to have been an apparition. But as I do not believe in borderland theories, any more than I believe that a man whose heart is nearly cut in twain can again breathe and live, I could only stand aghast, bewildered and utterly dumfounded.

Hidden from them by a low thorn-bush, I stood in silent stupefaction as they passed by. That it was no chimera of the imagination was proved by the fact that their footsteps sounded upon the path, and just as they had passed I heard Courtenay address his wife by name. The transformation of her countenance from the ineffable picture of grief and sorrow to the calm, sweet expression of content had been marvellous, to say the least—an event stranger, indeed, than any I had ever before witnessed. In the wild writings of the old romancers the dead have sometimes been resuscitated, but never in this workaday world of ours. There is a finality in death that is decisive.

Yet, as I here write these lines, I stake my professional reputation that the man I saw was the same whom I had seen dead in that upper room in Kew. I knew his gait, his cough, and his countenance too well to mistake his identity.

That night's adventure was certainly the most startling, and at the same time the most curious, that ever befel a man. Thus I became seized with curiosity, and at risk of detection crept forth from my hiding-place and looked out after them. To betray my presence would be to bar from myself any chance of learning the secret of it all; therefore I was compelled to exercise the greatest caution. Mary mourned the loss of her husband towards the world, and yet met him in secret at night—wandering with him by that solitary bye-path along which no villager ever passed after dark, and lovers avoided because of the popular tradition that a certain unfortunate Lady of the Manor of a century ago "walked" there. In the fact of the mourning so well feigned I detected the concealment of some remarkable secret.

The situation was, without doubt, an extraordinary one. The man upon whose body I had made a post-mortem examination was alive and well, walking with his wife, although for months before his assassination he had been a bed-ridden invalid. Such a thing was startling, incredible! Little wonder was it that at first I could scarce believe my own eyes. Only when I looked full into his face and recognised his features, with all their senile peculiarities, did the amazing truth become impressed upon me.

Around the bend in the river I stole stealthily after them, in order to watch their movements, trying to catch their conversation, although, unfortunately, it was in too low an undertone. He never released her arm or changed his affectionate attitude towards her, but appeared to be relating to her some long and interesting chain of events to which she listened with rapt attention.

Along the river's edge, out in the open moonlight, it was difficult to follow them without risk of observation. Now and then the elder-bushes and drooping willows afforded cover beneath their deep shadow, but in places where the river wound through the open water-meadows my presence might at any moment be detected. Therefore the utmost ingenuity and caution were necessary.

Having made the staggering discovery, I was determined to thoroughly probe the mystery. The tragedy of old Mr. Courtenay's death had resolved itself into a romance of the most mysterious and startling character. As I crept forward over the grass, mostly on tiptoe, so as to avoid the sound of my footfalls, I tried to form some theory to account for the bewildering circumstance, but could discern absolutely none.

Mary was still wearing her mourning; but about her head was wrapped a white silk shawl, and on her shoulders a small fur cape, for the spring night was chilly. Her husband had on a dark overcoat and soft felt hat of the type he always wore, and carried in his hand a light walking-stick. Once or twice he halted when he seemed to be impressing his words the more forcibly upon her, and then I was compelled to stop also and to conceal myself. I would have given much to overhear the trend of their conversation, but strive how I would I was unable. They seemed to fear eavesdroppers, and only spoke in low half-whispers.

I noticed how old Mr. Courtenay kept from time to time glancing around him, as though in fear of detection; hence I was in constant dread lest he should look behind him and discover me slinking along their path. I am by no means an adept at following persons, but in this case the stake was so great—the revelation of some startling and unparalleled mystery—that I strained every nerve and every muscle to conceal my presence while pushing forward after them.

Picture to yourself for a moment my position. The whole of my future happiness, and consequently my prosperity in life, was at stake at that instant. To clear up the mystery successfully might be to clear my love of the awful stigma upon her. To watch and to listen was the only way; but the difficulties in the dead silence of the night were well-nigh insurmountable, for I dare not approach sufficiently near to catch a single word. I had crept on after them for about a mile, until we were approaching the tumbling waters of the weir. The dull roar swallowed up the sound of their voices, but it assisted me, for I had no further need to tread noiselessly.

On nearing the lock-keeper's cottage, a little white-washed house wherein the inmates were sleeping soundly, they made a wide detour around the meadow, in order to avoid the chance of being seen. Mary was well known to the old lock-keeper who had controlled those great sluices for thirty years or more, and she knew that at night he was often compelled to be on duty, and might at that very moment be sitting on the bench outside his house, smoking his short clay.

I, however, had no such fear. Stepping lightly upon the grass beside the path I went past the house and continued onward by the riverside, passing at once into the deep shadow of the willows, which effectually concealed me.

The pair were walking at the same slow, deliberate pace beneath the high hedge on the further side of the meadow, evidently intending to rejoin the river-path some distance further up. This gave me an opportunity to get on in front of them, and I seized it without delay; for I was anxious to obtain another view of the face of the man whom I had for months believed to be in his grave.

Keeping in the shadow of the trees and bushes that overhung the stream, I sped onward for ten minutes or more until I came to the boundary of the great pasture, passing through the swing gate by which I felt confident that they must also pass. I turned to look before leaving the meadow, and could just distinguish their figures. They had turned at right angles, and, as I had expected, were walking in my direction.

Forward I went again, and after some hurried search discovered a spot close to the path where concealment behind a great old tree seemed possible; so at that coign of vantage I waited breathlessly for their approach. The roaring of the waters behind would, I feared, prevent any of their words from reaching me; nevertheless, I waited anxiously.

A great barn owl flapped lazily past, hooting weirdly as it went; then all nature became still again, save the dull sound of the tumbling flood. Ambler Jevons, had he been with me, would, no doubt, have acted differently. But it must be remembered that I was the merest tyro in the unravelling of a mystery, whereas, with him, it was a kind of natural occupation. And yet would he believe me when I told him that I had actually seen the dead man walking there with his wife?

I was compelled to admit within myself that such a statement from the lips of any man would be received with incredulity. Indeed, had such a thing been related to me, I should have put the narrator down as either a liar or a lunatic.

At last they came. I remained motionless, standing in the shadow, not daring to breathe. My eyes were fixed upon him, my ears strained to catch every sound.

He said something to her. What it was I could not gather. Then he pushed open the creaking gate to allow her to pass. Across the moon's face had drifted a white, fleecy cloud; therefore the light was not so brilliant as half an hour before. Still, I could see his features almost as plainly as I see this paper upon which I am penning my strange adventure, and could recognise every lineament and peculiarity of his countenance.

Having passed through the gate, he took her ungloved hand with an air of old-fashioned gallantry and raised it to his lips. She laughed merrily in rapturous content, and then slowly, very slowly, they strolled along the path that ran within a few feet of where I stood.

My heart leapt with excitement. Their voices sounded above the rushing of the waters, and they were lingering as though unwilling to walk further.

"Ethelwynn has told me," he was saying. "I can't make out the reason of his coldness towards her. Poor girl! she seems utterly heart-broken."

"He suspects," his wife replied.

"But what ground has he for suspicion?"

I stood there transfixed. They were talking of myself!

They had halted quite close to where I was, and in that low roar had raised their voices so that I could distinguish every word.

"Well," remarked his wife, "the whole affair was mysterious, that you must admit. With his friend, a man named Jevons, he has been endeavouring to solve the problem."

"A curse on Ambler Jevons!" he blurted forth in anger, as though he were well acquainted with my friend.

"If between them they managed to get at the truth it would be very awkward," she said.

"No fear of that," he laughed in full confidence. "A man once dead and buried, with a coroner's verdict upon him, is not easily believed to be alive and well. No, my dear; rest assured that these men will never get at our secret—never."

I smiled within myself. How little did he dream that the man of whom he had been speaking was actually overhearing his words!

"But Ethelwynn, in order to regain her place in the doctor's heart, may betray us," his wife remarked dubiously.

"She dare not," was the reply. "From her we have nothing whatever to fear. As long as you keep up the appearance of deep mourning, are discreet in all your actions, and exercise proper caution on the occasions when we meet, our secret must remain hidden from all."

"But I am doubtful of Ethelwynn. A woman as fondly in love with a man, as she is with Ralph, is apt to throw discretion to the winds," the woman observed. "Recollect that the breach between them is on our account, and that a word from her could expose the whole thing, and at the same time bring back to her the man for whose lost love she is pining. It is because of that I am in constant fear."

"Your apprehensions are entirely groundless," he declared in a decisive voice. "She's the only other person in the secret besides ourselves; but to betray us would be fatal to her."

"She may consider that she has made sufficient self-sacrifice?"

"Then all the greater reason why she should remain silent. She has her reputation to lose by divulging."

By his argument she appeared only half-convinced, for I saw upon her brow a heavy, thoughtful expression, similar to that I had noticed when sitting opposite her at dinner. The reason of her constant preoccupation was that she feared that her sister might give me the clue to her secret.

That a remarkable conspiracy had been in progress was now made quite plain; and, further, one very valuable fact I had ascertained was that Ethelwynn was the only other person who knew the truth, and yet dared not reveal it.

This man who stood before me was old Mr. Courtenay, without a doubt. That being so, who could have been the unfortunate man who had been struck to the heart so mysteriously?

So strange and complicated were all the circumstances, and so cleverly had the chief actors in the drama arranged its details, that Courtenay himself was convinced that for others to learn the truth was utterly impossible. Yet it was more than remarkable that he sought not to disguise his personal appearance if he wished to remain dead to the world. Perhaps, however, being unknown in that rural district—for he once had told me that he had never visited his wife's home since his marriage— he considered himself perfectly safe from recognition. Besides, from their conversation I gathered that they only met on rare occasions, and certainly Mary kept up the fiction of mourning with the greatest assiduity.

I recollected what old Mrs. Mivart had told me of her daughter's erratic movements; of her short mysterious absences with her dressing-bag and without a maid. It was evident that she made flying visits in various directions in order to meet her "dead" husband.

Courtenay spoke again, after a brief silence, saying:

"I had no idea that the doctor was down here, or I should have kept away. To be seen by him would expose the whole affair."

"I was quite ignorant of his visit until I went in to dinner and found him already seated at table," she answered. "But he will leave to-morrow.

He said to-night that to remain away from his patients for a single day was very difficult."

"Is he down here in pursuance of his inquiries, do you think?" suggested her husband.

"He may be. Mother evidently knew of his impending arrival, but told me nothing. I was annoyed, for he was the very last person I wished to meet."

"Well, he'll go in the morning, so we have nothing to fear. He's safe enough in bed, and sleeping soundly—confound him!"

The temptation was great to respond aloud to the compliment; but I refrained, laughing within myself at the valuable information I was obtaining.

XVIII

Words of the Dead

Justice is always vigilant—it stops not to weigh causes or motives, but overtakes the criminal, no matter whether his deeds be the suggestion of malice or the consequence of provoked revenge. I was all eagerness to face the pair in the full light and demand an explanation, yet I hesitated, fearing lest precipitation might prevent me gaining knowledge of the truth.

That they had no inclination to walk further was evident, for they still stood there in conversation, facing each other and speaking earnestly. I listened attentively to every word, my heart thumping so loudly that I wondered they did not hear its excited pulsations.

"You've seen nothing of Sir Bernard?" she was saying.

"Sir Bernard!" he echoed. "Why, of course not. To him I am dead and buried, just as I am to the rest of the world. My executors have proved my will at Somerset House, and very soon you will receive its benefits. To meet the old doctor would be to reveal the whole thing."

"It is all so strange," she said with a low sigh, "that sometimes, when I am alone, I can't believe it to be true. We have deceived the world so completely."

"Of course. That was my intention."

"But could it not have been done without the sacrifice of that man's life?" she queried. "Remember! The crime of murder was committed."

"You are only dreaming!" he replied, in a hard voice. "A mystery was necessary for our success."

"And it is a mystery which has entirely baffled the police in every particular."

"As I intended it should. I laid my plans with care, so that there should be no hitch or point by which Scotland Yard could obtain a clue."

"But our future life?" she murmured. "When may I return again to you? At present I am compelled to feign mourning, and present a perfect picture of interesting widowhood; but—but I hate this playing at death."

"Have patience, dear," he urged in a sympathetic tone. "For the moment we must remain entirely apart, holding no communication with each other save in secret, on the first and fifteenth day of every month as we arranged. As soon as I find myself in a position of safety we will disappear together, and you will leave the world wondering at the second mystery following upon the first."

"In how long a time do you anticipate?" she asked, looking earnestly into his eyes.

"A few months at most," was his answer. "If it were possible you should return to me at once; but you know how strange and romantic is my life, compelled to disguise my personality, and for ever moving from place to place, like the Wandering Jew. To return to me at present is quite impossible. Besides—you are in the hands of the executors; and before long must be in evidence in order to receive my money."

"Money is useless to me without happiness," she declared, in a voice of complaint. "My position at present is one of constant dread."

"Whom and what do you fear?"

"I believe that Dr. Boyd has some vague suspicion of the truth," she responded, after a pause.

"What?" he cried, in quick surprise. "Tell me why. Explain it all to me."

"There is nothing to explain—save that to-night he seemed to regard my movements with suspicion."

"Ah! my dear, your fears are utterly groundless," he laughed. "What can the fellow possibly know? He is assured that I am dead, for he signed my certificate and followed me to my grave at Woking. A man who attends his friend's funeral has no suspicion that the dead is still living, depend upon it. If there is any object in this world that is convincing it is a corpse."

"I merely tell you the result of my observations," she said. "In my opinion he has come here to learn what he can."

"He can learn nothing," answered the "dead" man. "If it were his confounded friend Jevons, now, we might have some apprehension; for the ingenuity of that man is, I've heard, absolutely astounding. Even Scotland Yard seeks his aid in the solving of the more difficult criminal problems."

"I tell you plainly that I fear Ethelwynn may expose us," his wife went on slowly, a distinctly anxious look upon her countenance. "As you know, there is a coolness between us, and rather than risk losing the doctor altogether she may make a clean breast of the affair."

"No, no, my dear. Rest assured that she will never betray us," answered Courtenay, with a light reassuring laugh. "True, you are not very friendly, yet you must recollect that she and I are friends. Her interests are identical with our own; therefore to expose us would be to expose herself at the same time."

"A woman sometimes acts without forethought."

"Quite true; but Ethelwynn is not one of those. She's careful to preserve her own position in the eyes of her lover, knowing quite well that to tell the truth would be to expose her own baseness. A man may overlook many offences in the woman he loves, but this particular one of which she is guilty a man never forgives."

His words went deep into my heart. Was not this further proof that the crime—for undoubtedly a crime had been accomplished in that house at Kew—had been committed by the hand of the woman I so fondly loved? All was so amazing, so utterly bewildering, that I stood there concealed by the tree, motionless as though turned to stone.

There was a motive wanting in it all. Yet I ask you who read this narrative of mine if, like myself, you would not have been staggered into dumbness at seeing and hearing a man whom you had certified to be dead, moving and speaking, and, moreover, in his usual health?

"He loves her!" his wife exclaimed, speaking of me. "He would forgive her anything. My own opinion is that if we would be absolutely secure it is for us to heal the breach between them."

He remained thoughtful for a few moments, apparently in doubt as to the wisdom of acting upon her suggestion. Surely in the situation was an element of humour, for, happily, I was being forearmed.

"It might possibly be good policy," he remarked at last. "If we could only bring them together again he would cease his constant striving to solve the enigma. We know well that he can never do that; nevertheless his constant efforts are as annoying as they are dangerous."

"That's just my opinion. There is danger to us in his constant inquiries, which are much more ingenious and careful than we imagine."

"Well, my child," he said, "you've stuck to me in this in a manner that few women would have dared. If you really think it necessary to bring Boyd and Ethelwynn together again you must do it entirely alone, for I could not possibly appear on the scene. He must never meet me, or the whole thing would be revealed."

"For your sake I am prepared to make the attempt," she said. "The fact of being Ethelwynn's sister gives me freedom to speak my mind to him."

"And to tell him some pretty little fiction about her?" he added, laughing.

"Yes. It will certainly be necessary to put an entirely innocent face on recent events in order to smooth matters over," she admitted, joining in his laughter.

"Rather a difficult task to make the affair at Kew appear innocent," he observed. "But you're really a wonderful woman, Mary. The way you've acted your part in this affair is simply marvellous. You've deceived everyone—even that old potterer, Sir Bernard himself."

"I've done it for your sake," was her response. "I made a promise, and I've kept it. Up to the present we are safe, but we cannot take too many precautions. We have enemies and scandal-seekers on every side."

"I admit that," he replied, rather impatiently, I thought. "If you think it a wise course you had better lose no time in placing Ethelwynn's innocence before her lover. You will see him in the morning, I suppose?"

"Probably not. He leaves by the eight o'clock train," she said. "When my plans are matured I will call upon him in London."

"And if any woman can deceive him, you can, Mary," he laughed. "In those widow's weeds of yours you could deceive the very devil himself!"

Mrs. Courtenay's airy talk of deception threw an entirely fresh light upon her character. Hitherto I had held her in considerable esteem as a woman who, being bored to death by the eccentricities of her invalid husband, had sought distraction with her friends in town, but nevertheless honest and devoted to the man she had wedded. But these words of hers caused doubt to arise within my mind. That she had been devoted to her husband's interest was proved by the clever imposture she was practising; indeed it seemed to me very much as if those frequent visits to town had been at the "dead" man's suggestion and with his entire consent. But the more I reflected upon the extraordinary details of the tragedy and its astounding dénouement, the more hopeless and maddening became the problem.

"I shall probably go to town to-morrow," she exclaimed, after smiling at his declaration. "Where are you in hiding just now?"

"In Birmingham. A large town is safer than a village. I return by the six o'clock train, and go again into close concealment."

"But you know people in Birmingham, don't you? We stayed there once with some people called Tremlett, I recollect."

"Ah, yes," he laughed. "But I am careful to avoid them. The district in which I live is far removed from them. Besides, I never by any chance go out by day. I'm essentially a nocturnal roamer."

"And when shall we meet again?"

"By appointment, in the usual way."

"At the usual place?" she asked.

"There can be no better, I think. It does not take you from home, and I am quite unknown down here."

"If any of the villagers ever discovered us they might talk, and declare that I met a secret lover," she laughed.

"If you are ever recognised, which I don't anticipate is probable, we can at once change our place of meeting. At present there is no necessity for changing it."

"Then, in the meantime, I will exercise my woman's diplomacy to effect peace between Ethelwynn and the doctor," she said. "It is the only way by which we can obtain security."

"For the life of me I can't discern the reason of his coolness towards her," remarked my "dead" patient.

"He suspects her."

"Of what?"

"Suspects the truth. She has told me so."

Old Henry Courtenay grunted in dissatisfaction.

"Hasn't she tried to convince him to the contrary?" he asked. "I was always under the impression that she could twist him round her finger—so hopelessly was he in love with her."

"So she could before this unfortunate affair."

"And now that he suspects the truth he's disinclined to have any more to do with her—eh? Well," he added, "after all, it's only natural. She's not so devilish clever as you, Mary, otherwise she would never have allowed herself to fall beneath suspicion. She must have somehow blundered."

"To-morrow I shall go to town," she said in a reflective voice. "No time should be lost in effecting the reconciliation between them."

"You are right," he declared. "You should commence at once. Call and talk with him. He believes so entirely in you. But promise me one thing; that you will not go to Ethelwynn," he urged.

"Why not?"

"Because it is quite unnecessary," he answered. "You are not good friends; therefore your influence upon the doctor should be a hidden one. She will believe that he has returned to her of his own free will; hence our position will be rendered the stronger. Act diplomatically. If she believes that you are interesting yourself in her affairs it may anger her."

"Then you suggest that I should call upon the doctor in secret, and try and influence him in her favour without her being aware of it?"

"Exactly. After the reconciliation is effected you may tell her. At present, however, it is not wise to show our hand. By your visit to the doctor you may be able to obtain from him how much he knows, and what are his suspicions. One thing is certain, that with all his shrewdness he doesn't dream the truth."

"Who would?" she asked with a smile. "If the story were told, nobody would believe it."

"That's just it! The incredibility of the whole affair is what places us in such a position of security; for as long as I lie low and you continue to act the part of the interesting widow, nobody can possibly get at the truth."

"I think I've acted my part well, up to the present," she said, "and I hope to continue to do so. To influence the doctor will be a difficult task, I fear. But I'll do my utmost, because I see that by the reconciliation Ethelwynn's lips would be sealed."

"Act with discretion, my dear," urged the old man. "But remember that Boyd is not a man to be trifled with—and as for that accursed friend of his, Ambler Jevons, he seems second cousin to the very King of Darkness himself."

"Never fear," she laughed confidently. "Leave it to me—leave all to me."

And then, agreeing that it was time they went back, they turned, retraced their steps, and passing through the small gate into the meadow, were soon afterwards lost to sight.

Truly my night's adventure had been as strange and startling as any that has happened to living man, for what I had seen and heard opened up a hundred theories, each more remarkable and tragic than the other, until I stood utterly dumfounded and aghast.

XIX

Jevons Grows Mysterious

On coming down to breakfast on the following morning I found Mrs. Mivart awaiting me alone. The old lady apologised for Mary's non-appearance, saying that it was her habit to have her tea in her room, but that she sent me a message of farewell.

Had it been at all possible I would have left by a later train, for I was extremely anxious to watch her demeanour after last night's clandestine meeting, but with such a crowd of patients awaiting me it was imperative to leave by the first train. Even that would not bring me to King's Cross before nearly eleven o'clock.

"Well now, doctor," Mrs. Mivart commenced rather anxiously when we were seated, and she had handed me my coffee. "You saw Mary last night, and had an opportunity of speaking with her. What is your opinion? Don't hesitate to tell me frankly, for I consider that it is my duty to face the worst."

"Really!" I exclaimed, looking straight at her after a moment's reflection. "To speak candidly I failed to detect anything radically wrong in your daughter's demeanour."

"But didn't you notice, doctor, how extremely nervous she is; how in her eyes there is a haunting, suspicious look, and how blank is her mind upon every other subject but the great calamity that has befallen her?"

"I must really confess that these things were not apparent to me," I answered. "I watched her carefully, but beyond the facts that she is greatly unnerved by the sad affair and that she is mourning deeply for her dead husband, I can discover nothing abnormal."

"You are not of opinion, then, that her mind is growing unbalanced by the strain?"

"Not in the least," I reassured her. "The symptoms she betrays are but natural in a woman of her nervous, highly-strung temperament."

"But she unfortunately grieves too much," remarked the old lady with a sigh. "His name is upon her lips at every hour. I've tried to distract her and urged her to accompany me abroad for a time, but all to no purpose. She won't hear of it."

I alone knew the reason of her refusal. In conspiracy with her "dead" husband it was impossible to be apart from him for long together. The undue accentuation of her daughter's feigned grief had alarmed the old lady—and justly so. Now that I recollected, her conduct at table on the previous night was remarkable, having regard to the true facts of the case. I confess I had myself been entirely deceived into believing that her sorrow at Henry Courtenay's death was unbounded. In every detail her acting was perfect, and bound to attract sympathy among her friends and arouse interest among strangers. I longed to explain to the quiet, charming old lady what I had seen during my midnight ramble; but such a course was, as yet, impossible. Indeed, if I made a plain statement, such as I have given in the foregoing pages, surely no one would believe me. But every man has his romance, and this was mine.

Unable to reveal Mary's secret, I was compelled reluctantly to take leave of her mother, who accompanied me out to where the dog-cart was in waiting.

"I scarcely know, doctor, how to thank you sufficiently," the dear old lady said as I took her hand. "What you have told me reassures me. Of late I have been extremely anxious, as you may imagine."

"You need feel no anxiety," I declared. "She's nervous and run down—that's all. Take her away for a change, if possible. But if she refuses, don't force her. Quiet is the chief medicine in her case. Good-bye."

She pressed my hand again in grateful acknowledgment, and then I mounted into the conveyance and was driven to the station.

On the journey back to town I pondered long and deeply. Of a verity my short visit to Mrs. Mivart had been fraught with good results, and I was contemplating seeking Ambler Jevons at the earliest possible moment and relating to him my astounding discovery. The fact that old Courtenay was still living was absolutely beyond my comprehension. To endeavour to form any theory, or to try and account for the bewildering phenomenon, was utterly useless. I had seen him, and had overheard his words. I could surely believe my eyes and ears. And there it ended. The why and wherefore I put aside for the present, remembering Mary's promise to him to come to town and have an interview with me.

Surely that meeting ought to be most interesting. I awaited it with the most intense anxiety, and yet in fear lest I might be led by her clever imposture to blurt out what I knew. I felt myself on the eve of a startling revelation; and my expectations were realized to the full, as the further portion of this strange romance will show.

WILLIAM LE QUEUX

I know that many narratives have been written detailing the remarkable and almost inconceivable machinations of those who have stained their hands with crime, but I honestly believe that the extraordinary features of my own life-romance are as strange as, if not stranger than, any hitherto recorded. Even my worst enemy could not dub me egotistical, I think; and surely the facts I have set down here are plain and unvarnished, without any attempt at misleading the reader into believing that which is untrue. Mine is a plain chronicle of a chain of extraordinary circumstances which led to an amazing dénouement.

From King's Cross to Guy's is a considerable distance, and when I alighted from the cab in the courtyard of the hospital it was nearly mid-day. Until two o'clock I was kept busy in the wards, and after a sandwich and a glass of sherry I drove to Harley Street, where I found Sir Bernard in his consulting-room for the first time for a month.

"Ah! Boyd," he cried merrily, when I entered. "Thought I'd surprise you to-day. I felt quite well this morning, so resolved to come up and see Lady Twickenham and one or two others. I'm not at home to patients, and have left them to you."

"Delighted to see you better," I declared, wringing his hand. "They were asking after you at the hospital to-day. Vernon said he intended going down to see you to-morrow."

"Kind of him," the old man laughed, placing his thin hands together, after rubbing and readjusting his glasses. "You were away last night; out of town, they said."

"Yes, I wanted a breath of fresh air," I answered, laughing. I did not care to tell him where I had been, knowing that he held my love for Ethelwynn as the possible ruin of my career.

His curiosity seemed aroused; but, although he put to me an ingenious question, I steadfastly refused to satisfy him. I recollected too well his open condemnation of my love on previous occasions. Now that the "murdered" man was proved to be still alive, I surely had no further grounds for my suspicion of Ethelwynn. That she had, by her silence, deceived me regarding her engagement to Mr. Courtenay was plain, but the theory that it was her hand that had assassinated him was certainly disproved. Thus, although the discovery of the "dead" man's continued existence deepened the mystery a thousandfold, it nevertheless dispelled from my heart a good deal of the suspicion regarding my well-beloved; and, in consequence, I was not desirous that any further hostile word should be uttered against her.

While Sir Bernard went out to visit her ladyship and two or three other nervous women living in the same neighbourhood, I seated myself in his chair and saw the afternoon callers one after another. I fear that the advice I gave during those couple of hours was not very notable for its shrewdness or brilliancy. As in other professions, so in medicine, when one's brain is overflowing with private affairs, one cannot attend properly to patients. On such occasions one is apt to ask the usual questions mechanically, hear the replies and scribble a prescription of some harmless formula. On the afternoon in question I certainly believe myself guilty of such lapse of professional attention. Yet even we doctors are human, although our patients frequently forget that fact. The medico is a long-suffering person, even in these days of scarcity of properly-qualified men—the first person called on emergency, and the very last to be paid!

It was past five o'clock before I was able to return to my rooms, and on arrival I found upon my table a note from Jevons. It was dated from the Yorick Club, a small but exceedingly comfortable Bohemian centre in Bedford Street, Covent Garden, and had evidently been written hurriedly on the previous night:—

"I hear you are absent in the country. That is unfortunate. But as soon as you receive this, lose no time in calling at the Hennikers' and making casual inquiries regarding Miss Mivart. Something has happened, but what it is I have failed to discover. You stand a better chance. Go at once. I must leave for Bath to-night. Address me at the Royal Hotel, G. W. Station.

AMBLER JEVONS

What could have transpired? And why had my friend's movements been so exceedingly erratic of late, if he had not been following some clue? Would that clue lead him to the truth, I wondered? Or was he still suspicious of Ethelwynn's guilt?

Puzzled by this vague note, and wondering what had occurred, and whether the trip to Bath was in connection with it, I made a hasty toilet and drove in a hansom to the Hennikers'.

Mrs. Henniker met me in the drawing-room, just as gushing and charming as ever. She was one of those many women in London who seek to hang on to the skirts of polite society by reason of a distant connexion being a countess—a fact of which she never failed to remind the stranger before half-an-hour's acquaintance. She found it always a pleasant manner in which to open a conversation at dinner, dance, or soirée: "Oh! do you happen to know my cousin, Lady Nassington?" She never sufficiently realised it as bad form, and therefore in her own circle was known among the women, who jeered at her behind her back, as "The Cousin of Lady Nassington." She was daintily dressed, and evidently just come in from visiting, for she still had her hat on when she entered.

"Ah!" she cried, with her usual buoyant air. "You truant! We've all been wondering what had become of you. Busy, of course! Always the same excuse! Find something fresh. You used it a fortnight ago to refuse my invitation to take pot-luck with us."

I laughed at her unconventional greeting, replying, "If I say something fresh it must be a lie. You know, Mrs. Henniker, how hard I'm kept at it, with hospital work and private practice."

"That's all very well," she said, with a slight pout of her well-shaped mouth—for she was really a pretty woman, even though full of airs and caprices. "But it doesn't excuse you for keeping away from us altogether."

"I don't keep away altogether," I protested. "I've called now."

She pulled a wry face, in order to emphasise her dissatisfaction at my explanation, and said:

"And I suppose you are prepared to receive castigation? Ethelwynn has begun to complain because people are saying that your engagement is broken off."

"Who says so?" I inquired rather angrily, for I hated all the tittle-tattle of that little circle of gossips who dawdle over the tea-cups of Redcliffe Square and its neighbourhood. I had attended a good many of them professionally at various times, and was well acquainted with all their ways and all their exaggerations. The gossiping circle in flat-land about Earl's Court was bad enough, but the Redcliffe Square set, being slightly higher in the social scale, was infinitely worse.

"Oh! all the ill-natured people are commenting upon your apparent coolness. Once, not long ago, you used to be seen everywhere with Ethelwynn, and now no one ever sees you. People form a natural conclusion, of course," said the fair-haired, fussy little woman, whose married state gave her the right to censure me on my neglect.

"Ethelwynn is, of course, still with you?" I asked, in anger that outsiders should seek to interfere in my private affairs.

"She still makes our house her home, not caring to go back to the dulness of Neneford," was her reply. "But at present she's away visiting one of her old schoolfellows—a girl who married a country banker and lives near Hereford."

"Then she's in the country?"

"Yes, she went three days ago. I thought she had written to you. She told me she intended doing so."

I had received no letter from her. Indeed, our recent correspondence had been of a very infrequent and formal character. With a woman's quick perception she had noted my coldness and had sought to show equal callousness. With the knowledge of Courtenay's continued existence now in my mind, I was beside myself with grief and anger at having doubted her. But how could I act at that moment, save in obedience to my friend Jevons' instructions? He had urged me to go and find out some details regarding her recent life with the Hennikers; and with that object I remarked:

"She hasn't been very well of late, I fear. The change of air should do her good."

"That's true, poor girl. She's seemed very unwell, and I've often told her that only one doctor in the world could cure her malady—yourself."

I smiled. The malady was, I knew too well, the grief of a disappointed love, and a perfect cure for that could only be accomplished by reconciliation. I was filled with regret that she was absent, for I longed there and then to take her to my breast and whisper into her ear my heart's outpourings. Yes; we men are very foolish in our impetuosity.

"How long will she be away?"

"Why?" inquired the smartly-dressed little woman, mischievously. "What can it matter to you?"

"I have her welfare at heart, Mrs. Henniker," I answered seriously.

"Then you have a curious way of showing your solicitude on her behalf," she said bluntly, smiling again. "Poor Ethelwynn has been pining day after day for a word from you; but you seldom, if ever, write, and when you do the coldness of your letters adds to her burden of grief. I knew always when she had received one by the traces of secret tears upon her cheeks. Forgive me for saying so, Doctor, but you men, either in order to test the strength of a woman's affection, or perhaps out of mere caprice, often try her patience until the strained thread snaps, and she who was a good and pure woman becomes reckless of everything— her name, her family pride, and even her own honour."

Her words aroused my curiosity.

"And you believe that Ethelwynn's patience is exhausted?" I asked, anxiously.

Her eyes met mine, and I saw a mysterious expression in them. There is always something strange in the eyes of a pretty woman who is hiding a secret.

"Well, Doctor," she answered, in a voice quite calm and deliberate, "you've already shown yourself so openly as being disinclined to further associate yourself publicly with poor Ethelwynn, because of the tragedy that befell the household, that you surely cannot complain if you find your place usurped by a new and more devoted lover."

"What!" I cried, starting up, fiercely. "What is this you tell me? Ethelwynn has a lover?"

"I have nothing whatever to do with her affairs, Doctor," said the tantalising woman, who affected all the foibles of the smarter set. "Now that you have forsaken her she is, of course, entirely mistress of her own actions."

"But I haven't forsaken her!" I blurted forth.

She only smiled superciliously, with the same mysterious look—an expression that I cannot define, but by which I knew that she had told me the crushing truth. Ethelwynn, believing that I had cast her aside, had allowed herself to be loved by another!

Who was the man who had usurped my place? I deserved it all, without a doubt. You, reader, have already in your heart condemned me as being hard and indifferent towards the woman I once loved so truly and so well. But, in extenuation, I would ask you to recollect how grave were the suspicions against her—how every fact seemed to prove conclusively that her sister's husband had died by her hand.

I saw plainly in Mrs. Henniker's veiled words a statement of the truth; and, after obtaining from her Ethelwynn's address near Hereford, bade her farewell and blindly left the house.

XX

My New Patient

In the feverish restlessness of the London night, with its rumbling market-wagons and the constant tinkling of cab-bells, so different to the calm, moonlit stillness of the previous night in rural England, I wrote a long explanatory letter to my love.

I admitted that I had wronged her by my apparent coldness and indifference, but sought to excuse myself on the ground of the pressure of work upon me. She knew well that I was not a rich man, and in that slavery to which I was now tied I had an object—the object I had placed before her in the dawning days of our affection—namely, the snug country practice with an old-fashioned comfortable house in one of the quiet villages or smaller towns in the Midlands. In those days she had been just as enthusiastic about it as I had been. She hated town life, I knew; and even if the wife of a country doctor is allowed few diversions, she can always form a select little tea-and-tennis circle of friends.

The fashion nowadays is for girls of middle-class to regard the prospect of becoming a country doctor's wife with considerable hesitation—"too slow," they term it; and declare that to live in the country and drive in a governess-cart is synonymous with being buried. Many girls marry just as servants change their places—in order "to better themselves;" and alas! that parents encourage this latter-day craze for artificiality and glitter of town life that so often fascinates and spoils a bride ere the honeymoon is over. The majority of girls to-day are not content to marry the hard-working professional man whose lot is cast in the country, but prefer to marry a man in town, so that they may take part in the pleasures of theatres, variety and otherwise, suppers at restaurants, and the thousand and one attractions provided for the reveller in London. They have obtained their knowledge of "life" from the society papers, and they see no reason why they should not taste of those pleasures enjoyed by their wealthier sisters, whose goings and comings are so carefully chronicled. The majority of girls have a desire to shine beyond their own sphere; and the attempt, alas! is accountable for very many of the unhappy marriages. This may sound prosy, I know, but the reader will forgive when he reflects upon the cases in point which arise to his memory—cases of personal friends, perhaps even of relations, to whom marriage was a failure owing to this uncontrollable desire on the part of the woman to assume a position to which neither birth nor wealth entitled her.

To the general rule, however, my love was an exception. Times without number had she declared her anxiety to settle in the country; for, being country born and bred, she was an excellent horsewoman, and in every essential a thorough English girl of the Grass Country, fond of a run with either fox or otter hounds; therefore, in suburban life at Kew, she had been entirely out of her element.

In that letter I wrote, composing it slowly and carefully—for like most medical men I am a bad hand at literary composition—I sought her forgiveness, and asked for an immediate interview. The wisdom of being so precipitous never occurred to me. I only know that in those night hours over my pipe I resolved to forget once and for all that letter I had discovered among the "dead" man's effects, and determined that, while I sought reconciliation with Ethelwynn, I would keep an open and watchful eye upon Mary and her fellow conspirator.

The suggestion that Ethelwynn, believing herself forsaken, had accepted the declarations of a man she considered more worthy than myself, lashed me to a frenzy of madness. He should never have her, whoever he might be. She had been mine, and should remain so, come what might. I added a postscript, asking her to wire me permission to travel down to Hereford to see her; then, sealing up the letter, I went out along the Marylebone Road and posted it in the pillar-box, which I knew was cleared at five o'clock in the morning.

It was then about three o'clock, calm, but rather overcast. The Marylebone Road had at last become hushed in silence. Wagons and cabs had both ceased, and save for a solitary policeman here and there the long thoroughfare, so full of traffic by day, was utterly deserted. I retraced my steps slowly towards the corner of Harley Street, and was about to open the door of the house wherein I had "diggings" when I heard a light, hurried footstep behind me, and turning, confronted the figure of a slim woman of middle height wearing a golf cape, the hood of which had been thrown over her head in lieu of a hat.

"Excuse me, sir," she cried, in a breathless voice, "but are you Doctor Boyd?"

I replied that such was my name.

"Oh, I'm in such distress," she said, in the tone of one whose heart is full of anguish. "My poor father!"

"Is your father ill?" I inquired, turning from the door and looking full at her. I was standing on the step, and she was on the pavement, having evidently approached from the opposite direction. She stood with her back to the street lamp, so I could discern nothing of her features. Only her voice told me that she was young.

"Oh, he's very ill," she replied anxiously. "He was taken queer at eleven o'clock, but he wouldn't hear of me coming to you. He's one of those men who don't like doctors."

"Ah!" I remarked; "there are many of his sort about. But they are compelled to seek our aid now and then. Well, what can I do for you? I suppose you want me to see him—eh?"

"Yes, sir, if you'd be so kind. I know its awfully late; but, as you've been out, perhaps you wouldn't mind running round to our house. It's quite close, and I'll take you there." She spoke with the peculiar drawl and dropped her "h's" in the manner of the true London-bred girl.

"I'll come if you'll wait a minute," I said, and then, leaving her outside, I entered the house and obtained my thermometer and stethoscope.

When I rejoined her and closed the door I made some inquiries about the sufferer's symptoms, but the description she gave me was so utterly vague and contradictory that I could make nothing out of it. Her muddled idea of his illness I put down to her fear and anxiety for his welfare.

She had no mother, she told me; and her father had, of late, given way just a little to drink. He "used" the Haycock, in Edgware Road; and she feared that he had fallen among a hard-drinking set. He was a pianoforte-maker, and had been employed at Brinsmead's for eighteen years. Since her mother died, six years ago, however, he had never been the same.

"It was then that he took to drink?" I hazarded.

"Yes," she responded. "He was devoted to her. They never had a wry word."

"What has he been complaining of? Pains in the head—or what?"

"Oh, he's seemed thoroughly out of sorts," she answered after some slight hesitation, which struck me as peculiar. She was greatly agitated regarding his illness, yet she could not describe one single symptom clearly. The only direct statement she made was that her father had

WILLIAM LE QUEUX

certainly not been drinking on the previous night, for he had remained indoors ever since he came home from the works, as usual, at seven o'clock.

As she led me along the Marylebone Road, in the same direction as that I had just traversed—which somewhat astonished me—I glanced surreptitiously at her, just at the moment when we were approaching a street lamp, and saw to my surprise that she was a sad-faced girl whose features were familiar. I recognised her in a moment as the girl who had been my fellow passenger from Brighton on that Sunday night. Her hair, however, was dishevelled, as though she had turned out from her bed in too great alarm to think of tidying it. I was rather surprised, but did not claim acquaintance with her. She led me past Madame Tussaud's, around Baker Street Station, and then into the maze of those small cross-streets that lie between Upper Baker Street and Lisson Grove until she stopped before a small, rather respectable-looking house, half-way along a short side-street, entering with a latch-key.

In the narrow hall it was quite dark, but she struck a match and lit a cheap paraffin lamp which stood there in readiness, then led me upstairs to a small sitting-room on the first floor, a dingy, stuffy little place of a character which showed me that she and her father lived in lodgings. Having set the lamp on the table, and saying that she would go and acquaint the invalid with my arrival, she went out, closing the door quietly after her. The room was evidently the home of a studious, if poor, man, for in a small deal bookcase I noticed, well-kept and well-arranged, a number of standard works on science and theology, as well as various volumes which told me mutely that their owner was a student, while upon the table lay a couple of critical reviews, the "Saturday" and "Spectator."

I took up the latter and glanced it over in order to pass the time, for my conductress seemed to be in consultation with her father. My eye caught an article that interested me, and I read it through, forgetting for a moment all about my call there. Fully ten minutes elapsed, when of a sudden I heard the voice of a man speaking somewhat indistinctly in a room above that in which I was sitting. He seemed to be talking low and gruffly, so that I was unable to distinguish what was said. At last, however, the girl returned, and, asking me to follow her, conducted me to a bedroom on the next floor.

The only illumination was a single night-light burning in a saucer, casting a faint, uncertain glimmer over everything, and shaded with an open book so that the occupant of the bed lay in deepest shadow. Unlike what one would have expected to find in such a house, an iron bedstead with brass rail, the bed was a great old-fashioned one with heavy wool damask hangings; and advancing towards it, while the girl retired and closed the door after her, I bent down to see the invalid.

In the shadow I could just distinguish on the pillow a dark-bearded face whose appearance was certainly not prepossessing.

"You are not well?" I said, inquiringly, as our eyes met in the dim half-light. "Your daughter is distressed about you."

"Yes, I'm a bit queer," he growled. "But she needn't have bothered you."

"Let me remove the shade from the light, so that I can see your face," I suggested. "It's too dark to see anything."

"No," he snapped; "I can't bear the light. You can see quite enough of me here."

"Very well," I said, reluctantly, and taking his wrist in one hand I held my watch in the other.

"I fancy you'll find me a bit feverish," he said in a curious tone, almost as though he were joking, and by his manner I at once put him down as one of those eccentric persons who are sceptical of any achievements of medical science.

I was holding his wrist and bending towards the light, in order to distinguish the hands of my watch, when a strange thing happened.

There was a deafening explosion close behind me, which caused me to jump back startled. I dropped the man's hand and turned quickly in the direction of the sound; but, as I did so, a second shot from a revolver held by an unknown person was discharged full in my face.

The truth was instantly plain. I had been entrapped for my watch and jewellery—like many another medical man in London has been before me; doctors being always an easy prey for thieves. The ruffian shamming illness sprang from his bed fully dressed, and at the same moment two other blackguards, who had been hidden in the room, flung themselves upon me ere I could realize my deadly peril.

The whole thing had been carefully planned, and it was apparent that the gang were quite fearless of neighbours overhearing the shots. The place bore a bad reputation, I knew; but I had never suspected that a man might be fired at from behind in that cowardly way.

So sudden and startling were the circumstances that I stood for a moment motionless, unable to fully comprehend their intention. There was but one explanation. These men intended to kill me!

Without a second's hesitation they rushed upon me, and I realized with heart-sinking that to attempt to resist would be utterly futile. I was entirely helpless in their hands!

XXI

Woman's Wiles

Look sharp!" cried the black-bearded ruffian who had feigned illness. "Give him a settler, 'Arry. He wants his nerves calmin' a bit!"

The fellow had seized my wrists, and I saw that one of the men who had sprung from his place of concealment was pouring some liquid from a bottle upon a sponge. I caught a whiff of its odour—an odour too familiar to me—the sickly smell of chloroform.

Fortunately I am pretty athletic, and with a sudden wrench I freed my wrists from the fellow's grip, and, hitting him one from the shoulder right between the eyes, sent him spinning back against the chest of drawers. To act swiftly was my only chance. If once they succeeded in pressing that sponge to my nostrils and holding it there, then all would be over; for by their appearance I saw they were dangerous criminals, and not men to stick at trifles. They would murder me.

As I sent down the man who had shammed illness, his two companions dashed towards me with imprecations upon their lips; but with lightning speed I sprang towards the door and placed my back against it. So long as I could face them I intended to fight for life. Their desire was, I knew, to attack me from behind, as they had already done. I had surely had a narrow escape from their bullets, for they had fired at close range.

At Guy's many stories have been told of similar cases where doctors, known to wear valuable watches, diamond rings or scarf pins, have been called at night by daring thieves and robbed; therefore I always, as precaution, placed my revolver in my pocket when I received a night call to a case with which I was not acquainted.

I had not disregarded my usual habit when I had placed my thermometer and stethoscope in my pocket previous to accompanying the girl; therefore it reposed there fully loaded, a fact of which my assailants were unaware.

In much quicker time than it takes to narrate the incident I was again pounced upon by all three, the man with the sponge in readiness to dash it to my mouth and nostrils.

But as they sprang forward to seize me, I raised my hand swiftly, took aim, and fired straight at the holder of the sponge, the bullet passing through his shoulder and causing him to drop the anæsthetic as though it were a live coal, and to spring several feet from the ground.

"God! I'm shot!" he cried.

But ere the words had left his mouth I fired a second chamber, inflicting a nasty wound in the neck of the fellow with the black beard.

"Shoot! shoot!" he cried to the third man, but it was evident that in the first struggle, when I had been seized, the man's revolver had dropped on the carpet, and in the semi-darkness he could not recover it.

Recognising this, I fired a pot shot in the man's direction; then, opening the door, sprang down the stairs into the hall. One of them followed, but the other two, wounded as they were, did not care to face my weapon again. They saw that I knew how to shoot, and probably feared that I might inflict a fatal hurt.

As I approached the front door, and was fumbling with the lock, the third man flung himself upon me, determined that I should not escape. With great good fortune, however, I managed to unbolt the door, and after a desperate struggle, in which he endeavoured to wrest the weapon from my hand, I succeeded at last in gripping him by the throat, and after nearly strangling him flung him to the ground and escaped into the street, just as his associates, hearing his cries of distress, dashed downstairs to his assistance.

Without doubt it was the narrowest escape of my life that I have ever had, and so excited was I that I dashed down the street hatless until I emerged into Lisson Grove. Then, and only then, it occurred to me that, having taken no note of the house, I should be unable to recognise it and denounce it to the police. But when one is in peril of one's life all other thoughts or instincts are submerged in the one frantic effort of self-preservation. Still, it was annoying to think that such scoundrels should be allowed to go scot free.

Breathless, excited, and with nerves unstrung, I opened my door with my latch-key and returned to my room, where the reading-lamp had burned low, for it had been alight all through the night. I mixed myself a stiff brandy and soda, tossed it off, and then turned to look at myself in the glass.

The picture I presented was disreputable and unkempt. My hair was ruffled, my collar torn open from its stud, and one sleeve of my coat had been torn out, so that the lining showed through. I had a nasty scratch across the neck, too, inflicted by the fingernails of one of the blackguards, and from the abrasion blood had flowed and made a mess of my collar.

Altogether I presented a very brilliant and entertaining spectacle. But my watch, ring and scarf-pin were in their places. If robbery had been their motive, as no doubt it had been, then they had profited nothing, and two of them had been winged into the bargain. The only mode by which their identity could by chance be discovered was in the event of those wounds being troublesome. In that case they would consult a medical man; but as they would, in all probability, go to some doctor in a distant quarter of London, the hope of tracing them by such means was but a slender one.

Feeling a trifle faint I sat in my chair, resting for a quarter of an hour or so; then, becoming more composed, I put out the study lights, and after a refreshing wash went to bed.

The morning's reflections were somewhat disconcerting. A deliberate and dastardly attempt had been made upon my life; but with what motive? The young woman, whose face was familiar, had, I recollected, asked most distinctly whether I was Doctor Boyd—a fact which showed that the trap had been prepared. I now saw the reason why she was unable to describe the man's sham illness, and during the morning, while at work in the hospital wards, my suspicions became aroused that there had been some deeper motive in it all than the robbery of my watch or scarf-pin. Human life had been taken for far less value than that of my jewellery, I knew; nevertheless, the deliberate shooting at me while I felt the patient's pulse showed a determination to assassinate. By good fortune, however, I had escaped, and resolved to exercise more care in future when answering night calls to unknown houses.

Sir Bernard did not come to town that day; therefore I was compelled to spend the afternoon in the severe consulting-room at Harley Street, busy the whole time. Shortly before six o'clock, utterly worn out, I strolled round to my rooms to change my coat before going down to the Savage Club to dine with my friends—for it was Saturday night, and I seldom missed the genial house-dinner of that most Bohemian of institutions.

Without ceremony I threw open the door of my sitting-room and entered, but next instant stood still, for, seated in my chair patiently awaiting me was the slim, well-dressed figure of Mary Courtenay. Her widow's weeds became her well; and as she rose with a rustle of silk, a bright laugh rippled from her lips, and she said:

WILLIAM LE QUEUX

"I know I'm an unexpected visitor, Doctor, but you'll forgive my calling in this manner, won't you?"

"Forgive you? Of course," I answered; and with politeness which I confess was feigned, I invited her to be seated. True to the promise made to her husband, she had lost no time in coming to see me, but I was fortunately well aware of the purport of her errand.

"I had no idea you were in London," I said, by way of allowing her to explain the object of her visit, for, in the light of the knowledge I had gained on the Nene bank two nights previously, her call was of considerable interest.

"I'm only up for a couple of days," she answered. "London has not the charm for me that it used to have," and she sighed heavily, as though her mind were crowded by bitter memories. Then raising her veil, and revealing her pale, handsome face, she said bluntly, "The reason of my call is to talk to you about Ethelwynn."

"Well, what of her?" I asked, looking straight into her face and noticing for the first time a curious shifty look in her eyes, such as I had never before noticed in her. She tried to remain calm, but, by the nervous twitching of her fingers and lower lip, I knew that within her was concealed a tempest of conflicting emotions.

"To speak quite frankly, Ralph," she said in a calm, serious voice, "I don't think you are treating her honourably, poor girl. You seem to have forsaken her altogether, and the neglect has broken her heart."

"No, Mrs. Courtenay; you misunderstand the situation," I protested. "That I have neglected her slightly I admit; nevertheless the neglect was not wilful, but owing to my constant occupation in my practice."

"She's desperate. Besides, it's common talk that you've broken off the engagement."

"Gossip does not affect me; therefore why should she take any heed of it?"

"Well, she loves you. That you know quite well. You surely could not have been deceived in those days at Kew, for her devotion to you was absolute and complete." She was pleading her sister's cause just as Courtenay had directed her. I felt annoyed that she should thus endeavour to impose upon me, yet saw the folly of betraying the fact that I knew her secret. My intention was to wait and watch.

"I called at the Hennikers' a couple of days ago, but Ethelwynn is no longer there. She's gone into the country, it seems," I remarked.

"Where to?" she asked quickly.

"She's visiting someone near Hereford."

"Oh!" she exclaimed, as though a sudden light dawned upon her. "I know, then. Why, I wonder, did she not tell me. I intended to call on her this evening, but it is useless. I'm glad to know, for I don't care much for Mrs. Henniker. She's such a very shallow woman."

"Ethelwynn seems to have wandered about a good deal since the sad affair at Kew," I observed.

"Yes, and so have I," she responded. "As you are well aware, the blow was such a terrible one to me that—that somehow I feel I shall never get over it—never!" I saw tears, genuine tears, welling in her eyes. If she could betray emotion in that manner she was surely a wonderful actress.

"Time will efface your sorrow," I said, in a voice meant to be sympathetic. "In a year or two your grief will not be so poignant, and the past will gradually fade from your memory. It is always so."

She shook her head mournfully.

"No," she said, "for in addition to my grief there is the mystery of it all—a mystery that grows each day more and more inscrutable."

I glanced sharply at her in surprise. Was she trying to mislead me, or were her words spoken in real earnest? I could not determine.

"Yes," I acquiesced. "The mystery is as complete as ever."

"Has no single clue been found, either by the police or by your friend—Jevons is, I think, his name?" she asked, with keen anxiety.

"One or two points have, I believe, been elucidated," I answered; "but the mystery still remains unsolved."

"As it ever will be," she added, with a sigh which appeared to me to be one of satisfaction, rather than of regret. "The details were so cleverly arranged that the police have been baffled in every endeavour. Is not that so?"

I nodded in the affirmative.

"And your friend Jevons? Has he given up all hope of any satisfactory discovery?"

"I really don't know," I answered. "I've not seen him for quite a long time. And in any case he has told me nothing regarding the result of his investigations. It is his habit to be mute until he has gained some tangible result."

A puzzled, apprehensive expression crossed her white brow for a moment; then it vanished into a pleasant smile, as she asked in confidence:

WILLIAM LE QUEUX

"Now, tell me, Ralph, what is your own private opinion of the situation?"

"Well, it is both complicated and puzzling. If we could discover any reason for the brutal deed we might get a clue to the assassin; but as far as the police have been able to gather, it seems that there is an entire absence of motive; hence the impossibility of carrying the inquiries further."

"Then the investigation is actually dropped?" she exclaimed, unable to further conceal her anxiety.

"I presume it is," I replied.

Her chest heaved slightly, and slowly fell again. By its movement I knew that my answer allowed her to breathe more freely.

"You also believe that your friend Jevons has been compelled, owing to negative results, to relinquish his efforts?" she asked.

"Such is my opinion. But I have not seen him lately in order to consult him."

In silence she listened to my answer, and was evidently reassured by it; yet I could not, for the life of me, understand her manner—at one moment nervous and apprehensive, and at the next full of an almost imperious self-confidence. At times the expression in her eyes was such as justified her mother in the fears she had expressed to me. I tried to diagnose her symptoms, but they were too complicated and contradictory.

She spoke again of her sister, returning to the main point upon which she had sought the interview. She was a decidedly attractive woman, with a face rendered more interesting by her widow's garb.

But why was she masquerading so cleverly? For what reason had old Courtenay contrived to efface his identity so thoroughly? As I looked at her, mourning for a man who was alive and well, I utterly failed to comprehend one single fact of the astounding affair. It staggered belief!

"Let me speak candidly to you, Ralph," she said, after we had been discussing Ethelwynn for some little time. "As you may readily imagine, I have my sister's welfare very much at heart, and my only desire is to see her happy and comfortable, instead of pining in melancholy as she now is. I ask you frankly, have you quarrelled?"

"No, we have not," I answered promptly.

"Then if you have not, your neglect is all the more remarkable," she said. "Forgive me for speaking like this, but our intimate acquaintanceship in the past gives me a kind of prerogative to speak my mind. You won't be offended, will you?" she asked, with one of those sweet smiles of hers that I knew so well.

"Offended? Certainly not, Mrs. Courtenay. We are too old friends for that."

"Then take my advice and see Ethelwynn again," she urged. "I know how she adores you; I know how your coldness has crushed all the life out of her. She hides her secret from mother, and for that reason will not come down to Neneford. See her, and return to her; for it is a thousand pities that two lives should be wrecked so completely by some little misunderstanding which will probably be explained away in a dozen words. You may consider this appeal an extraordinary one, made by one sister on behalf of another, but when I tell you that I have not consulted Ethelwynn, nor does she know that I am here on her behalf, you will readily understand that I have both your interests equally at heart. To me it seems a grievous thing that you should be placed apart in this manner; that the strong love you bear each other should be crushed, and your future happiness be sacrificed. Tell me plainly," she asked in earnestness. "You love her still—don't you?"

"I do," was my frank, outspoken answer, and it was the honest truth.

XXII

A Message

T he pretty woman in her widow's weeds stirred slightly and settled her
skirts, as though my answer had given her the greatest satisfaction.

"Then take my advice, Ralph," she went on. "See her again before it
is too late."

"You refer to her fresh lover—eh?" I inquired bitterly.

"Her fresh lover?" she cried in surprise. "I don't understand you.
Who is he, pray?"

"I'm in ignorance of his name."

"But how do you know of his existence? I have heard nothing of
him, and surely she would have told me. All her correspondence, all her
poignant grief, and all her regrets have been of you."

"Mrs. Henniker gave me to understand that my place in your sister's
heart has been filled by another man," I said, in a hard voice.

"Mrs. Henniker!" she cried in disgust. "Just like that evil-tongued
mischief-maker! I've told you already that I detest her. She was my
friend once—it was she who allured me from my husband's side. Why
she exercises such an influence over poor Ethelwynn, I can't tell. I do
hope she'll leave their house and come back home. You must try and
persuade her to do so."

"Do you think, then, that the woman has lied?" I asked.

"I'm certain of it. Ethelwynn has never a thought for any man save
yourself. I'll vouch for that."

"But what object can she have in telling me an untruth?"

The widow smiled.

"A very deep one, probably. You don't know her as well as I do, or you
would suspect all her actions of ulterior motive."

"Well," I said, after a pause, "to tell the truth, I wrote to Ethelwynn
last night with a view to reconciliation."

"You did!" she cried joyously. "Then you have anticipated me, and my
appeal to you has been forestalled by your own conscience—eh?"

"Exactly," I laughed. "She has my letter by this time, and I am
expecting a wire in reply. I have asked her to meet me at the earliest
possible moment."

"Then you have all my felicitations, Ralph," she said, in a voice that seemed to quiver with emotion. "She loves you—loves you with a fiercer and even more passionate affection than that I entertained towards my poor dead husband. Of your happiness I have no doubt, for I have seen how you idolised her, and how supreme was your mutual content when in each other's society. Destiny, that unknown influence that shapes our ends, has placed you together and forged a bond between you that is unbreakable—the bond of perfect love."

There seemed such a genuine ring in her voice, and she spoke with such solicitude for our welfare, that in the conversation I entirely forgot that after all she was only trying to bring us together again in order to prevent her own secret from being exposed.

At some moments she seemed the perfection of honesty and integrity, without the slightest affectation of interest or artificiality of manner, and it was this fresh complexity of her character that utterly baffled me. I could not determine whether, or not, she was in earnest.

"If it is really destiny I suppose that to try and resist it is quite futile," I remarked mechanically.

"Absolutely. Ethelwynn will become your wife, and you have all my good wishes for prosperity and happiness."

I thanked her, but pointed out that the matrimonial project was, as yet, immature.

"How foolish you are, Ralph!" she said. "You know very well that you'd marry her to-morrow if you could."

"Ah! if I could," I repeated wistfully. "Unfortunately my position is not yet sufficiently well assured to justify my marrying. Wedded poverty is never a pleasing prospect."

"But you have the world before you. I've heard Sir Bernard say so, times without number. He believes implicitly in you as a man who will rise to the head of your profession."

I laughed dubiously, shaking my head.

"I only hope that his anticipations may be realized," I said. "But I fear I'm no more brilliant than a hundred other men in the hospitals. It takes a smart man nowadays to boom himself into notoriety. As in literature and law, so in the medical profession, it isn't the clever man who rises to the top of the tree. More often it is a second-rate man, who has private influence, and has gauged the exact worth of self-advertisement. This is an age of reputations quickly made, and just as rapidly lost. In the professional world a new man rises with every moon."

"But that need not be so in your case," she pointed out. "With Sir Bernard as your chief, you are surely in an assured position."

Taking her into my confidence, I told her of my ideal of a snug country practice—one of those in which the assistant does the night-work and attends to the club people, while there is a circle of county people as patients. There are hundreds of such practices in England, where a doctor, although scarcely known outside his own district, is in a position which Harley Street, with all its turmoil of fashionable fads and fancies, envies as the elysium of what life should be. The village doctor of Little Perkington may be an ignorant old buffer; but his life, with its three days' hunting a week, its constant invitations to shoot over the best preserves, and its free fishing whenever in the humour, is a thousand times preferable to the silk-hatted, frock-coated existence of the fashionable physician.

I had long ago talked it all over with Ethelwynn, and she entirely agreed with me. I had not the slightest desire to have a consulting-room of my own in Harley Street. All I longed for was a life in open air and rural tranquillity; a life far from the tinkle of the cab-bell and the milkman's strident cry; a life of ease and bliss, with my well-beloved ever at my side. The unfortunate man compelled to live in London is deprived of half of God's generous gifts.

"Though this unaccountable coldness has fallen between you," Mary said, looking straight at me, "you surely cannot have doubted the strength of her affection?"

"But Mrs. Henniker's insinuation puzzles me. Besides, her recent movements have been rather erratic, and almost seem to bear out the suggestion."

"That woman is utterly unscrupulous!" she cried angrily. "Depend upon it that she has some deep motive in making that slanderous statement. On one occasion she almost caused a breach between myself and my poor husband. Had he not possessed the most perfect confidence in me, the consequences might have been most serious for both of us. The outcome of a mere word, uttered half in jest, it came near ruining my happiness for ever. I did not know her true character in those days."

"I had no idea that she was a dangerous woman," I remarked, rather surprised at this statement. Hitherto I had regarded her as quite a harmless person, who, by making a strenuous effort to obtain a footing in good society, often rendered herself ridiculous in the eyes of her friends.

"Her character!" she echoed fiercely. "She's one of the most evil-tongued women in London. Here is an illustration. While posing as Ethelwynn's friend, and entertaining her beneath her roof, she actually insinuates to you the probability of a secret lover! Is it fair? Is it the action of an honest, trustworthy woman?"

I was compelled to admit that it was not. Yet, was this action of her own, in coming to me in those circumstances, in any way more straightforward? Had she known that I was well aware of the secret existence of her husband, she would assuredly never have dared to speak in the manner she had. Indeed, as I sat there facing her, I could scarcely believe it possible that she could act the imposture so perfectly. Her manner was flawless; her self-possession marvellous.

But the motive of it all—what could it be? The problem had been a maddening one from first to last.

I longed to speak out my mind then and there; to tell her of what I knew, and of what I had witnessed with my own eyes. Yet such a course was useless. I was proceeding carefully, watching and noting everything, determined not to blunder.

Had you been in my place, my reader, what would you have done? Recollect, I had witnessed a scene on the river-bank that was absolutely without explanation, and which surpassed all human credence. I am a matter-of-fact man, not given to exaggerate or to recount incidents that have not occurred, but I confess openly and freely that since I had walked along that path I hourly debated within myself whether I was actually awake and in the full possession of my faculties, or whether I had dreamt the whole thing.

Yet it was no dream. Certain solid facts convinced me of its stern, astounding reality. The man upon whose body I had helped to make an autopsy was actually alive.

In reply to my questions my visitor told me that she was staying at Martin's, in Cork Street—a small private hotel which the Mivarts had patronised for many years—and that on the following morning she intended returning again to Neneford.

Then, after she had again urged me to lose no time in seeing Ethelwynn, and had imposed upon me silence as to what had passed between us, I assisted her into a hansom, and she drove away, waving her hand in farewell.

The interview had been a curious one, and I could not in the least understand its import. Regarded in the light of the knowledge I had

WILLIAM LE QUEUX

gained when down at Neneford, it was, of course, plain that both she and her "dead" husband were anxious to secure Ethelwynn's silence, and believed they could effect this by inducing us to marry. The conspiracy was deeply-laid and ingenious, as indeed was the whole of the amazing plot. Yet, some how, when I reflected upon it on my return from the club, I could not help sitting till far into the night trying to solve the remarkable enigma.

A telegram from Ethelwynn had reached me at the Savage at nine o'clock, stating that she had received my letter, and was returning to town the day after to-morrow. She had, she said, replied to me by that night's post.

I felt anxious to see her, to question her, and to try, if possible, to gather from her some fact which would lead me to discern a motive in the feigned death of Henry Courtenay. But I could only wait in patience for the explanation. Mary's declaration that her sister possessed no other lover besides myself reassured me. I had not believed it of her from the first; yet it was passing strange that such an insinuation should have fallen from the lips of a woman who now posed as her dearest friend.

Next day, Sir Bernard came to town to see two unusual cases at the hospital, and afterwards drove me back with him to Harley Street, where he had an appointment with a German Princess, who had come to London to consult him as a specialist. As usual, he made his lunch off two ham sandwiches, which he had brought with him from Victoria Station refreshment-room and carried in a paper bag. I suggested that we should eat together at a restaurant; but the old man declined, declaring that if he ate more than his usual sandwiches for luncheon when in town he never had any appetite for dinner.

So I left him alone in his consulting-room, munching bread and ham, and sipping his wineglassful of dry sherry.

About half-past three, just before he returned to Brighton, I saw him again as usual to hear any instructions he wished to give, for sometimes he saw patients once, and then left them in my hands. He seemed wearied, and was sitting resting his brow upon his thin bony hands. During the day he certainly had been fully occupied, and I had noticed that of late he was unable to resist the strain as he once could.

"Aren't you well?" I asked, when seated before him.

"Oh, yes," he answered, with a sigh. "There's not much the matter with me. I'm tired, I suppose, that's all. The eternal chatter of those confounded women bores me to death. They can't tell their symptoms without going into all the details of family history and domestic infelicity," he snapped. "They think me doctor, lawyer, and parson rolled into one."

I laughed at his criticism. What he said was, indeed, quite true. Women often grew confidential towards me, at my age; therefore I could quite realize how they laid bare all their troubles to him.

"Oh, by the way!" he said, as though suddenly recollecting. "Have you met your friend Ambler Jevons lately?"

"No," I replied. "He's been away for some weeks, I think. Why?"

"Because I saw him yesterday in King's Road. He was driving in a fly, and had one eye bandaged up. Met with an accident, I should think."

"An accident!" I exclaimed in consternation. "He wrote to me the other day, but did not mention it."

"He's been trying his hand at unravelling the mystery of poor Courtenay's death, hasn't he?" the old man asked.

"I believe so?"

"And failed—eh?"

"I don't think his efforts have been crowned with very much success, although he has told me nothing," I said.

In response the old man grunted in dissatisfaction. I knew how disgusted he had been at the bungling and utter failure of the police inquiries, for he was always declaring Scotland Yard seemed to be useless, save for the recovery of articles left in cabs.

He glanced at his watch, snatched up his silk hat, buttoned his coat, and, wishing me good-bye, went out to catch the Pullman train.

Next day about two o'clock I was in one of the wards at Guy's, seeing the last of my patients, when a telegram was handed to me by one of the nurses.

I tore it open eagerly, expecting that it was from Ethelwynn, announcing the hour of her arrival at Paddington.

But the message upon which my eyes fell was so astounding, so appalling, and so tragic that my heart stood still.

The few words upon the flimsy paper increased the mystery to an even more bewildering degree than before!

XXIII

THE MYSTERY OF MARY

The astounding message, despatched from Neneford and signed by Parkinson, the butler, ran as follows:—

"Regret to inform you that Mrs. Courtenay was found drowned in the river this morning. Can you come here? My mistress very anxious to see you."

Without a moment's delay I sent a reply in the affirmative, and, after searching in the "A.B.C.," found that I had a train at three o'clock from King's Cross. This I took, and after an anxious journey arrived duly at the Manor, all the blinds of which were closely drawn.

Parkinson, white-faced and agitated, a thin, nervous figure in a coat too large for him, had been watching my approach up the drive, and held open the door for me.

"Ah, Doctor!" the old fellow gasped. "It's terrible—terrible! To think that poor Miss Mary should die like that!"

"Tell me all about it," I demanded, quickly. "Come!" and I led the way into the morning room.

"We don't know anything about it, sir; it's all a mystery," the grey-faced old man replied. "When one of the housemaids went up to Miss Mary's room at eight o'clock this morning to take her tea, as usual, she received no answer to her knock. Thinking she was asleep she returned half-an-hour later, only to find her absent, and that the bed had not been slept in. We told the mistress, never thinking that such an awful fate had befallen poor Miss Mary. Mistress was inclined to believe that she had gone off on some wild excursion somewhere, for of late she's been in the habit of going away for a day or two without telling us. At first none of us dreamed that anything had happened, until, just before twelve o'clock, Reuben Dixon's lad, who'd been out fishing, came up, shouting that poor Miss Mary was in the water under some bushes close to the stile that leads into Monk's Wood. At first we couldn't believe it; but, with the others, I flew down post-haste, and there she was, poor thing, under the surface, with her dress caught in the bushes that droop into the water. Her hat was gone, and her hair, unbound, floated out, waving with the current. We at once got a boat and took her out, but she was quite dead. Four men from the village carried her up here, and they've placed her in her own room."

"The police know about it, of course?"

"Yes, we told old Jarvis, the constable. He's sent a telegram to Oundle, I think."

"And what doctor has seen her?"

"Doctor Govitt. He's here now."

"Ah! I must see him. He has examined the body, I suppose?"

"I expect so, sir. He's been a long time in the room."

"And how is it believed that the poor young lady got into the water?" I asked, anxious to obtain the local theory.

"It's believed that she either fell in or was pushed in a long way higher up, because half-a-mile away, not far from the lock, there's distinct marks in the long grass, showing that somebody went off the path to the brink of the river. And close by that spot they found her black silk shawl."

"She went out without a hat, then?" I remarked, recollecting that when she had met her husband in secret she had worn a shawl. Could it be possible that she had met him again, and that he had made away with her? The theory seemed a sound one in the present circumstances.

"It seems to me, sir, that the very fact of her taking her shawl showed that she did not intend to be out very long," the butler said.

"It would almost appear that she went out in the night in order to meet somebody," I observed.

The old man shook his head sorrowfully, saying:

"Poor Miss Mary's never been the same since her husband died, Doctor. She was often very strange in her manner. Between ourselves, I strongly suspect it to be a case of deliberate suicide. She was utterly broken down by the awful blow."

"I don't see any motive for suicide," I remarked. Then I asked, "Has she ever been known to meet anyone on the river-bank at night?"

Old Parkinson was usually an impenetrable person. He fidgeted, and I saw that my question was an awkward one for him to answer without telling a lie.

"The truth will have to be discovered about this, you know," I went on. "Therefore, if you have any knowledge likely to assist us at the inquest it is your duty to explain."

"Well, sir," he answered, after a short pause, "to tell the truth, in this last week there have been some funny rumours in the village."

"About what?"

"People say that she was watched by Drake, Lord Nassington's gamekeeper, who saw her at two o'clock in the morning walking arm-in-arm with an old gentleman. I heard the rumour down at the Golden Ball, but I wouldn't believe it. Why, Mr. Courtenay's only been dead a month or two. The man Drake is a bragging fellow, and I think most people discredit his statement."

"Well," I said, "it might possibly have been true. It seems hardly conceivable that she should go wandering alone by the river at night. She surely had some motive in going there. Was she only seen by the gamekeeper on one occasion?"

"Only once. But, of course, he soon spread it about the village, and it formed a nice little tit-bit of gossip. As soon as I heard it I took steps to deny it."

"It never reached the young lady's ears?"

"Oh, no," the old servant answered. "We were careful to keep the scandal to ourselves, knowing how it would pain her. She's had sufficient trouble in her life, poor thing." And with tears in his grey old eyes, he added: "I have known her ever since she was a child in her cradle. It's awful that her end should come like this."

He was a most trustworthy and devoted servant, having spent nearly thirty years of his life in the service of the family, until he had become almost part of it. His voice quivered with emotion when he spoke of the dead daughter of the house, but he knew that towards me it was not a servant's privilege to entirely express the grief he felt.

I put other questions regarding the dead woman's recent actions, and he was compelled to admit that they had, of late, been quite unaccountable. Her absences were frequent, and she appeared to sometimes make long and mysterious journeys in various directions, while her days at home were usually spent in the solitude of her own room. Some friends of the family, he said, attributed it to grief at the great blow she had sustained, while others suspected that her mind had become slightly unhinged. I recollected, myself, how strange had been her manner when she had visited me, and inwardly confessed to being utterly mystified.

Doctor Govitt I found to be a stout middle-aged man, of the usual type of old-fashioned practitioner of a cathedral town, whose methods and ideas were equally old-fashioned. Before I entered the room where the unfortunate woman was lying, he explained to me that life had evidently been extinct about seven hours prior to the discovery of the body.

"There are no marks of foul play?" I inquired anxiously.

"None, as far as I've been able to find—only a scratch on the left cheek, evidently inflicted after death."

"What's your opinion?"

"Suicide. Without a doubt. The hour at which she fell into the water is shown by her watch. It stopped at 2.28."

"You have no suspicion of foul play?"

"None whatever."

I did not reply; but by the compression of my lips I presume he saw that I was dubious.

"Ah! I see you are suspicious," he said. "Of course, in tragic circumstances like these the natural conclusion is to doubt. The poor young lady's husband was mysteriously done to death, and I honestly believe that her mind gave way beneath the strain of grief. I've attended her professionally two or three times of late, and noted certain abnormal features in her case that aroused my suspicions that her brain had become unbalanced. I never, however, suspected her of suicidal tendency."

"Her mother, Mrs. Mivart, did," I responded. "She told me so only a few days ago."

"I know, I know," he answered. "Of course, her mother had more frequent and intimate opportunities for watching her than we had. In any case it is a very dreadful thing for the family."

"Very!" I said.

"And the mystery surrounding the death of Mr. Courtenay—was it never cleared up? Did the police never discover any clue to the assassin?"

"No. Not a single fact regarding it, beyond those related at the inquest, has ever been brought to light."

"Extraordinary—very extraordinary!"

I went with him into the darkened bedroom wherein lay the body, white and composed, her hair dishevelled about her shoulders, and her white waxen hands crossed about her breast. The expression upon her countenance—that face that looked so charming beneath its veil of widowhood as she had sat in my room at Harley Place—was calm and restful, for indeed, in the graceful curl of the lips, there was a

WILLIAM LE QUEUX

kind of half-smile, as though, poor thing, she had at last found perfect peace.

Govitt drew up the blind, allowing the golden sunset to stream into the room, thereby giving me sufficient light to make my examination. The latter occupied some little time, my object being to discover any marks of violence. In persons drowned by force, and especially in women, the doctor expects to find red or livid marks upon the wrists, arms or neck, where the assailant had seized the victim. Of course, these are not always discernible, for it is easier to entice the unfortunate one to the water's edge and give a gentle push than grapple in violence and hurl a person into the stream by main force. The push leaves no trace; therefore, the verdict in hundreds of cases of wilful murder has been "Suicide," or an open one, because the necessary evidence of foul play has been wanting.

Here was a case in point. The scratch on the face that Govitt had described was undoubtedly a post-mortem injury, and, with the exception of another slight scratch on the ball of the left thumb, I could find no trace whatever of violence. And yet, to me, the most likely theory was that she had again met her husband in secret, and had lost her life at his hands. To attribute a motive was utterly impossible. I merely argued logically within myself that it could not possibly be a case of suicide, for without a doubt she had met clandestinely the eccentric old man whom the world believed to be dead.

But if he were alive, who was the man who had died at Kew?

The facts within my knowledge were important and startling; yet if I related them to any second person I felt that my words would be scouted as improbable, and my allegations would certainly not be accepted. Therefore I still kept my own counsel, longing to meet Jevons and hear the result of his further inquiries.

Mrs. Mivart I found seated in her own room, tearful and utterly crushed. Poor Mary's end had come upon her as an overwhelming burden of grief, and I stood beside her full of heartfelt sympathy. A strong bond of affection had always existed between us; but, as I took her inert hand and uttered words of comfort, she only shook her head sorrowfully and burst into a torrent of tears. Truly the Manor was a dismal house of mourning.

To Ethelwynn I sent a telegram addressed to the Hennikers, in order that she should receive it the instant she arrived in town. Briefly I explained the tragedy, and asked her to come down to the Manor at once, feeling assured that Mrs. Mivart, in the hour of her distress, desired her daughter at her side. Then I accompanied the local constable, and the three police officers who had come over from Oundle, down to the riverside.

The brilliant afterglow tinged the broad, brimming river with a crimson light, and the trees beside the water already threw heavy shadows, for the day was dying, and the glamour of the fading sunset and the dead stillness of departing day had fallen upon everything. Escorted by a small crowd of curious villagers, we walked along the footpath over the familiar ground that I had traversed when following the pair. Eagerly we searched everywhere for traces of a struggle, but the only spot where the long grass was trodden down was at a point a little beyond the ferry. Yet as far as I could see there was no actual sign of any struggle. It was merely as though the grass had been flattened by the trailing of a woman's skirt across it. Examination showed, too, imprints of Louis XV. heels in the soft clay bank. One print was perfect, but the other, close to the edge, gave evidence that the foot had slipped, thus establishing the spot as that where the unfortunate young lady had fallen into the water. When examining the body I had noticed that she was wearing Louis XV. shoes, and also that there was still mud upon the heels. She had always been rather proud of her feet, and surely there is nothing which sets off the shape of a woman's foot better than the neat little shoe, with its high instep and heel.

We searched on until twilight darkened into night, traversing that path every detail of which had impressed itself so indelibly upon my brain. We passed the stile near which I had stood hidden in the bushes and overheard that remarkable conversation between the "dead" man and his wife. All the memories of that never-to-be-forgotten night returned to me. Alas! that I had not questioned Mary when she had called upon me on the previous day.

She had died, and her secret was lost.

WILLIAM LE QUEUX

XXIV

ETHELWYNN IS SILENT

At midnight I was seated in the drawing-room of the Manor. Before me, dressed in plain black which made her beautiful face look even paler than it was, sat my love, bowed, despondent, silent. The household, although still astir, was hushed by the presence of the dead; the long old room itself, usually so bright and pleasant, seemed full of dark shadows, for the lamp, beneath its yellow shade, burned but dimly, and everywhere there reigned an air of mourning.

Half-demented by grief, my love had arrived in hot haste about ten o'clock, and, rushing to poor Mary's room, had thrown herself upon her knees beside the poor inanimate clay; for, even though of late differences might have existed between them, the sisters were certainly devoted to each other. The scene in that room was an unhappy one, for although Ethelwynn betrayed nothing by her lips, I saw by her manner that she was full of remorse over the might-have-beens, and that she was bitterly reproaching herself for some fact of which I had no knowledge.

Of the past we had not spoken. She had been too full of grief, too utterly overcome by the tragedy of the situation. Her mournful figure struck a sympathetic chord in my heart. Perhaps I had misjudged her; perhaps I had attributed to her sinister motives that were non-existent. Alas! wherever mystery exists, little charity enters man's heart. Jealousy dries up the milk of human kindness.

"Dearest," I said, rising and taking her slim white hand that lay idly in her lap, "in this hour of your distress you have at least one person who would console and comfort you—one man who loves you."

She raised her eyes to mine quickly, with a strange, eager look. Her glance was as though she did not fully realize the purport of my words. I knew myself to be a sad blunderer in the art of love, and wondered if my words were too blunt and abrupt.

"Ah!" she sighed. "If only I believed that those words came direct from your heart, Ralph!"

"They do," I assured her. "You received my letter at Hereford—you read what I wrote to you?"

"Yes," she answered. "I read it. But how can I believe in you further, after your unaccountable treatment? You forsook me without giving any reason. You can't deny that."

"I don't seek to deny it," I said. "On the contrary, I accept all the blame that may attach to me. I only ask your forgiveness," and bending to her in deep earnestness, I pressed the small hand that was within my grasp.

"But if you loved me, as you declare you have always done, why did you desert me in that manner?" she inquired, her large dark eyes turned seriously to mine.

I hesitated. Should I tell her the truth openly and honestly?

"Because of a fact which came to my knowledge," I answered, after a long pause.

"What fact?" she asked with some anxiety.

"I made a discovery," I said ambiguously.

"Regarding me?"

"Yes, regarding yourself," I replied, with my eyes fixed full upon hers. I saw that she started at my words, her countenance fell, and she caught her breath quickly.

"Well, tell me what it is," she asked in a hard tone, a tone which showed me that she had steeled herself for the worst.

"Forgive me if I speak the truth," I exclaimed. "You have asked me, and I will be perfectly frank with you. Well, I discovered amongst old Mr. Courtenay's papers a letter written by you several years ago which revealed the truth."

"The truth!" she gasped, her face blanched in an instant. "The truth of what?"

"That you were once engaged to become his wife."

Her breast heaved quickly, and I saw that my words had relieved her of some grave apprehension. When I declared that I knew "the truth" she believed that I spoke of the secret of Courtenay's masquerading. The fact of her previous engagement was, to her, of only secondary importance, for she replied:

"Well, and is that the sole cause of your displeasure?"

I felt assured, from the feigned flippancy of her words, that she held knowledge of the strange secret.

"It was the main cause," I said. "You concealed the truth from me, and lived in that man's house after he had married Mary."

"I had a reason for doing so," she exclaimed, in a quiet voice. "I did not live there by preference."

WILLIAM LE QUEUX

"You were surely not forced to do so."

"No; I was not forced. It was a duty." Then, after a pause, she covered her face with her hands and suddenly burst into tears, crying, "Ah, Ralph! If you could know all—all that I have suffered, you would not think ill of me! Appearances have been against me, that I know quite well. The discovery of that letter must have convinced you that I was a schemer and unworthy, and the fact that I lived beneath the roof of the man who had cast me off added colour to the theory that I had conceived some deep plot. Probably," she went on, speaking between her sobs, "probably you even suspected me of having had a hand in the terrible crime. Tell me frankly," she asked, gripping my arm, and looking up into my face. "Did you ever suspect me of being the assassin?"

I paused. What could I reply? Surely it was best to be open and straightforward. So I told her that I had not been alone in the suspicion, and that Ambler Jevons had shared it with me.

"Ah! that accounts for his marvellous ingenuity in watching me. For weeks past he has seemed to be constantly near me, making inquiries regarding my movements wherever I went. You both suspected me. But is it necessary that I should assert my innocence of such a deed?" she asked. "Are you not now convinced that it was not my hand that struck down old Mr. Courtenay?"

"Forgive me," I urged. "The suspicion was based upon ill-formed conclusions, and was heightened by your own peculiar conduct after the tragedy."

"That my conduct was strange was surely natural. The discovery was quite as appalling to me as to you; and, knowing that somewhere among the dead man's papers my letters were preserved, I dreaded lest they should fall into the hands of the police and thereby connect me with the crime. It was fear that my final letter should be discovered that gave my actions the appearance of guilt."

I took both her hands in mine, and fixing my gaze straight into those dear eyes wherein the love-look shone—that look by which a man is able to read a woman's heart—I asked her a question.

"Ethelwynn," I said, calmly and seriously, "we love each other. I know I've been suspicious without cause and cruel in my neglect; nevertheless the separation has quickened my affection, and has shown that to me life without you is impossible. You, darling, are the only woman who has entered my life. I have championed no woman save yourself; by no ties have I been bound to any woman in this world. This I would have you believe, for it is the truth. I could not lie to you if I would; it is the truth—God is my witness."

She made me no answer. Her hands trembled, and she bowed her head so that I could not see her face.

"Will you not forgive, dearest?" I urged. The great longing to speak out my mind had overcome me, and having eased myself of my burden I stood awaiting her response. "Will you not be mine again, as in the old days before this chain of tragedy fell upon your house?"

Again she hesitated for several minutes. Then, of a sudden, she lifted her tear-stained face towards me, all rosy with blushes and wearing that sweet look which I had known so well in the happy days bygone.

"If you wish it, Ralph," she faltered, "we will forget that any breach between us has ever existed. I desire nothing else; for, as you well know, I love no one else but you. I have been foolish, I know. I ought to have explained the girlish romantic affection I once entertained for that man who afterwards married Mary. In those days he was my ideal. Why, I cannot tell. Girls in their teens have strange caprices, and that was mine. Just as schoolboys fall violently in love with married women, so are schoolgirls sometimes attracted towards aged men. People wonder when they hear of May and December marriages; but they are not always from mercenary motives, as is popularly supposed. Nevertheless I acted wrongly in not telling you the truth from the first. I am alone to blame."

So much she said, though with many a pause, and with so keen a self-reproach in her tone that I could hardly bear to hear her, when I interrupted—

"There is mutual blame on both sides. Let us forget it all," and I bent until my lips met hers and we sealed our compact with a long, clinging caress.

"Yes, dear heart. Let us forget it," she whispered. "We have both suffered—both of us," and I felt her arms tighten about my neck. "Oh, how you must have hated me!"

"No," I declared. "I never hated you. I was mystified and suspicious, because I felt assured that you knew the truth regarding the tragedy at Kew, and remained silent."

She looked into my eyes, as though she would read my soul.

"Unfortunately," she answered, "I am not aware of the truth."

"But you are in possession of certain strange facts—eh?"

"That I am in possession of facts that lead me to certain conclusions, is the truth. But the clue is wanting. I have been seeking for it through all these months, but without success."

"Cannot we act in accord in this matter, dearest? May I not be acquainted with the facts which, with your intimate knowledge of the Courtenay household, you were fully acquainted with at the time of the tragedy?" I urged.

"No, Ralph," she replied, shaking her head, and at the same time pressing my hand. "I cannot yet tell you anything."

"Then you have no confidence in me?" I asked reproachfully.

"It is not a question of confidence, but one of honour," she replied.

"But you will at least satisfy my curiosity upon one point?" I exclaimed. "You will tell me the reason you lived beneath Courtenay's roof?"

"You know the reason well. He was an invalid, and I went there to keep Mary company."

I smiled at the lameness of her explanation. It was, however, an ingenious evasion of the truth, for, after all, I could not deny that I had known this through several years. Old Courtenay, being practically confined to his room, had himself suggested Ethelwynn bearing his young wife company.

"Answer me truthfully, dearest. Was there no further reason?"

She paused; and in her hesitation I detected a desire to deceive, even though I loved her so fondly.

"Yes, there was," she admitted at last, bowing her head.

"Explain it."

"Alas! I cannot. It is a secret."

"A secret from me?"

"Yes, dear heart!" she cried, clutching my hands with a wild movement. "Even from you."

My face must have betrayed the annoyance that I felt, for the next second she hastened to soften her reply by saying:

"At present it is impossible for me to explain. Think! Poor Mary is lying upstairs. I can say nothing at present—nothing—you understand."

"Then afterwards—after the burial—you will tell me what you know?"

"Until I discover the truth I am resolved to maintain silence. All I can tell you is that the whole affair is so remarkable and astounding that its explanation will be even more bewildering than the tangled chain of circumstances."

"Then you are actually in possession of the truth," I remarked with some impatience. "What use is there to deny it?"

"At present I have suspicions—grave ones. That is all," she protested.

"What is your theory regarding poor Mary's death?" I asked, hoping to learn something from her.

"Suicide. Of that there seems not a shadow of doubt."

I was wondering if she knew of the "dead" man's existence. Being in sisterly confidence with Mary, she probably did.

"Did it ever strike you," I asked, "that the personal appearance of Mr. Courtenay changed very considerably after death. You saw the body several times after the discovery. Did you notice the change?"

She looked at me sharply, as though endeavouring to discern my meaning.

"I saw the body several times, and certainly noticed a change in the features. But surely the countenance changes considerably if death is sudden?"

"Quite true," I answered. "But I recollect that, in making the post-mortem, Sir Bernard remarked upon the unusual change. He seemed to have grown fully ten years older than when I had seen him alive four hours before."

"Well," she asked, "is that any circumstance likely to lead to a solution of the mystery? I don't exactly see the point."

"It may," I answered ambiguously, puzzled at her manner and wondering if she were aware of that most unaccountable feature of the conspiracy.

"How?" she asked.

But as she had steadfastly refused to reveal her knowledge to me, or the reason of her residence beneath Courtenay's roof, I myself claimed the right to be equally vague.

We were still playing at cross-purposes; therefore I urged her to be frank with me. But she strenuously resisted all my persuasion.

"No. With poor Mary lying dead I can say nothing. Later, when I have found the clue for which I am searching, I will tell you what I know. Till then, no word shall pass my lips."

I knew too well that when my love made up her mind it was useless to try and turn her from her purpose. She was no shallow, empty-headed girl, whose opinion could be turned by any breath of the social wind or any invention of the faddists; her mind was strong and well-balanced, so that she always had the courage of her own convictions. Her sister, on the contrary, had been one of those giddy women who follow every frill and furbelow of Fashion, and who take up all the latest crazes with a seriousness worthy of better objects. In temperament, in disposition, in character, and in strength of mind they had been the exact opposite of each other; the one sister flighty and thoughtless, the other patient and forbearing, with an utter disregard for the hollow artificialities of Society.

"But in this matter we may be of mutual assistance to each other," I urged, in an effort to persuade her. "As far as I can discern, the mystery contains no fewer than seven complete and distinct secrets. To obtain the truth regarding one would probably furnish the key to the whole."

"Then you think that poor Mary's untimely death is closely connected with the tragedy at Kew?" she asked.

"Most certainly. But I do not share your opinion of suicide."

"What? You suspect foul play?" she cried.

I nodded in the affirmative.

"You believe that poor Mary was actually murdered?" she exclaimed, anxiously. "Have you found marks of violence, then?"

"No, I have found nothing. My opinion is formed upon a surmise."

"What surmise?"

I hesitated whether to tell her all the facts that I had discovered, for I was disappointed and annoyed that she should still preserve a dogged silence, now that a reconciliation had been brought about.

"Well," I answered, after a pause, "my suspicion of foul play is based upon logical conclusions. I have myself been witness of one most astonishing fact—namely, that she was in the habit of meeting a certain man clandestinely at night, and that their favourite walk was along the river bank."

"What!" she cried, starting up in alarm, all the colour fading from her face. "You have actually seen them together?"

"I have not only seen them, but I have overheard their conversation," I answered, surprised at the effect my words had produced upon her.

"Then you already know the truth!" she cried, in a wild voice that was almost a shriek. "Forgive me—forgive me, Ralph!" And throwing herself suddenly upon her knees she looked up into my face imploringly, her white hands clasped in an attitude of supplication, crying in a voice broken by emotion: "Forgive me, Ralph! Have compassion upon me!" and she burst into a flood of tears which no caress or tender effort of mine could stem.

I adored her with a passionate madness that was beyond control. She was, as she had ever been, my ideal—my all in all. And yet the mystery surrounding her was still impenetrable; an enigma that grew more complicated, more impossible of solution.

XXV

Forms a Bewildering Enigma

"Found Drowned" was the verdict of the twelve respectable villagers who formed the Coroner's jury to inquire into the tragic death of young Mrs. Courtenay. It was the only conclusion that could be arrived at in the circumstances, there being no marks of violence, and no evidence to show how the unfortunate lady got into the river.

Ambler Jevons, who had seen a brief account of the affair in the papers, arrived hurriedly in time to attend the inquest; therefore it was not until the inquiry was over that we were enabled to chat. His appearance had changed during the weeks of his absence: his face seemed thinner and wore a worried, anxious expression.

"Well, Ralph, old fellow, this turns out to be a curious business, doesn't it?" he exclaimed, when, after leaving the public room of the Golden Ball, wherein the inquiry had been held, we had strolled on through the long straggling village of homely cottages with thatched roofs, and out upon the white, level highroad.

"Yes," I admitted. "It's more than curious. Frankly, I have a distinct suspicion that Mary was murdered."

"That's exactly my own opinion," he exclaimed quickly. "There's been foul play somewhere. Of that I'm certain."

"And do you agree with me, further, that it is the outcome of the tragedy at Kew?"

"Most certainly," he said. "That both husband and wife should be murdered only a few months after one another points to motives of revenge. You'll remember how nervous old Courtenay was. He went in constant fear of his life, it was said. That fact proves conclusively that he was aware of some secret enemy."

"Yes. Now that you speak of it, I recollect it quite well," I remarked, adding, "But where, in the name of Fortune, have you been keeping yourself during all these weeks of silence?"

"I've been travelling," he responded rather vaguely. "I've been going about a lot."

"And keeping watch on Ethelwynn during part of the time," I laughed.

"She told you, eh?" he exclaimed, rather apprehensively. "I didn't know that she ever recognised me. But women are always sharper than men. Still, I'm sorry that she saw me."

"There's no harm done—providing you've made some discovery regarding the seven secrets that compose the mystery," I said.

"Seven secrets!" he repeated thoughtfully, and then was silent a few moments, as though counting to himself the various points that required elucidation. "Yes," he said at last, "you're right, Ralph, there are seven of them—seven of the most extraordinary secrets that have ever been presented to mortal being as part of one and the same mystery."

He did not, of course, enumerate them in his mind, as I had done, for he was not aware of all the facts. The Seven Secrets, as they presented themselves to me, were: First, the identity of the secret assassin of Henry Courtenay; second, the manner in which that extraordinary wound had been caused; thirdly, the secret of Ethelwynn, held by Sir Bernard; fourthly, the secret motive of Ethelwynn in remaining under the roof of the man who had discarded her in favour of her sister; fifthly, the secret of Courtenay's reappearance after burial; sixthly, the secret of the dastardly attempt on my life by those ruffians of Lisson Grove; and, seventhly, the secret of Mary Courtenay's death. Each and every one of the problems was inscrutable. Others, of which I was unaware, had probably occurred to my friend. To him, just as to me, the secrets were seven.

"Now, be frank with me, Ambler," I said, after a long pause. "You've gained knowledge of some of them, haven't you?"

By his manner I saw that he was in possession of information of no ordinary character.

He paused, and slowly twisted his small dark moustache, at last admitting—

"Yes, Ralph, I have."

"What have you discovered?" I cried, in fierce eagerness. "Tell me the result of your inquiries regarding Ethelwynn. It is her connection with the affair which occupies my chief thoughts."

"For the present, my dear fellow, we must leave her entirely out of it," my friend said quietly. "To tell you the truth, after announcing my intention to give up the affair as a mystery impenetrable, I set to work and slowly formed a theory. Then I drew up a deliberate plan of campaign, which I carried out in its entirety."

"And the result?"

"Its result—" he laughed. "Well, when I'd spent several anxious weeks in making the most careful inquiries, I found, to my chagrin, that I was upon an entirely wrong scent, and that the person I suspected of being the assassin at Kew was innocent. There was no help for it but to begin all over again, and I did so. My inquiries then led me in an entirely opposite direction. I followed my new and somewhat startling theory, and found to my satisfaction that I had at length struck the right trail. Through a whole fortnight I worked on night and day, often snatching a few hours of sleep in railway carriages, and sometimes watching through the whole night—for when one pursues inquiries alone it is frequently imperative to keep watchful vigil. To Bath, to Hereford, to Edinburgh, to Birmingham, to Newcastle, and also to several places far distant in the South of England I travelled in rapid succession, until at last I found a clue, but one so extraordinary that at first I could not give it credence. Ten days have passed, and even now I refuse to believe that such a thing could be. I'm absolutely bewildered by it."

"Then you believe that you've at last gained the key to the mystery?" I said, eagerly drinking in his words.

"It seems as though I have. Yet my information is so very vague and shadowy that I can really form no decisive opinion. It is this mysterious death of Mrs. Courtenay that has utterly upset all my theories. Tell me plainly, Ralph, what causes you to suspect foul play? This is not a time for prevarication. We must be open and straightforward to each other. Tell me the absolute truth."

Should I tell him frankly of the amazing discovery I had made? I feared to do so, lest he should laugh me to scorn. The actual existence of Courtenay seemed too incredible. And yet as he was working to solve the problem, just as I was, there seemed every reason why we should be aware of each other's discoveries. We had both pursued independent inquiries into the Seven Secrets until that moment, and it was now high time we compared results.

"Well, Jevons," I exclaimed, hesitatingly, at last, "I have during the week elucidated one fact, a fact so strange that, when I tell you, I know you will declare that I was dreaming. I myself cannot account for it in the least. But that I was witness of it I will vouch. The mystery is a remarkable one, but what I've discovered adds to its inscrutability."

"Tell me," he urged quickly, halting and turning to me in eagerness. "What have you found out?"

"Listen!" I said. "Hear me through, until you discredit my story." Then, just as I have already written down the strange incidents in the foregoing chapters, I related to him everything that had occurred since the last evening he sat smoking with me in Harley Place.

He heard me in silence, the movements of his face at one moment betraying satisfaction, and at the next bewilderment. Once or twice he grunted, as though dissatisfied, until I came to the midnight incident beside the river, and explained how I had watched and what I had witnessed.

"What?" he cried, starting in sudden astonishment. "You actually saw him? You recognised Henry Courtenay!"

"Yes. He was walking with his wife, sometimes arm-in-arm."

He did not reply, but stood in silence in the centre of the road, drawing a geometrical design in the dust with the ferrule of his stick. It was his habit when thinking deeply.

I watched his dark countenance—that of a man whose whole thought and energy were centred upon one object.

"Ralph," he said at last, "what time is the next train to London?"

"Two-thirty, I think."

"I must go at once to town. There's work for me there—delicate work. What you've told me presents a new phase of the affair," he said in a strange, anxious tone.

"Does it strengthen your clue?" I asked.

"In a certain degree—yes. It makes clear one point which was hitherto a mystery."

"And also makes plain that poor Mrs. Courtenay met with foul play?" I suggested.

"Ah! For the moment, this latest development of the affair is quite beyond the question. We must hark back to that night at Richmond Road. I must go at once to London," he added, glancing at his watch. "Will you come with me?"

"Most willingly. Perhaps I can help you."

"Perhaps; we will see."

So we turned and retraced our steps to the house of mourning, where, having pleaded urgent consultations with patients, I took leave of Ethelwynn. We were alone, and I bent and kissed her lips in order to show her that my love and confidence had not one whit abated. Her countenance brightened, and with sudden joy she flung her arms around my neck and returned my caress, pleading—"Ralph! You will forgive—you will forgive me, won't you?"

WILLIAM LE QUEUX

"I love you, dearest!" was all that I could reply; and it was the honest truth, direct from a heart overburdened by mystery and suspicion.

Then with a last kiss I turned and left her, driving with Ambler Jevons to catch the London train.

XXVI

AMBLER JEVONS IS BUSY

The sleepy-eyed tea-blender of Mark Lane remained plunged in a deep reverie during the greater part of the journey to town, and on arrival at King's Cross declined to allow me to accompany him. This disappointed me. I was eager to pursue the clue, but no amount of persuasion on my part would induce him to alter his decision.

"At present I must continue alone, old fellow," he answered kindly. "It is best, after all. Later on I may want your help."

"The facts I've told you are of importance, I suppose?"

"Of the greatest importance," he responded. "I begin to see light through the veil. But if what I suspect is correct, then the affair will be found to be absolutely astounding."

"Of that I'm certain," I said. "When will you come in and spend an hour?"

"As soon as ever I can spare time," he answered. "To-morrow, or next day, perhaps. At present I have a very difficult task before me. Good-bye for the present." And hailing a hansom he jumped in and drove away, being careful not to give the address to the driver while within my hearing. Ambler Jevons had been born with the instincts of a detective. The keenness of his intellect was perfectly marvellous.

On leaving him I drove to Harley Street, where I found Sir Bernard busy with patients, and in rather an ill-temper, having been worried unusually by some smart woman who had been to consult him and had been pouring into his ear all her domestic woes.

"I do wish such women would go and consult somebody else," he growled, after he had been explaining her case to me. "Same symptoms as all of them. Nerves—owing to indigestion, late hours, and an artificial life. Wants me to order her to Carlsbad or somewhere abroad—so that she can be rid of her husband for a month or so. I can see the reason plain enough. She's got some little game to play. Faugh!" cried the old man, "such women only fill one with disgust."

I went on to tell him of the verdict upon the death of Mrs. Courtenay, and his manner instantly changed to one of sympathy.

"Poor Henry!" he exclaimed. "Poor little woman! I wonder that

WILLIAM LE QUEUX

nothing has transpired to give the police a clue. To my mind, Boyd, there was some mysterious element in Courtenay's life that he entirely hid from his friends. In later years he lived in constant dread of assassination."

"Yes, that has always struck me as strange," I remarked.

"Has nothing yet been discovered?" asked my chief. "Didn't the police follow that manservant Short?"

"Yes, but to no purpose. They proved to their own satisfaction that he was innocent."

"And your friend Jevons—the tea-dealer who makes it a kind of hobby to assist the police. What of him? Has he continued his activity?"

"I believe so. He has, I understand, discovered a clue."

"What has he found?" demanded the old man, bending forward in eagerness across the table. He had been devoted to his friend Courtenay, and was constantly inquiring of me whether the police had met with any success.

"At present he will tell me nothing," I replied.

Sir Bernard gave vent to an exclamation of dissatisfaction, observing that he hoped Jevons' efforts would meet with success, as it was scandalous that a double tragedy of that character could occur in a civilized community without the truth being revealed and the assassin arrested.

"There's no doubt that the tragedy was a double one," I observed. "Although the jury have returned a verdict of 'Found Drowned' in the widow's case, the facts, even as far as at present known, point undoubtedly to murder."

"To murder!" he cried. "Then is it believed that she's been wilfully drowned?"

"That is the local surmise."

"Why?" he asked, with an eager look upon his countenance, for he took the most intense interest in every feature of the affair.

"Well, because it is rumoured that she had been seen late one night walking along the river-bank, near the spot where she was found, accompanied by a strange man."

"A strange man?" he echoed, his interest increased. "Did anyone see him sufficiently close to recognise him?"

"I believe not," I answered, hesitating at that moment to tell him all I knew. "The local police are making active inquiries, I believe."

"I wonder who it could have been?" Sir Bernard exclaimed reflectively. "Mrs. Courtenay was always so devoted to poor Henry, that the story of the stranger appears to me very like some invention of the villagers. Whenever a tragedy occurs in a rural district all kinds of absurd canards are started. Probably that's one of them. It is only natural for the rustic mind to connect a lover with a pretty young widow."

"Exactly. But I have certain reasons for believing the clandestine meeting to have taken place," I said.

"What causes you to give credence to the story?"

"Statements made to me," I replied vaguely. "And further, all the evidence points to murder."

"Then why did the jury return an open verdict?"

"It was the best thing they could do in the circumstances, as it leaves the police with a free hand."

"But who could possibly have any motive for the poor little woman's death?" he asked, with a puzzled, rather anxious expression upon his grey brow.

"The lover may have wished to get rid of her," I suggested.

"You speak rather ungenerously, Boyd," he protested. "Remember, we don't know for certain that there was a lover in the case, and we should surely accept the rumours of country yokels with considerable hesitation."

"I make no direct accusation," I said. "I merely give as my opinion that she was murdered by the man she was evidently in the habit of meeting. That's all."

"Well, if that is so, then I hope the police will be successful in making an arrest," declared the old physician. "Poor little woman! When is the funeral?"

"The day after to-morrow."

"I must send a wreath. How sad it is! How very sad!" And he sighed sympathetically, and sat staring with fixed eyes at the dark green wall opposite.

"It's time you caught your train," I remarked, glancing at the clock.

"No," he answered. "I'm dining at the House of Commons to-night with my friend Houston. I shall remain in town all night. I so very seldom allow myself any dissipation," and he smiled rather sadly.

Truly he led an anchorite's life, going to and fro with clockwork regularity, and denying himself all those diversions in Society which are ever at the command of a notable man. Very rarely did he accept an invitation to dine, and the fact that he lived down at Hove was in order to have a good excuse to evade people. He was a great man, with all a great man's little eccentricities.

The two following days passed uneventfully. Each evening, about ten, Ambler Jevons came in to smoke and drink. He stayed an hour, apparently nervous, tired, and fidgety in a manner quite unusual; but to my inquiries regarding the success of his investigations he remained dumb.

"Have you discovered anything?" I asked, eagerly, on the occasion of his second visit.

He hesitated, at length answering—

"Yes—and no. I must see Ethelwynn without delay. Telegraph and ask her to meet you here. I want to ask her a question."

"Do you still suspect her?"

He shrugged his shoulders with an air of distinct vagueness.

"Wire to her to-night," he urged. "Your man can take the message down to the Charing Cross office, and she'll get it at eight o'clock in the morning. The funeral is over, so there is nothing to prevent her coming to town."

I was compelled to agree to his suggestion, although loth to again bring pain and annoyance to my love. I knew how she had suffered when, a few days ago, I had questioned her, and I felt convinced by her manner that, although she had refused to speak, she herself was innocent. Her lips were sealed by word of honour.

According to appointment Jevons met me when I had finished my next morning's work at Guy's, and we took a glass of sherry together in a neighbouring bar. Then at his invitation I accompanied him along the Borough High Street and Newington Causeway to the London Road, until we came to a row of costermongers' barrows drawn up beside the pavement. Before one of these, piled with vegetables ready for the Saturday-night market, he stopped, and was immediately recognised by the owner—a tall, consumptive-looking man, whose face struck me somehow as being familiar.

"Well, Lane?" my companion said. "Busy, eh?"

"Not very, sir," was the answer, with the true cockney twang. "Trade ain't very brisk. There's too bloomin' many of us 'ere nowadays."

Leaving my side my companion advanced towards the man and whispered some confidential words that I could not catch, at the same time pulling something from his breast-pocket and showing it to him.

"Oh, yes, sir. No doubt abawt it!" I heard the man exclaim.

Then, in reply to a further question from Jevons, he said:

"'Arry 'Arding used to work at Curtis's. So I fancy that 'ud be the place to find out somethink. I'm keepin' my ears open, you bet," and he winked knowingly.

Where I had seen the man before I could not remember. But his face was certainly familiar.

When we left him and continued along the busy thoroughfare of cheap shops and itinerant vendors I asked my friend who he was, to which he merely replied:

"Well, he's a man who knows something of the affair. I'll explain later. In the meantime come with me to Gray's Inn Road. I have to make a call there," and he hailed a hansom, into which we mounted.

Twenty minutes later we alighted before a dingy-looking barber's shop and inquired for Mr. Harding—an assistant who was at that moment shaving a customer of the working class. It was a house where one could be shaved for a penny, but where the toilet accessories were somewhat primitive.

While I stood on the threshold Ambler Jevons asked the barber's assistant if he had ever worked at Curtis's, and if, while there, he knew a man whose photograph he showed him.

"Yes, sir," answered the barber, without a moment's hesitation. "That's Mr. Slade. He was a very good customer, and Mr. Curtis used always to attend on him himself."

"Slade, you say, is his name?" repeated my friend.

"Yes, sir."

Then, thanking him, we re-entered the cab and drove to an address in a street off Shaftesbury Avenue.

"Slade! Slade!" repeated Ambler Jevons to himself as we drove along. "That's the name I've been in search of for weeks. If I am successful I believe the Seven Secrets will resolve themselves into one of the most remarkable conspiracies of modern times. I must, however, make this call alone, Ralph. The presence of a second person may possibly prevent the man I'm going to see from making a full and straightforward statement. We must not risk failure in this inquiry, for I anticipate that it may give us the key to the whole situation. There's a bar opposite the Palace Theatre. I'll set you down there, and you can wait for me. You don't mind, do you?"

"Not at all, if you'll promise to explain the result of your investigations afterwards."

WILLIAM LE QUEUX

"You shall know everything later," he assured me, and a few minutes afterwards I alighted at the saloon bar he had indicated, a long lounge patronised a good deal by theatrical people.

He was absent nearly half-an-hour, and when he returned I saw from his face that he had obtained some information that was eminently satisfactory.

"I hope to learn something further this afternoon," he said before we parted. "If I do I shall be with you at four." Then he jumped into a hansom and disappeared. Jevons was a strange fellow. He rushed hither and thither, telling no one his business or his motives.

About the hour he had named he was ushered into my room. He had made a complete change in his appearance, wearing a tall hat and frock coat, with a black fancy waistcoat whereon white flowers were embroidered. By a few artistic touches he had altered the expression of his features too— adding nearly twenty years to his age. His countenance was one of those round, flexible ones that are so easily altered by a few dark lines.

"Well, Ambler?" I said anxiously, when we were alone. "What have you discovered?"

"Several rather remarkable facts," was his philosophic response. "If you care to accompany me I can show you to-night something very interesting."

"Care to accompany you?" I echoed. "I'm only too anxious."

He glanced at his watch, then flinging himself into the chair opposite me, said, "We've an hour yet. Have you got a drop of brandy handy?"

Then for the first time I noticed that the fresh colour of his cheeks was artificial, and that in reality he was exhausted and white as death. The difficulty in speaking that I had attributed to excitement was really due to exhaustion.

Quickly I produced the brandy, and gave him a stiff peg, which he swallowed at a single gulp. His eyes were no longer sleepy-looking, but there was a quick fire in them which showed me that, although suppressed, there burned within his heart a fierce desire to get at the truth. Evidently he had learned something since I left him, but what it was I could not gather.

I looked at the clock, and saw it was twenty minutes past six. He noticed my action, and said:

"If we start in an hour we shall have sufficient time."

Ambler Jevons was never communicative. But as he sat before me his brows were knit in deep thought, his hands chafed with suppressed agitation, and he took a second brandy-and-soda, an unusual indulgence, which betrayed an absent mind.

At length he rose, carefully brushed his silk hat, settled the hang of his frock-coat before the glass, tugged at his cravat, and then, putting on his light overcoat, announced his readiness to set out.

About half-an-hour later our cab set us down in Upper Street, Islington, close to the Agricultural Hall, and, proceeding on foot a short distance, we turned up a kind of court, over the entrance of which a lamp was burning, revealing the words "Lecture Hall."

Jevons produced two tickets, whereupon we were admitted into a long, low room filled by a mixed audience consisting of men. Upon the platform at the further end was a man of middle age, with short fair beard, grey eyes, and an alert, resolute manner—a foreigner by his dress—and beside him an Englishman of spruce professional appearance—much older, slightly bent, with grey countenance and white hair.

We arrived just at the moment of the opening of the proceedings. The Englishman, whom I set down to be a medical man, rose, and in introducing the lecturer beside him, said:

"I have the honour, ladies and gentlemen, to introduce to you Doctor Paul Deboutin—who, as most of you know, is one of the most celebrated medical men in Paris, professor at the Salpêtrière, and author of many works upon nervous disorders. The study of the latter is not, unfortunately, sufficiently taken up in this country, and it is in order to demonstrate the necessity of such study that my friends and myself have invited Doctor Deboutin to give this lecture before an audience of both medical men and the laity. The doctor asks me to apologise to you for his inability to express himself well in English, but personally I have no fear that you will misunderstand him."

Then he turned, introduced the lecturer, and re-seated himself.

I was quite unprepared for such a treat. Deboutin, as every medical man is aware, is the first authority on nervous disorders, and his lectures have won for him a world-wide reputation. I had read all his books, and being especially struck with "Névroses et Idées Fixes," a most convincing work, had longed to be present at one of his demonstrations. Therefore, forgetful that I was there for some unknown reason, I settled myself to listen.

Rapidly and clearly he spoke in fairly good English, with a decision that showed him to be perfect master at once of his subject and of the phrases with which he intended to clothe his thoughts. He briefly

WILLIAM LE QUEUX

outlined the progress of his experiments at the Salpêtrière, and at the hospitals of Lyons and Marseilles, then without long preliminary, proceeded to demonstrate a most interesting case.

A girl of about twenty-five, with a countenance only relieved from ugliness by a fine pair of bright dark eyes, was led in by an assistant and seated in a chair. She was of the usual type seen in the streets of Islington, poorly dressed with some attempt at faded finery—probably a workgirl in some city factory. She cast an uneasy glance upon the audience, and then turned towards the doctor, who drew his chair towards the patient so that her knees nearly touched his.

It was a case of nervous "Hémianopsie," or one-eyed vision, he explained.

Now the existence of this has always been denied, therefore the experiment was of the most intense interest to every medical man present.

First the doctor, after ordering the patient to look him straight in the face, held a pencil on the left side of her head, and found that, in common with most of us, she was conscious of its presence without moving her eyes, even when it was almost at the level of her ear. Then he tried the same experiment on the right side of the face, when it was at once plain that the power of lateral vision had broken down—for she answered, "No, sir. No, no," as he moved the pencil to and fro with the inquiry whether she could see it. Nevertheless he demonstrated that the power of seeing straight was quite unimpaired, and presently he gave to his assistant a kind of glass hemisphere, which he placed over the girl's head, and by which he measured the exact point on its scale where the power of lateral vision ceased.

This being found and noted, Professor Deboutin placed his hand upon the patient's eyes, and with a brief "You may sleep now, my girl," in broken English, she was asleep in a few seconds.

Then came the lecture. He verbally dissected her, giving a full and lucid explanation of the nervous system, from the spinal marrow and its termination in the coccyx, up to the cortex of the brain, in which he was of opinion that there was in that case a lesion—probably curable—amply accounting for the phenomenon present. So clear, indeed, were his remarks that even a layman could follow them.

At last the doctor awoke the patient, and was about to proceed with another experiment when his quick eye noticed a hardly-perceptible flutter of the eyelids. "Ah, you are tired," he said. "It is enough." And he conducted her to the little side door that gave exit from the platform.

The next case was one of the kind which is always the despair of doctors—hysteria. A girl, accompanied by her mother, a neatly-dressed, respectable-looking body, was led forward, but her hands were trembling, and her face working so nervously that the doctor had to reassure her. With a true cockney accent she said that she lived in Mile End, and worked at a pickle factory. Her symptoms were constant headache, sudden falls, and complete absence of sensation in her left hand, which greatly interfered with her work. Some of the questions were inconvenient—until, in answer to one regarding her father, she gave a cry that "Poor father died last year," and broke into an agony of weeping. In a moment the doctor took up an anthropometric instrument from the table, and made a movement as though to touch her presumably insensible hand.

"Ah, you'll hurt me!" she said. Presently, while her attention was attracted in another direction, he touched the hand with the instrument, when she drew it back with a yell of pain, showing that the belief that her hand was insensible was entirely due to hysteria. He analysed her case just as he had done the first, and declared that by a certain method of treatment, too technical to be here explained, a complete cure could be effected.

Another case of hysteria followed, and then a terrible exhibition of a wild-haired woman suffering from what the lecturer described as a "crise des nerfs," which caused her at will to execute all manner of horrible contortions as though she were possessed. She threw herself on the floor on her back, with her body arched so that it rested only on her head and heels, while she delivered kicks at those in front of her, not with her toes, but with her heels. Meanwhile her face was so congested as to appear almost black.

The audience were, I think, relieved when the poor unfortunate woman, calmed by Deboutin's method of suggestion, was led quietly away, and her place taken by a slim, red-haired girl of more refined appearance than the others, but with a strange stony stare as though unconscious of her surroundings. She was accompanied by a short, wizened-faced old lady, her grandmother.

At this juncture the chairman rose and said:

"This case is of great interest, inasmuch as it is a discovery made by my respected colleague, whom we all know by repute, Sir Bernard Eyton."

The mention of my chief's name was startling. I had no idea he

WILLIAM LE QUEUX

had taken any interest in the French methods. Indeed, he had always declared to me that Charcot and his followers were a set of charlatans.

"We have the pleasure of welcoming Sir Bernard here this evening," continued the chairman; "and I shall ask him to kindly explain the case."

With apparent reluctance the well-known physician rose, after being cordially welcomed to the platform by the French savant, adjusted his old-fashioned glasses, and commenced to introduce the subject. His appearance there was certainly quite unexpected, but as I glanced at Ambler I saw a look of triumph in his face. We were sitting at the back of the hall, and I knew that Sir Bernard, being short-sighted, could not recognise us at the distance.

"I am here at Doctor Fulton's invitation to meet our great master, Professor Deboutin, of whom for many years I have been a follower." Then he went on to express the pleasure it gave him to demonstrate before them a case which he declared was not at all uncommon, although hitherto unsuspected by medical men.

Behind the chair of the new-comer stood the strange-looking old lady—who answered for her grand-daughter, the latter being mute. Her case was one, Sir Bernard explained, of absence of will. With a few quick questions he placed the history of the case before his hearers. There was a bad family history—a father who drank, and a mother who suffered from epilepsy. At thirteen the girl had received a sudden fright owing to a practical joke, and from that moment she gradually came under the influence of some hidden unknown terror so that she even refused to eat altogether. The strangest fact, however, was that she could still eat and speak in secret, although in public she was entirely dumb, and no amount of pleasure or pain would induce her to utter a sound.

"This," explained Sir Bernard, "is one of the many cases of absence of will, partial or entire, which has recently come beneath my notice. My medical friends, and also Professor Deboutin, will agree that at the age the patient received her fright many girls are apt to tend towards what the Charcot School term 'aboulie,' or, in plain English, absence of will. Now one of the most extraordinary symptoms of this is terror. Terror," he said, "of performing the simplest functions of nature; terror of movement, terror of eating—though sane in every other respect. Some there are, too, in whom this terror is developed upon one point only, and in such the inequality of mental balance can, as a rule, only be detected by one who has made deep research in this particular branch of nervous disorders."

The French professor followed with a lengthy discourse, in which he bestowed the highest praise upon Sir Bernard for his long and patient experiments, which, he said, had up to the present been conducted in secret, because he feared that if it were known he had taken up that branch of medical science he might lose his reputation as a lady's doctor.

Then, just as the meeting was being brought to a conclusion, Jevons touched me on the shoulder, and we both slipped out.

"Well," he asked. "What do you think of it all?"

"I've been highly interested," I replied. "But how does this further our inquiries, or throw any light on the tragedy?"

"Be patient," was his response, as we walked together in the direction of the Angel. "Be patient, and I will show you."

XXVII

Mr. Lane's Romance

The Seven Secrets, each distinct from each other and yet connected; each one in itself a complete enigma, formed a problem of which even Ambler Jevons himself could not discover the solution.

Contrary to his usual methods, he allowed me to accompany him in various directions, making curious inquiries that had apparently nothing to connect them with the mystery of the death of Mr. and Mrs. Courtenay.

In reply to a wire I had sent to Ethelwynn came a message saying that her mother was entirely prostrated, therefore she could not at present leave her. This, when shown to Ambler, caused him to purse his lips and raise his shoulders with that gesture of suspicion which was a peculiarity of his. Was it possible that he actually suspected her?

The name of Slade seemed ever in Jevons' mind. Indeed, most of his inquiries were regarding some person of that name.

One evening, after dining together, he took me in a cab across the City to the Three Nuns Hotel, at Aldgate—where, in the saloon bar, we sat drinking. Before setting out he had urged me to put on a shabby suit of clothes and a soft hat, so that in the East End we should not attract attention as "swells." As for his own personal appearance, it was certainly not that of the spruce city man. He was an adept at disguises, and on this occasion wore a reefer jacket, a peaked cap, and a dark violet scarf in lieu of collar, thus presenting the aspect of a seafarer ashore. He smoked a pipe of the most approved nautical type, and as we sat together in the saloon he told me sea stories, in order that a group of men sitting near might overhear.

That he had some object in all this was quite certain, but what it was I could not gather.

Suddenly, after an hour, a little under-sized old man of dirty and neglected appearance, who had been drinking at the bar, shuffled up to us, and whispered something to Ambler that I did not catch. The words, nevertheless, caused my companion to start, and, disregarding the fresh whiskey and soda he had just ordered, he rose and walked out—an example which I followed.

"Lanky sent me, sir," the old man said, addressing Ambler, when we were out in the street. "He couldn't come hisself. 'E said you'd like to know the news."

"Of course, I was waiting for it," replied my companion, alert and eager.

"Well," he said, "I suppose I'd better tell yer the truth at once, sir."

"Certainly. What is it?"

"Well, Lanky's dead."

"Dead?" cried Ambler. "Impossible. I was waiting for him."

"I know. This morning in the Borough Market he told me to come 'ere and find you, because he wasn't able to come. 'E had a previous engagement. Lanky's engagements were always interestin'," he added, with a grim smile.

"Well, go on," said Ambler, eagerly. "What followed?"

"'E told me to go down to Tait Street and see 'im at eight o'clock, as 'e had a message for you. I went, and when I got there I found 'im lying on the floor of his room stone dead."

"You went to the police, of course?"

"No, I didn't; I came here to see you instead. I believe the poor bloke's been murdered. 'E was a good un, too—poor Lanky Lane!"

"What!" I exclaimed. "Is that man Lane dead?"

"It seems so," Jevons responded. "If he is, then there we have further mystery."

"If you doubt it, sir, come with me down to Shadwell," the old man said in his cockney drawl. "Nobody knows about it yet. I ought to have told the p'lice, but I know you're better at mysterious affairs than the silly coppers in Leman Street."

Jevons' fame as an investigator of crime had spread even to that class known as the submerged tenth. How fashions change! A year or two ago it was the mode in Society to go "slumming." To-day only social reformers and missionaries make excursions to the homes of the lower class in East London. A society woman would not to-day dare admit that she had been further east than Leadenhall Street.

"Let's go and see what has really happened," Ambler said to me. "If Lane is dead, then it proves that his enemy is yours."

"I can't see that. How?" I asked.

"You will see later. For the moment we must occupy ourselves with his death, and ascertain whether it is owing to natural causes or to foul play. He was a heavy drinker, and it may have been that."

WILLIAM LE QUEUX

"No," declared the little old man, "Lanky wasn't drunk to-day—that I'll swear. I saw 'im in Commercial Road at seven, talkin' to a feller wot's in love wiv 'is sister."

"Then how do you account for this discovery of yours?" asked my companion.

"I can't account for it, guv'nor. I simply found 'im lying on the floor, and it give me a shock, I can tell yer. 'E was as cold as ice."

"Let's go and see ourselves," Ambler said: so together we hurried through the Whitechapel High Street, at that hour busy with its costermonger market, and along Commercial Road East, arriving at last in the dirty, insalubrious thoroughfare, a veritable hive of the lowest class of humanity, Tait Street, Shadwell.

Up the dark stairs of one of the dirtiest of the dwellings our conductor guided us, lighting our steps with wax vestas, struck upon the wall, and on gaining the third floor of the evil-smelling place he pushed open a door, and we found ourselves in an unlit room.

"Don't move, gentlemen," the old man urged. "You may fall over 'im. 'E's right there, just where you're standin'. I'll light the lamp."

Then he struck another match, and by its fickle light we saw the body of Lane, the street-hawker, lying full length only a yard from us, just as our conductor had described.

The cheap and smelling paraffin lamp being lit, I took a hasty glance around the poor man's home. There was but little furniture save the bed, a chair or two, and a rickety table. Upon the latter was one of those flat bottles known as a "quartern." Our first attention, however, was to the prostrate man. A single glance was sufficient to show that he was dead. His eyes were closed, his hands clenched, and his body was bent as though he had expired in a final paroxysm of agony. The teeth, too, were hard set, and there were certain features about his appearance that caused me to entertain grave suspicion from the first. His thin, consumptive face, now blanched, was strangely drawn, as though the muscles had suddenly contracted, and there was an absence of that composure one generally expects to find in the faces of those who die naturally.

As a medical man I very soon noted sufficient appearances to tell me that death had been due either to suicide or foul play. The former seemed to me the most likely.

"Well?" asked Ambler, rising from his knees when I had concluded the examination of the dead man's skinny, ill-nourished body. "What's your opinion, Ralph?"

"He's taken poison," I declared.

"Poison? You believe he's been poisoned."

"It may have been wilful murder, or he may have taken it voluntarily," I answered. "But it is most evident that the symptoms are those of poisoning."

Ambler gave vent to a low grunt, half of satisfaction, half of suspicion. I knew that grunt well. When on the verge of any discovery he always emitted that guttural sound.

"We'd better inform the police," I remarked. "That's all we can do. The poor fellow is dead."

"Dead! Yes, we know that. But we must find out who killed him."

"Well," I said, "I think at present, Ambler, we've quite sufficient on our hands without attempting to solve any further problems. The poor man may have been in despair and have taken poison wilfully."

"In despair!" echoed the old man. "No fear. Lanky was happy enough. 'E wasn't the sort of fellow to hurry hisself out o' the world. He liked life too jolly well. Besides, he 'ad a tidy bit o' money in the Savin's Bank. 'E was well orf once, wer' Lanky. Excuse me for interruptin'."

"Well, if he didn't commit suicide," I remarked, "then, according to all appearances, poison was administered to him wilfully."

"That appears to be the most feasible theory," Ambler said. "Here we have still a further mystery."

Of course, the post-mortem appearances of poisoning, except in a few instances, are not very characteristic. As every medical man is aware, poison, if administered with a criminal intent, is generally in such a dose as to take immediate effect—although this is by no means necessary, as there are numerous substances which accumulate in the system, and when given in small and repeated quantities ultimately prove fatal—notably, antimony. The diagnosis of the effects of irritant poisons is not so difficult as it is in the case of narcotics or other neurotics, where the symptoms are very similar to those produced by apoplexy, epilepsy, tetanus, convulsions, or other forms of disease of the brain. Besides, one of the most difficult facts we have to contend with in such cases is that poison may be found in the body, and yet a question may arise as to its having been the cause of death.

XXVIII

"Poor Mrs. Courtenay"

Ambler appeared to be much concerned regarding the poor man's death. When we had first met beside his vegetable barrow in the London Road he certainly seemed a hard-working, respectable fellow, with a voice rendered hoarse and rough by constantly shouting his wares. But by the whispered words that had passed I knew that Ambler was in his confidence. The nature of this I had several times tried to fathom.

His unexpected death appeared to have upset all Ambler's plans. He grunted and took a tour round the poorly-furnished chamber.

"Look here!" he said, halting in front of me. "There's been foul play here. We must lose no time in calling the police—not that they are likely to discover the truth."

"Why do you say that?"

"Because the poor fellow has been the victim of a secret assassin."

"Then you suspect a motive?"

"I believe that there is a motive why his lips should be closed—a strange and remote one." Then, turning to the old fellow who had been the dead man's friend, he asked: "Do you know anyone by the name of Slade?"

"Slade?" repeated the croaking old fellow. "Slade? No, sir. I don't recollect anyone of that name. Is it a man or a woman?"

"Either."

"No, sir."

"Do you know if Lanky Lane ever had visitors here—I mean visitors not of his own class?"

"I never 'eard of none. Lanky wasn't the sort o' chap to trouble about callers. He used to spend 'is nights in the Three Nuns wiv us; but he'd sit 'ours over two o' gin. 'E saved 'is money, 'e did."

"But look here," exclaimed Ambler, seriously. "Are you quite certain that you've never seen him with any stranger at nights?"

"Never to my knowledge."

"Well," my companion said, "you'd better go and call the police."

When the old fellow had shuffled away down the rickety stairs, Ambler, turning to me, said abruptly:

"That fellow is lying; he knows something about this affair."

I had taken up the empty dram bottle and smelt it. The spirit it had contained was rum—which had evidently been drunk from the bottle, as there was no glass near. A slight quantity remained, and this I placed aside for analysis if necessary.

"I can't see what this poor fellow has to do with the inquiry upon which we are engaged, Ambler," I remarked. "I do wish you'd be more explicit. Mystery seems to heap upon mystery."

"Yes. You're right," he said reflectively. "Slowly—very slowly, I am working out the problem, Ralph. It has been a long and difficult matter; but by degrees I seem to be drawing towards a conclusion. This," and he pointed to the man lying dead, "is another of London's many mysteries, but it carries us one step further."

"I can't, for the life of me, see what connection the death of this poor street hawker has with the strange events of the immediate past."

"Remain patient. Let us watch the blustering inquiries of the police," he laughed. "They'll make a great fuss, but will find out nothing. The author of this crime is far too wary."

"But this man Slade?" I said. "Of late your inquiries have always been of him. What is his connection with the affair?"

"Ah, that we have yet to discover. He may have no connection, for aught I know. It is mere supposition, based upon a logical conclusion."

"What motive had you in meeting this man here to-night?" I inquired, hoping to gather some tangible clue to the reason of his erratic movements.

"Ah! that's just the point," he responded. "If this poor fellow had lived he would have revealed to me a secret—we should have known the truth!"

"The truth!" I gasped. "Then at the very moment when he intended to confess to you he has been struck down."

"Yes. His lips have been sealed by his enemy—and yours. Both are identical," he replied, and his lips snapped together in that peculiar manner that was his habit. I knew it was useless to question him further.

Indeed, at that moment heavy footsteps sounded upon the stairs, and two constables, conducted by the shuffling old man, appeared upon the scene.

"We have sent for you," Ambler explained. "This man is dead—died suddenly, we believe."

"Who is he, sir?" inquired the elder of the pair, bending over the prostrate man, and taking up the smoky lamp in order to examine his features more carefully.

"His name is Lane—a costermonger, known as Lanky Lane. The man with you is one of his friends, and can tell you more about him than I can."

"Is he dead?" queried the second constable, touching the thin, pallid face.

"Certainly," I answered. "I'm a doctor, and have already made an examination. He's been dead some time."

My name and address was taken, together with that of my companion. When, however, Ambler told the officers his name, both were visibly impressed. The name of Jevons was well known to the police, who held him in something like awe as a smart criminal investigator.

"I know Inspector Barton at Leman Street—your station, I suppose?" he added.

"Yes, sir," responded the first constable. "And begging your pardon, sir, I'm honoured to meet you. We all heard how you beat the C. I. Department in the Bowyer Square Mystery, and how you gave the whole information to Sergeant Payling without taking any of the credit to yourself. He got all the honour, sir, and your name didn't appear at the Old Bailey."

Jevons laughed. He was never fond of seeing his name in print. He made a study of the ways and methods of the criminal, but only for his own gratification. The police knew him well, but he hid his light under the proverbial bushel always.

"What is your own opinion of the affair, sir?" the officer continued, ready to take his opinion before that of the sergeant of the Criminal Investigation Department attached to his station.

"Well," said Ambler, "it looks like sudden death, doesn't it? Perhaps it's poison."

"Suicide?"

"Murder, very possibly," was Jevons' quiet response.

"Then you really think there's a mystery, sir?" exclaimed the constable quickly.

"It seems suspiciously like one. Let us search the room. Come along Ralph," he added, addressing me. "Just lend a hand."

There was not much furniture in the place to search, and before long, with the aid of the constable's lantern, we had investigated every nook and cranny.

Only one discovery of note was made, and it was certainly a strange one.

Beneath a loose board, near the fireplace, Jevons discovered the dead man's hoard. It consisted of several papers carefully folded together. We examined them, and found them to consist of a hawker's licence, a receipt for the payment for a barrow and donkey, a post-office savings bank book, showing a balance of twenty-six pounds four shillings, and several letters from a correspondent unsigned. They were type-written, in order that the handwriting should not be betrayed, and upon that flimsy paper used in commercial offices. All of them were of the highest interest. The first, read aloud by Ambler, ran as follows:—

Dear Lane,

I have known you a good many years, and never thought you were such a fool as to neglect a good thing. Surely you will reconsider the proposal I made to you the night before last in the bar of the Elephant and Castle? You once did me a very good turn long ago, and now I am in a position to put a good remunerative bit of business in your way. Yet you are timid that all may not turn out well! Apparently you do not fully recognise the stake I hold in the matter, and the fact that any exposure would mean ruin to me. Surely I have far more to lose than you have. Therefore that, in itself, should be sufficient guarantee to you. Reconsider your reply, and give me your decision to-morrow night. You will find me in the saloon bar of the King Lud, in Ludgate Hill, at eight o'clock. Do not speak to me there, but show yourself, and then wait outside until I join you. Have a care that you are not followed. That hawk Ambler Jevons has scent of us. Therefore, remain dumb and watchful.

Z.

"That's curious," I remarked. "Whoever wrote that letter was inciting Lane to conspiracy, and at the same time held you in fear, Ambler."

My companion laughed again—a quiet self-satisfied laugh. Then he commenced the second letter, type-written like the first, but evidently upon another machine.

Dear Lane,

Your terms seem exorbitant. I quite understand that at least four or five of you must be in the affair, but the price asked is ridiculous. Besides, I didn't like Bennett's tone when he spoke to me yesterday. He was almost threatening. What have you told him? Recollect that each of us knows something to the detriment of the other, and even in these days of so-called equality the man with money is always the best. You must contrive to shut Bennett's mouth. Give him money, if he wants it—up to ten pounds. But, of course, do not say that it comes from me. You can, of course, pose as my friend, as you have done before. I shall be at the usual place to-night.

Z.

"Looks as though there's been some blackmailing," one of the constables remarked. "Who's Bennett?"

"I expect that's Bobby Bennett who works in the Meat Market," replied the atom of a man who had accosted us at Aldgate. "He was a friend of Lanky's, and a bad 'un. I've 'eard say that 'e 'ad a record at the Old Bailey."

"What for?"

"'Ousebreakin'."

"Is he working now?" Ambler inquired.

"Yes. I saw 'im in Farrin'don Street yesterday."

"Ah!" remarked the constable. "We shall probably want to have a chat with him. But the chief mystery is the identity of the writer of these letters. At all events it is evident that this poor man Lane knew something to his detriment, and was probably trying to make money out of that knowledge."

"Not at all an unusual case," I said.

Jevons grunted, and appeared to view the letters with considerable satisfaction. Any documentary evidence surrounding a case of mysterious death is always of interest. In this case, being of such a suspicious nature, it was doubly so.

"Are you quite decided not to assist me?" *another letter ran. It was likewise type-written, and from the same source.* "Recollect you did so once, and were well paid for it. You had enough to keep you in luxury for years had you not so foolishly frittered it away on your so-called friends. Any of the latter would give you away to the police to-morrow for a five-pound note. This, however, is my last appeal to you. If you help me I shall give you one hundred pounds, which is not bad payment for an hour's work. If you do not, then you will not hear from me again.

Z.

"Seems a bit brief, and to the point," was the elder constable's remark. "I wonder what is the affair mentioned by this mysterious correspondent? Evidently the fellow intended to bring off a robbery, or something, and Lane refused to give his aid."

"Apparently so," replied Ambler, fingering the last letter remaining in his hand. "But this communication is even of greater interest," he added, turning to me and showing me writing in a well-known hand.

"I know that writing!" I cried. "Why—that letter is from poor Mrs. Courtenay!"

"It is," he said, quietly. "Did I not tell you that we were on the eve of a discovery, and that the dead man lying there could have told us the truth?"

XXIX

The Police are at Fault

A mbler Jevons read the letter, then handed it to me without comment.

It was written upon the note-paper I knew so well, stamped with the neat address "Neneford," in black, but bearing no date. What I read was as follows:—

Sir,

I fail to comprehend the meaning of your words when you followed me into the train at Huntingdon last night. I am in no fear of any catastrophe; therefore I can only take your offer of assistance as an attempt to obtain money from me. If you presume to address me again I shall have no other course than to acquaint the police.

Yours truly
Mary Courtenay

"Ah!" I exclaimed. "Then he warned her, and she misunderstood his intention."

"Without a doubt," said Ambler, taking the letter from my hand. "This was written probably only a few days before her death. That man," and he glanced at the prostrate body, "was the only one who could give us the clue by which to unravel the mystery."

But the dead man's lips had closed, and his secret was held for ever. Only those letters remained to connect him with the river tragedy; or rather to show that he had communicated with the unfortunate Mrs. Courtenay.

In company we walked to Leman Street Police Station, one of the chief centres of the Metropolitan Police in the East End, and there, in an upper office, Ambler had a long consultation with the sergeant of the Criminal Investigation Department.

I described the appearance of the body, and stated my suspicions of poisoning, all of which the detective carefully noted before going forth to make his own examination. My address was taken, so that I might assist at the post-mortem, and then, shortly after midnight I drove back westward through the City with Ambler at my side.

He spoke little, and when in Oxford Street, just at the corner of Newman Street, he descended, wished me a hurried good-night, and disappeared into the darkness. He was often given to strange vagaries of erratic movement. It was as though some thought had suddenly occurred to him, and he acted at once upon it.

That night I scarcely closed my eyes. My brain was awhirl with thoughts of all the curious events of the past few months—the inexplicable presence of old Mr. Courtenay, and the subsequent death of Mary and of the only man who, according to Ambler, knew the remarkable secret.

Ethelwynn's strange words worried me. What could she mean? What did she know? Surely hers could not be a guilty conscience. Yet, in her words and actions I had detected that cowardice which a heavy conscience always engenders. One by one I dissected and analysed the Seven Secrets, but not in one single instance could I obtain a gleam of the truth.

While at the hospital next day I was served with a notice to assist at the post-mortem of the unfortunate Lane, whose body was lying in the Shadwell mortuary; and that same afternoon I met by appointment Doctor Tatham, of the London Hospital, who, as is well known, is an expert toxicologist.

To describe in technical detail the examination we made would not interest the general reader of this strange narrative. The average man or woman knows nothing or cares less for the duodenum or the pylorus; therefore it is not my intention to go into long and wearying detail. Suffice it to say that we preserved certain portions of the body for subsequent examination, and together were engaged the whole evening in the laboratory of the hospital. Tatham was well skilled in the minutiæ of the tests. The exact determination of the cause of death in cases of poisoning always depends partly on the symptoms noted before death, and partly on the appearances found after death. Regarding the former, neither of us knew anything; hence our difficulties were greatly increased. The object of the analyst is to obtain the substances which he has to examine chemically in as pure a condition as possible, so that there may be no doubt about the results of his tests; also, of course, to separate active substances from those that are inert, all being mixed together in the stomach and alimentary canal. Again, in dealing with such fluids as the blood, or the tissues of the body, their natural constituents must be got rid of before the foreign and poisonous body can be reached. There is this difficulty further to contend with: that some of the most poisonous of substances are of unstable composition and are readily altered by chemical reagents; to this group belong many vegetable and most animal poisons. These, therefore, must be treated differently from the more stable inorganic compounds. With an inorganic poison we may destroy all organic materials mixed with it, trusting to find the poison still recognisable after this process. Not so with an organic substance; that must be separated by other than destructive means.

Through the whole evening we tested for the various groups of poisons—corrosives, simple irritants, specific irritants and neurotics. It was a long and scientific search.

Some of the tests with which I was not acquainted I watched with the keenest interest, for, of all the medical men in London, Tatham was the most up to date in such analyses.

At length, after much work with acids, filtration, and distillation, we determined that a neurotic had been employed, and that its action on the vasomotor system of the nerves was very similar, if not identical, with nitrate of amyl.

Further than that, even Tatham, expert in such matters, could not proceed. Hours of hard work resulted in that conclusion, and with it we were compelled to be satisfied.

In due course the inquest was held at Shadwell, and with Ambler I attended as a witness. The reporters, of course, expected a sensation; but, on the contrary, our evidence went to show that, as the poisonous substance was found in the "quartern" bottle on deceased's table, death was in all probability due to suicide.

Some members of the jury took an opposite view. Then the letters we had found concealed were produced by the police, and, of course, created a certain amount of interest. But to the readers of newspapers the poisoning of a costermonger at Shadwell is of little interest as compared with a similar catastrophe in that quarter of London vaguely known as "the West End." The letters were suspicious, and both coroner and jury accepted them as evidence that Lane was engaged upon an elaborate scheme of blackmail.

"Who is this Mary Courtenay, who writes to him from Neneford?" inquired the coroner of the inspector.

"Well, sir," the latter responded, "the writer herself is dead. She was found drowned a few days ago near her home under suspicious circumstances."

Then the reporters commenced to realize that something extraordinary was underlying the inquiry.

"Ah!" remarked the coroner, one of the most acute officials of his class. "Then, in face of this, her letter seems to be more than curious. For aught we know the tragedy at Neneford may have been wilful murder; and we have now the suicide of the assassin?"

"That, sir, is the police theory," replied the inspector.

"Police theory be hanged!" exclaimed Ambler, almost loud enough to be heard. "The police know nothing of the case, and will never learn anything. If the jury are content to accept such an explanation, and brand poor Lane as a murderer, they must be allowed to do so."

I knew Jevons held coroners' juries in the most supreme contempt; sometimes rather unreasonably so, I thought.

"Well," the coroner said, "this is certainly remarkable evidence," and he turned the dead woman's letter over in his hand. "It is quite plain that the deceased approached the lady ostensibly to give her warning of some danger, but really to blackmail her; for what reason does not at present appear. He may have feared her threat to give information to the police; hence his crime, and subsequent suicide."

"Listen!" exclaimed Jevons in my ear. "They are actually trying the dead man for a crime he could not possibly have committed! They've got hold of the wrong end of the stick, as usual. Why don't they give a verdict of suicide and have done with it. We can't afford to waste a whole day explaining theories to a set of uneducated gentlemen of the Whitechapel Road. The English law is utterly ridiculous where coroners' juries are concerned."

The coroner heard his whispering, and looked towards us severely.

"We have not had sufficient time to investigate the whole of the facts connected with Mrs. Courtenay's mysterious death," the inspector went on. "You will probably recollect, sir, a mystery down at Kew some little time ago. It was fully reported in the papers, and created considerable sensation—an old gentleman was murdered under remarkable circumstances. Well, sir, the gentleman in question was Mrs. Courtenay's husband."

The coroner sat back in his chair and stared at the officer who had spoken, while in the court a great sensation was caused. Mention of the

Kew Mystery brought its details vividly back to the minds of everyone. Yes. After all, the death of that poor costermonger, Lanky Lane, was of greater public interest than the representatives of the Press anticipated.

"Are you quite certain of this?" the coroner queried.

"Yes, sir. I am here by the direction of the Chief Inspector of Scotland Yard to give evidence. I was engaged upon the case at Kew, and have also made inquiries into the mystery at Neneford."

"Then you have suspicion that the deceased was—well, a person of bad character?"

"We have."

"Fools!" growled Ambler. "Lane was a policeman's 'nose,' and often obtained payment from Scotland Yard for information regarding the doings of a certain gang of thieves. And yet they actually declare him to be a bad character. Preposterous!"

"Do you apply for an adjournment?"

"No, sir. We anticipate that the verdict will be suicide—the only one possible in face of the evidence."

And then, as though the jury were compelled to act upon the inspector's suggestion, they returned a simple verdict. "That the deceased committed suicide by poisoning while of unsound mind."

XXX

SIR BERNARD'S DECISION

For fully a week I saw nothing of Ambler.

Sir Bernard was unwell, and remained down at Hove; therefore I was compelled to attend to his practice. There were several serious cases, the patients being persons of note; thus I was kept very busy.

My friend's silence was puzzling. I wrote to him, but received no response. A wire to his office in the City elicited the fact that Mr. Jevons was out of town. Probably he was still pursuing the inquiry he had so actively taken up. Nevertheless, I was dissatisfied that he should leave me so entirely in the dark as to his intentions and discoveries.

Ethelwynn came to town for the day, and I spent several hours shopping with her. She was strangely nervous, and all the old spontaneous gaiety seemed to have left her. She had read in the papers of the curious connection between the death of the man Lane and that of her unfortunate sister; therefore our conversation was mainly upon the river mystery. Sometimes she seemed ill at ease with me, as though fearing some discovery. Perhaps, however, it was merely my fancy.

I loved her. She was all the world to me; and yet in her eyes I seemed to read some hidden secret which she was endeavouring, with all the power at her command, to conceal. In such circumstances there was bound to arise between us a certain reserve that we had not before known. Her conversation was carried on in a mechanical manner, as though distracted by her inner thoughts; and when, after having tea together in Bond Street, we drove to the station, and I saw her off on her return to Neneford, my mind was full of darkest apprehensions.

Yes. That interview convinced me more than ever that she was, in some manner, cognisant of the truth. The secret existence of old Mr. Courtenay, the man whom I myself had pronounced dead, was the crowning point of the strange affair; and yet I felt by some inward intuition that this fact was not unknown to her.

All the remarkable events of that moonlit night when I had followed husband and wife along the river-bank came back to me, and I saw vividly the old man's face, haggard and drawn, just as it had been in life. Surely there could be no stranger current of events than those which

WILLIAM LE QUEUX

formed the Seven Secrets. They were beyond explanation—all of them. I knew nothing. I had certainly seen results; but I knew not their cause.

Nitrate of amyl was not a drug which a costermonger would select with a view to committing suicide. Indeed, I daresay few of my readers, unless they are doctors or chemists, have ever before heard of it. Therefore my own conclusion, fully endorsed by the erratic Ambler, was that the poor fellow had been secretly poisoned.

Nearly a fortnight passed, and I heard nothing of Ambler. He was still "out of town." Day by day passed, but nothing of note transpired. Sir Bernard was still suffering from a slight touch of sciatica at home, and on visiting him one Sunday I found him confined to his bed, grumbling and peevish. He was eccentric in his miserly habits and his hatred of society, beyond doubt; and the absurdities which his enemies attributed to him were not altogether unfounded. But he had, at all events, the rare quality of entertaining for his profession a respect nearly akin to enthusiasm. Indeed, according to his views, the faculty possessed almost infallible qualities. In confidence he had more than once admitted to me that certain of his colleagues practising in Harley Street were amazing donkeys; but he would never have allowed anyone else to say so. From the moment a man acquired that diploma which gave him the right over life and death, that man became, in his eyes, an august personage for the world at large. It was a crime, he thought, for a patient not to submit to his decision, and certainly it must be admitted that his success in the treatment of nervous disorders had been most remarkable.

"You were at that lecture by Deboutin, of Paris, the other day!" he exclaimed to me suddenly, while I was seated at his bedside describing the work I had been doing for him in London. "Why didn't you tell me you were going there?"

"I went quite unexpectedly—with a friend."

"With whom?"

"Ambler Jevons."

"Oh, that detective fellow!" laughed the old physician. "Well," he added, "it was all very interesting, wasn't it?"

"Very—especially your own demonstrations. I had no idea that you were in correspondence with Deboutin."

He laughed; then, with a knowing look, said:

"Ah, my dear fellow, nowadays it doesn't do to tell anyone of your own researches. The only way is to spring it upon the profession as a great triumph: just as Koch did his cure for tuberculosis. One must create an impression, if only with a quack remedy. The day of the steady plodder is past; it's all hustle, even in medicine."

"Well, you certainly did make an impression," I said, smiling. "Your experiments were a revelation to the profession. They were talking of them at the hospital only yesterday."

"H'm. They thought me an old fogey, eh? But, you see, I've been keeping pace with the times, Boyd. A man to succeed nowadays must make a boom with something, it matters not what. For years I've been experimenting in secret, and some day I will show them further results of my researches—and they will come upon the profession like a thunderclap, staggering belief."

The old man chuckled to himself as he thought of his scientific triumph, and how one day he would give forth to the world a truth hitherto unsuspected.

We chatted for a long time, mostly upon technicalities which cannot interest the reader, until suddenly he said:

"I'm getting old, Boyd. These constant attacks I have render me unfit to go to town and sit in judgment on that pack of silly women who rush to consult me whenever they have a headache or an erring husband. I think that very soon I ought to retire. I've done sufficient hard work all the years since I was a 'locum' down in Oxfordshire. I'm worn out."

"Oh, no," I said. "You mustn't retire yet. If you did, the profession would lose one of its most brilliant men."

"Enough of compliments," he snapped, turning wearily on his pillow. "I'm sick to death of it all. Better to retire while I have fame, than to outlive it. When I give up you will step into my shoes, Boyd, and it will be a good thing for you."

Such a suggestion was quite unexpected. I had never dreamed that he contemplated handing over his practice to me. Certainly it would be a good thing for me if he did. It would give me a chance such as few men ever had. True, I was well known to his patients and had worked hard in his interests, but that he intended to hand his practice over to me I had never contemplated. Hence I thanked him most heartily. Yes, Sir Bernard had been my benefactor always.

"All the women know you," he went on in his snappish way. "You are the only man to take my place. They would come to you; but not to a new man. All I can hope is that they won't bore you with their domestic troubles—as they have done me," and he smiled.

WILLIAM LE QUEUX

"Oh," I said. "More than once I, too, have been compelled to listen to the domestic secrets of certain households. It really is astonishing what a woman will tell her doctor, even though he may be young."

The old man laughed again.

"Ah!" he sighed. "You don't know women as I know them, Boyd. You've got your experience to gain. Then you'll hold them in abhorrence—just as I do. They call me a woman-hater," he grunted. "Perhaps I am—for I've had cause to hold the feminine mind and the feminine passion equally in contempt."

"Well," I laughed, "there's not a man in London who is more qualified to speak from personal experience than yourself. So I anticipate a pretty rough time when I've had years of it, as you have."

"And yet you want to marry!" he snapped, looking me straight in the face. "Of course, you love Ethelwynn Mivart. Every man at your age loves. It is a malady that occurs in the 'teens and declines in the thirties. I should have thought that your affection of the heart had been about cured. It is surely time it was."

"It is true that I love Ethelwynn," I declared, rather annoyed, "and I intend to marry her."

"If you do, then you'll spoil all your chances of success. The class of women who are my patients would much rather consult a confirmed bachelor than a man who has a jealous wife hanging to his coat-tails. The doctor's wife must always be a long-suffering person."

I smiled; and then our conversation turned upon his proposed retirement, which was to take place in six months' time.

I returned to London by the last train, and on entering my room found a telegram from Ambler making an appointment to call on the following evening. The message was dated from Eastbourne, and was the first I had received from him for some days.

Next morning I sat in Sir Bernard's consulting-room as usual, receiving patients, and the afternoon I spent on the usual hospital round. About six o'clock Ambler arrived, drank a brandy and soda with a reflective air, and then suggested that we might dine together at the Cavour—a favourite haunt of his.

At table I endeavoured to induce him to explain his movements and what he had discovered; but he was still disinclined to tell me anything. He worked always in secret, and until facts were clear said nothing. It was a peculiarity of his to remain dumb, even to his most intimate friends concerning any inquiries he was making. He was a man of moods, with an active mind and a still tongue—two qualities essential to the successful unravelling of mysteries.

Having finished dinner we lit cigars, and took a cab back to my rooms. On passing along Harley Street it suddenly occurred to me that in the morning I had left a case of instruments in Sir Bernard's consulting-room, and that I might require them for one of my patients if called that night.

Therefore I stopped the cab, dismissed it, and knocked at Sir Bernard's door. Ford, on opening it, surprised me by announcing that his master, whom I had left in bed on the previous night, had returned to town suddenly, but was engaged.

Ambler waited in the hall, while I passed along to the door of the consulting-room with the intention of asking permission to enter, as I always did when Sir Bernard was engaged with a patient.

On approaching the door, however, I was startled by hearing a woman's voice raised in angry, reproachful words, followed immediately by the sound of a scuffle, and then a stifled cry. Without further hesitation I turned the handle.

The door was locked.

XXXI

Contains the Plain Truth

A sudden idea occurred to me, and I acted instantly upon its impulse. There was a second entrance through the morning room; and I dashed round to the other door, which fortunately yielded.

The sight that met my gaze was absolutely staggering. I stood upon the threshold aghast. Sir Bernard, his dark eyes starting from his ashen face, stood, holding a woman within his grasp, pinning her to the wall, and struggling to cover her mouth with his hands and prevent her cries from being overheard.

The woman was none other than Ethelwynn.

At my unexpected entry he released his hold, shrinking back with a wild, fierce look in his face, such as I had never before seen.

"Ralph!" cried my love, rushing forward and clinging to my neck. "Ralph! For God's sake save me from that fiend! Save me!"

I put my arm around her to protect her, at the same instant shouting to Jevons, who entered, as much astounded as myself. My love had evidently come to town and kept an appointment with the old man. The situation was startling, and required explanation.

"Tell me, Ethelwynn," I said, in a hard, stern voice. "What does all this mean?"

She drew herself up and tried to face me firmly, but was unable. I had burst in upon her unexpectedly, and she seemed to fear how much of the conversation I had overheard.

Noticing her silence, my friend Jevons addressed her, saying:

"Miss Mivart, you are aware of all the circumstances of the tragedy at Kew. Please explain them. Only by frank admission can you clear yourself, remember. To prevaricate further is quite useless."

She glanced at the cringing old fellow standing on the further side of the room—the man who had raised his hand against her. Then, with a sudden resolution, she spoke, saying:

"It is true that I am aware of many facts which have been until to-day kept secret. But now that I know the horrible truth they shall remain mysteries no longer. I have been the victim of a long and dastardly persecution, but I now hope to clear my honour before you, Ralph, and before my Creator." Then she paused, and, taking breath and drawing herself up straight with an air of determined resolution, went on:

"First, let us go back to the days soon after Mary's marriage. I think it was about a year after the wedding when I suddenly noticed a change in her. Her intellect seemed somehow weakened. Hitherto she had possessed a strong, well-defined character; this suddenly developed into a weak, almost childish balance of the brain. Instead of possessing a will of her own, she was no longer the mistress of her actions, but as easily led as an infant. Only to myself and to my mother was this change apparent. To all her friends and acquaintances she was just the same. About that time she consulted this man here—Sir Bernard Eyton, her husband's friend—regarding some other ailment, and he no doubt at once detected that her intellect had given way. Although devoted to her husband, nevertheless the influence of any friend of the moment was irresistible, and for that reason she drifted into the pleasure-seeking set in town."

"But the tragedy?" Jevons exclaimed. "Tell us of that. My own inquiries show that you are aware of it all. Mrs. Courtenay murdered her husband, I know."

"Mary—the assassin!" I gasped.

"Alas! it is too true. Now that my poor sister is dead, concealment is no longer necessary," my love responded, with a deep sigh. "Mary killed her husband. She returned home, entered the house secretly, and, ascending to his room, struck him to the heart."

"But the wound—how was it inflicted?" I demanded eagerly.

"With that pair of long, sharp-pointed scissors which used to be on poor Henry's writing-table. You remember them. They were about eight inches long, with ivory handles and a red morocco case. The wound puzzled you, but to me it seems plain that, after striking the blow, in an endeavour to extricate the weapon she opened it and closed it again, thereby inflicting those internal injuries that were so minutely described at the inquest. Well, on that night I heard a sound, and, fearing that the invalid wanted something, crept from my room. As I gained the door I met Mary upon the threshold. She stood facing me with a weird, fixed look, and in her hand was the weapon with which she had killed her husband. That awful moment is fixed indelibly upon my memory. I shall carry its recollection to the grave. I dashed quickly into the room, and to my horror saw what had occurred. Then my thoughts were for Mary—to conceal her guilt. Whispering to her

WILLIAM LE QUEUX

to obey me I led her downstairs, through the back premises, and so out into the street. A cab was passing, and I put her into it, telling the man to drive to the Hennikers', with whom she had been spending the evening. Then, cleaning the scissors of blood by thrusting them several times into the mould of a garden I was passing, I crossed the road and tossed them over the high wall into the thick undergrowth which flanks Kew Gardens. At that spot I felt certain that they would never be discovered. As quickly as possible I re-entered the house, secured the door by which I had made my exit, and returned again to my room with the awful knowledge of my sister's crime upon my conscience."

"What hour was that?"

"When I retired again to bed my watch showed that it was barely half-past one. At two o'clock Short, awakened by his alarum clock, made the discovery and aroused the house. What followed you know well enough. I need not describe it. You can imagine what I felt, and how guilty was my conscience with the awful knowledge of it all."

"The circumstances were certainly most puzzling," I remarked. "It almost appears as though matters were cleverly arranged in order to baffle detection."

"To a certain extent they undoubtedly were. I knew that the Hennikers would say nothing of poor Mary's erratic return to them. I did all in my power to withdraw suspicion from my sister, at the risk of it falling upon myself. You suspected me, Ralph. And only naturally—after that letter you discovered."

"But Mary's homicidal tendency seems to have been carefully concealed," I said. "I recollect having detected in her a strange vagueness of manner, but it never occurred to me that she was mentally weak. In the days immediately preceding the tragedy I certainly saw but little of her. She was out nearly every evening."

"She was not responsible for her actions for several weeks together sometimes," Sir Bernard interrupted. "I discovered it over a year ago."

"And you profited by your discovery!" my love cried, turning upon him fiercely. "The crime was committed at your instigation!" she declared.

"At my instigation!" he echoed, with a dry laugh. "I suppose you will say next that I hypnotised her—or some bunkum of that sort!"

"I'm no believer in hypnotic theories. They were exploded long ago," she answered. "But what I do believe—nay, what is positively proved from my poor sister's own lips by a statement made before witnesses—is that you were the instigator of the crime. You met her by appointment that night at Kew Bridge. You opened the door of the house for her, and you compelled her to go in and commit the deed. Although demented, she recollected it all in her saner moments. You told her terrible stories of old Mr. Courtenay, for whom you had feigned such friendship, and for weeks you urged her to kill him secretly until, in the frenzy of insanity to which you had brought her, she carried out your design with all that careful ingenuity that is so often characteristic of madness."

"You lie, woman!" the old man snapped. "I had nothing whatever to do with the affair! I was at home at Hove on that night."

"No! no! you were not," interrupted Jevons. "Your memory requires refreshing. Reflect a moment, and you'll find that you arrived at Brighton Station at seven o'clock next morning from Victoria. You spent the night in London; and further, you were recognised by a police inspector walking along the Chiswick Road as early as half-past three. I have not been idle, Sir Bernard, and have spent a good deal of time at Hove of late."

"What do you allege, then?" he cried in fierce anger, a dark, evil expression on his pale, drawn face. "I suppose you'll declare that I'm a murderer next!"

"I allege that, at your instigation, a serious and desperate attempt was made, a short time ago, upon the life of my friend Boyd by ruffians who were well paid by you."

"Another lie!" he blurted forth defiantly.

"What?" I cried. "Is that the truth, Ambler? Was I entrapped at the instigation of this man?"

"Yes. He had reasons for getting rid of you—as you will discern later."

"I tell you it's an untruth!" shouted the old man, in a frenzy of rage.

"Deny it if you will," answered my friend, with a nonchalant air. "It, however, may be interesting to you to know that the man 'Lanky Lane,' one of the desperate gang whom you bribed to call up Boyd on the night in question, is what is known at Scotland Yard as a policeman's 'nose,' or informer; and that he made a plain statement of the whole affair before he fell a victim to your carefully-laid plan by which his lips were sealed."

In an instant I recollected that the costermonger of the London Road was one of the ruffians.

The old man's lips compressed. He saw that he was cornered.

The revelation that to his clever cunning was due the many remarkable features of the mystery held me utterly bewildered. At first it seemed impossible; but as the discussion grew more heated, and the facts poured forth from the mouth of the woman I loved, and from the man who was my best friend, I became convinced that at last the whole of the mysterious affair would be elucidated.

One point, however, still puzzled me, namely, the inexplicable scene I had witnessed on the bank of the Nene.

I referred to it; whereupon Ambler Jevons drew from his breast-pocket two photographs, and, holding them before the eyes of the trembling old man, said:

"You recognise these? For a long time past I've been making inquiries into your keen interest in amateur theatricals. My information led me to Curtis's, the wigmakers; and they furnished me with this picture, showing you made up as as Henry Courtenay. It seems that, under the name of Slade, you furnished them with a portrait of the dead man and ordered the disguise to be copied exactly—a fact to which a dozen witnesses are prepared to swear. This caused me to wonder what game you were playing, and, after watching, I found that on certain nights you wore the disguise—a most complete and excellent one—and with it imposed upon the unfortunate widow of weak intellect. You posed as her husband, and she believed you to be him. So completely was the woman in your thrall that you actually led her to believe that Courtenay was not dead after all! You had a deeper game to play. It was a clever and daring piece of imposture. Representing yourself as her husband who, for financial reasons, had been compelled to disappear and was believed to be dead, you had formed a plan whereby to obtain the widow's fortune as soon as the executors had given her complete mastery of it. You had arranged it all with her. She was to pose as a widow, mourn your loss, and then sell the Devonshire estate and hand you the money, believing you to be her husband and rightly entitled to it. The terrible crime which the unfortunate woman had committed at your instigation had turned her brain, as you anticipated, and she, docile and half-witted, was entirely beneath your influence until—" and he paused.

"Until what?" I asked, utterly astounded at this remarkable explanation of what I had considered to be an absolutely inexplicable phenomenon.

He spoke again, quite calmly:

"Until this man, to his dismay, found that poor Mrs. Courtenay's intellect was regaining its strength. They met beside the river, and, her brain suddenly regaining its balance, she discovered the ingenious fraud he was imposing upon her." Turning to Sir Bernard, he said, "She tore off your disguise and declared that she would go to the police and tell the truth of the whole circumstances—how that you had induced her to go to the house in Kew and kill her husband. You saw that your game was up if she were not silenced; therefore, without further ado, you sent the poor woman to her last account."

"You lie!" the old man cried, his drawn face blanched to the lips. "She fell in—accidentally."

"She did not. You threw her in," declared Ambler Jevons, firmly. "I followed you there. I was witness of the scene between you; and, although too far off to save poor Mrs. Courtenay, I was witness of your crime!"

"You!" he gasped, glaring at my companion in fear, as though he foresaw the horror of his punishment.

"Yes!" responded Jevons, in his dry, matter-of-fact voice, his sleepy eyes brightening for a moment. "Since the day of the tragedy at Kew until this afternoon I have never relinquished the inquiry. The Seven Secrets I took one by one, and gradually penetrated them, at the same time keeping always near you and watching your movements when you least expected it. But enough—I never reveal my methods. Suffice it to say that in this I have succeeded by sheer patience and application. Every word of my allegation I am prepared to substantiate in due course at the Old Bailey." Then, after a second's pause, he looked straight at the culprit standing there, crushed and dumb before him, and declared: "Sir Bernard Eyton, you are a murderer!"

With my love's hand held in mine I stood speechless at those staggering revelations. I saw how Ethelwynn watched the contortions of the old doctor's face with secret satisfaction, for he had ever been her enemy, just as he had been mine. He had uttered those libellous hints regarding her with a view to parting us, so as to give him greater freedom to work his will with poor Mary. Then, when he had feared that through my love I had obtained knowledge of his dastardly offence, he had made an attempt upon my life by means of hired ruffians. The woman who had been in his drawing-room at Hove on the occasion of my visit was Mary, as I afterwards found out, and the attractive young person in the Brighton train had also been a caller at his house in connection with the attempt planned to be made upon me.

WILLIAM LE QUEUX

"You—you intend to arrest me?" Sir Bernard gasped at last, with some difficulty, his brow like ivory beneath the tight-drawn skin. A change had come over him, and he was standing with his back to a bookcase, swaying unsteadily as though he must fall.

"I certainly do," was Ambler Jevons' prompt response. "You have been the means of committing a double murder for the purposes of gain—because you knew that your friend Courtenay had left a will in your favour in the event of his wife's decease. That will has already been proved; but perhaps it may interest you to know that the latest and therefore the valid will is in my own possession, I having found it during a search of the dead man's effects in company with my friend Boyd. It is dated only a month before his death, and leaves the fortune to the widow, and in the event of her death to her sister Ethelwynn."

"To me!" cried my love, in surprise.

"Yes, Miss Ethelwynn. Everything is left to you unreservedly," he explained. Then, turning again to the clever impostor before him, he added: "You will therefore recognise that all your plotting, so well matured and so carefully planned that your demoniacal ingenuity almost surpasses the comprehension of man, has been in vain. By the neglect of one small detail, namely to sufficiently disguise your identity when dealing with Curtis, I have been enabled, after a long and tedious search, to fix you as the man who on several occasions was made up to present in the night the appearance of the dead Courtenay. The work has taken me many tedious weeks. I visited every wig-maker and half the hairdressers in London unsuccessfully until, by mere chance, the ruffian whom you employed to entrap my friend Boyd gave me a clue to the fact that Curtis made wigs as well as theatrical costumes. The inquiry has been a long and hazardous one," he went on. "But from the very first I was determined to get at the bottom of the mystery, cost me what it might—and I have fortunately succeeded." Then, turning again to the cringing wretch, upon whom the terrible denunciation had fallen as a thunderbolt, he added: "The forgiveness of man, Sir Bernard Eyton, you will never obtain. It has been ever law that the murderer shall die—and you will be no exception."

The effect of those words upon the guilty man was almost electrical. He drew himself up stiffly, his keen, wild eyes starting from his blanched face as he glared at his accuser. His lips moved. No sound, however, came from them. The muscles of his jaws seemed to suddenly become paralysed, for he was unable to close his mouth. He stood for a moment, an awful spectacle, the brand of Cain upon him. A strange gurgling sound escaped him, as though he were trying to articulate, but was unable; then he made wild signs with both his hands, clutched suddenly at the air, and fell forward in a fit.

I went to him, loosened his collar, and applied restoratives, but in ten minutes I saw that he was beyond human aid. What I had at first believed to be a fit was a sudden cessation of the functions of the heart—caused by wild excitement and the knowledge that punishment was upon him.

Within fifteen minutes of that final accusation the old man lay back upon the carpet lifeless, struck dead by natural causes at the moment that his crimes had become revealed.

Thus were the Seven Secrets explained; and thus were the Central Criminal Court and the public spared what would have been one of the most sensational trials of modern times.

The papers on Monday reported "with deepest regret" the sudden death from heart disease of Sir Bernard Eyton, whom they termed "one of the greatest and most skilful physicians of modern times."

JUST TWO YEARS HAVE PASSED since that memorable evening.

You, my reader, are probably curious to know whether I have succeeded in obtaining the quiet country practice that was my ideal. Well, yes, I have. And what is more, I have obtained in Ethelwynn a wife who is devoted to me and beloved by all the countryside—a wife who is the very perfection of all that is noble and good in woman. The Courtenay estate is ours; but I am not an idle man. Somehow I cannot be.

My practice? Where is it? Well, it is in Leicestershire. I dare not be more explicit, for Ethelwynn has urged me to conceal our identity, in order that we may not be remarked as a couple whose wooing was so strangely tragic and romantic.

Ambler Jevons still carries on his tea-blending business in the City, the most confirmed of bachelors, and the shrewdest of all criminal investigators. Even though we have been so intimate for years, and he often visits me at—I was nearly, by a slip, writing the name of the Leicestershire village—he has never explained to me his methods, and seldom, if ever, speaks of those wonderful successes by which Scotland Yard is so frequently glad to profit.

Only a few days ago, while we were sitting on the lawn behind my quaint old-fashioned house awaiting dinner, I chanced to remark upon the happiness which his ingenuity and perseverance had brought me; whereupon, turning to me with a slight, reflective smile, he replied:

"Ah, yes! Ralph, old fellow. I gave up that problem in despair fully a dozen times, and it was only because I knew that the future happiness of you both depended upon its satisfactory solution that I began afresh and strove on, determined not to be beaten. I watched carefully, not only Eyton, but Ethelwynn and yourself. I was often near you when you least suspected my presence. But that crafty old scoundrel was possessed of the ingenuity of Satan himself, combined with all the shrewd qualities that go to make a good detective; hence in every movement, every wile, and every action he was careful to cover himself, so that he could establish an *alibi* on every point. For that reason the work was extremely difficult. He was a veritable artist in crime. Yes," he added, "of the many inquiries I've taken up, the most curious and most complicated of them all was that of The Seven Secrets."

THE END

A Note About the Author

William Le Queux (1864–1927) was an Anglo-French journalist, novelist, and radio broadcaster. Born in London to a French father and English mother, Le Queux studied art in Paris and embarked on a walking tour of Europe before finding work as a reporter for various French newspapers. Towards the end of the 1880s, he returned to London where he edited *Gossip* and *Piccadilly* before being hired as a reporter for *The Globe* in 1891. After several unhappy years, he left journalism to pursue his creative interests. Le Queux made a name for himself as a leading writer of popular fiction with such espionage thrillers as *The Great War in England in 1897* (1894) and *The Invasion of 1910* (1906). In addition to his writing, Le Queux was a notable pioneer of early aviation and radio communication, interests he maintained while publishing around 150 novels over his decades long career.

A Note from the Publisher

Spanning many genres, from non-fiction essays to literature classics to children's books and lyric poetry, Mint Edition books showcase the master works of our time in a modern new package. The text is freshly typeset, is clean and easy to read, and features a new note about the author in each volume. Many books also include exclusive new introductory material. Every book boasts a striking new cover, which makes it as appropriate for collecting as it is for gift giving. Mint Edition books are only printed when a reader orders them, so natural resources are not wasted. We're proud that our books are never manufactured in excess and exist only in the exact quantity they need to be read and enjoyed.

bookfinity™

Discover more of your favorite classics with Bookfinity™.

- Track your reading with custom book lists.
- Get great book recommendations for your personalized Reader Type.
- Add reviews for your favorite books.
- AND MUCH MORE!

Visit **bookfinity.com** and take the fun Reader Type quiz to get started.

Enjoy our classic and modern companion pairings!

Classic & Modern